THE OPUS DICTUM

GARY MCAVOY

LITERATI
EDITIONS.

Printed in the United States of America
Hardcover ISBN: 978-1-954123-10-6
Paperback ISBN: 978-1-954123-09-0
eBook ISBN: 978-1-954123-08-3

Library of Congress Control Number: 2021923099

Published by:
Literati Editions
PO Box 5987
Bremerton WA 98312-5987
Email: info@LiteratiEditions.com
Visit the author's website: www.GaryMcAvoy.com

This is a work of fiction. Names, characters, businesses, organizations, places, long-standing institutions, agencies, public offices, events, locales and incidents are either the products of the author's imagination or have been used in a fictitious manner. Apart from historical references throughout the book, any resemblance to actual persons, living or dead, or actual events is purely coincidental.

All trademarks are property of their respective owners. Neither Gary McAvoy nor Literati Editions is associated with any product or vendor mentioned in this book.

BOOKS BY GARY MCAVOY

The Opus Dictum

The Vivaldi Cipher

The Magdalene Veil

The Magdalene Reliquary

The Magdalene Deception

And Every Word Is True

PROLOGUE

LONDON, ENGLAND – 18 JUNE 1982

anging from a long stretch of twisted orange rope knotted in the steel scaffolding beneath Blackfriars Bridge, the body of Roberto Calvi swung gently in the light morning breeze over the River Thames.

A young postal employee crossing the bridge on his way to work had discovered the body at seven thirty that Friday morning. Dialing 999 from a red telephone box at the end of the bridge, he reported the sighting to City of London Police, who promptly dispatched a crime scene unit.

With a River Police launch moored beneath the bridge, CSU officers lowered Calvi's body onto the deck of the vessel. Investigators were surprised to find Calvi's clothing had been stuffed with four large stones and a brick, and in his pockets they found close to $15,000 in several international currencies and a forged Italian passport. Adding to those oddities was the fact that his trademark mustache had been shaved off.

Italian banker Roberto Calvi had been in London since the tenth of June, having fled Italy to escape prosecution on charges of corruption related to his dealings with Banco Ambrosiano, Italy's largest privately owned bank of which Calvi was chairman.

Initially ruled a suicide—but later believed to have been an elaborately staged murder by Francesco "Frankie the Strangler" Di Carlo—Calvi's death was likely attributed to damaging knowledge he possessed about the inner workings of a secret Italian Masonic lodge known as Propaganda Due, or P2, and its close links with the Vatican Bank which, having a ten percent stake, was the largest shareholder of Banco Ambrosiano. Calvi's association with the Vatican was so intimate he had been known throughout the tight-knit financial community as "God's Banker."

Founded in 1877, Propaganda Due's primary goal was to defend the Catholic Church against the expected arrival of the Antichrist. The P2 lodge was nicknamed by its members as *"Frati Neri,"* or Black Friars, for the black robes they wore during secret ritualistic meetings. The obvious inference of Calvi's body hanging beneath a bridge of the same name was not lost on keen observers, who deemed it a symbolic warning from the mysterious yet powerful Masonic syndicate.

While membership in P2—or any Masonic

organization—was expressly forbidden by the Church under pain of excommunication, for centuries it secretly counted among its members a procession of cardinals, bishops, and priests. Complementing its distinctive symbols, secret signs and gestures, the global brotherhood of Freemasons offered its members privileged access to others in powerful positions from all walks of life, and the attraction of such admission sufficiently offset the Church's frail promise of punishment.

Besides, the very cardinals and bishops governing such oversight were themselves likely high-ranking Masons, deliberately placed in such positions by their predecessors.

When Roberto Calvi had arrived in London the week prior to his death, he had been seen carrying a bulging briefcase believed to hold incriminating details of accounts and transactions linking the pending catastrophic failure of Calvi's Banco Ambrosiano to a succession of powerful organizations: P2, the Sicilian Mafia, the Camorra, high-ranking Italian politicians, British and Italian secret services, the Vatican Bank—and a secretive, far right faction of Catholics known as Opus Deus, translated from Latin as "The Work of God."

Well-financed and unusually powerful for a relatively small but fiercely dedicated organization, Opus Deus was apparently intent on bailing out Banco Ambrosiano in exchange for a major stake in the operation. Indeed, the Vatican ended up paying almost $250 million to absolve its role in the fiasco, which involved illegal currency movements and possible financing of right-wing terrorist groups. Money moves in mysterious ways in such labyrinthine circles, and it was possible the Vatican had no idea its money was helping to underwrite terrorism.

Regardless, Roberto Calvi's briefcase held secrets too valuable to many formidable interests, and certain forces apparently believed he had to be stopped from ever revealing anything.

But after his death, the briefcase simply disappeared.

And since 1982, those same formidable forces held a persistent anxiousness that at any time, by anyone, devastating information could be uncovered that could bring down many a person or institution.

CHAPTER
ONE
PRESENT DAY

"*P*ronto, Vaticano.*"

Sister Teresa Drinkwater answered the incoming call on Line 12 of the Vatican switchboard. "*Si, signore,*" she replied to the caller's request. "I will put you through to Bishop Esposito's office now."

It was rush hour in the call center that morning as the six nuns handling the switchboard managed the constant flow of telephone communications into and out of Vatican City. Coming from various countries—Italy, Brazil, Poland, Philippines, India, the United States and others—the Sisters of the Pious Disciples of the Divine Master spoke a myriad of languages and personally handled more than half a million incoming calls each year.

Operator Sister Teresa served both as supervisor of the switchboard and as lead administrator for the Vatican's computer network. Which meant she actually belonged to the Daughters of St. Paul order, since the Paulines, as the order is called, includes among its ranks members who held technology vocations.

Another line lit up on her computer screen. It was an internal call from the office of the Prefect of the Secret Archives, Father Michael Dominic.

"*Pronto, Vaticano*," she answered. *Hello, Vatican.*

"Hey, Teri!" Father Dominic said cheerfully. "I was hoping you'd answer. How's your morning going?" Unlike some of the older priests who kept all communications cloaked in the formal piousness of their office, Father Dominic spoke easily to all those who served the church. A welcomed voice in what could be a long shift.

"Father Michael!" the young American nun replied with a bounce in her voice. "Funny you should ask. We're busier here than a hive of mosquitoes at a nudist colony."

Dominic laughed, as he always did at Teri's often earthy expressions.

"Who can I connect you with?" she asked him.

"Actually, I'm calling to speak with *you*," Dominic said. "I'd like to meet to discuss our computer system."

"Well, there goes my budget for this year. What did you have in mind?"

"Why don't we meet for lunch in the canteen, and I'll introduce you to my new assistant? We can talk more about it there."

"It's a date," Teri said. "See you then, Father." She punched the End Call button with her mouse and moved on to the next caller.

Knowing her fellow American, Father Dominic, was prefect of the Vatican Secret Archives, she could easily guess that his request would involve something in that realm. The truth was, it was hard turning down any of Dominic's requests, for she had developed kind of a crush on the handsome young priest. At 33, he turned the heads of many of the younger nuns here, despite their vows. Teri knew he was from New York and had been ordained at St. Patrick's Cathedral by his mentor, Cardinal Enrico Petrini, with whom he had long had a close relationship. Everyone in Vatican City knew that.

It was Ian Duffy's first week as Dominic's new assistant *scrittore* in the Secret Archives, replacing Toshi Kwan who had taken a job with IBM as their chief steganographer.

A young and ambitious technologist from Silicon Valley, Duffy was as Irish as they came: a strapping, six-foot tall hipster with a mop of red hair, fair skin, and the hint of a brogue accent inherited from his grandparents while growing up under their care in the Cupertino foothills of Northern California.

As an Apple alumnus—having been a big data developer at the tech giant for several years previous—Duffy was hired by Dominic not only to assist him in identifying and cataloging the millions of yet-unseen documents the Archives held, but also to create and manage a custom software program for storing and retrieving the vast amounts of digital information already recorded in the Archives. Expert in the use of frameworks and systems for distributed storage and processing, Duffy's mission was key to the Vatican's plan for upgrading worldwide access to specified datasets the

Archives manages, as well as the millions of images stored in the Vatican Apostolic Library's database.

"Ready for lunch, Ian?" Dominic asked. "We're meeting with the Vatican's network admin, Sister Teri, to talk about your new workstation."

"You bet, Michael!" Duffy replied enthusiastically. "I've already got my shopping list in hand." He grinned at the thought of the gleaming new Mac Pro he had in mind, with the latest Apple silicon chip and gobs of graphic processing power and storage capacity.

"Few things make me happier than having the best possible equipment other peoples' money can buy," he added, his green eyes bright with expectation.

Exiting the building through the Courtyard of the Library, Dominic and Duffy walked across the Via di Belvedere into the commercial sector of Vatican City. Entering the canteen, Dominic looked across the long room smelling of wonderful foods and bustling with activity, then spotted Sister Teresa in her blue and white habit seated alone at a table by the windows.

"Hi, Teri," he said, pulling out a chair. "I'd like you to meet Ian Duffy, my new assistant. Ian, this is Sister Teresa Drinkwater, better known as Teri."

"Drinkwater! What a great name," Duffy said. "I imagine you're always thirsty?"

"Oh, you've got a lively one here, Michael," she said, shaking hands with Duffy. "And is that a Gaelic accent I detect? Or is it just a speech impediment?"

Duffy looked at her with a droll face, then laughed.

"We're gonna get along just great," he enthused. "Yes, Teri, my family hails from Ireland."

"Alright, let's get some food first," the priest urged. As much as Dominic respected and relished the wisdom of the elder clergy he dealt with, he found the liveliness of younger ones, like Sister Teri and now Duffy, invigorating. He liked to think of his 33-year-old self as still young and vibrant. His routine morning run and hitting the gym kept him trim and in shape. But several events had made clear the heavy burden that came with being prefect of the Vatican Apostolic Archive, of being entrusted with the safety of the Vatican's vast array of documents. Burdens that could age a young priest before his time. Which was one reason he had pushed to employ Ian Duffy—the sooner the rich resources of the Vatican's documents were catalogued, the sooner they would be protected for all time.

The three moved to the end of the cafeteria line. Each loaded an orange tray with various dishes offered along the food line. After paying for their meals, they returned to the table, then said grace before picking up their forks.

"Did you hear the pope dropped in here recently?" Teri asked the others, her large green eyes open in amazement. "Just walked in the door alone, picked up a tray, waited in line like everyone else, then started loading up his plate! People were blown away. The Holy Father is such a good man."

"Yes, I read about it. That even made the Vatican newspaper," Dominic said. "Not that there's that much else to report here. But it did make the front page."

"How many people work in the Vatican?" Duffy asked.

Sister Teri's face lit up. "Pope John Paul II was asked that question by a reporter once. His answer was, 'About half'!"

Dominic and Duffy roared with laughter, not having heard the anecdote before.

"Vatican City has around two thousand employees," Dominic answered. "And three-quarters of them live outside the walls."

"So, where are you from, Teri?" Duffy asked as a fork full of pan-fried cod found its way to his mouth.

"San Francisco," she replied. "I used to work for Google as a network administrator until I chose to become a Pauline nun and devote my life to God's technology. I mean, work." She smiled coyly at the distinction.

"Ah, yes. The perils of the Paulines," Duffy quipped.

"As if I hadn't heard that one before," Teri groaned.

"This is going to be a long lunch," Dominic sighed. "I can see you two will be an unstoppable force together."

"Where are you from, Ian?" Teri asked.

"I'm from the Bay Area, too," he said. "I worked for Apple in Cupertino until Michael here offered me this plum assignment. We met through an old classmate of mine from Stanford who's now an investment manager at the Vatican Bank. Milo Banducci. Do you know him?"

Teri wiped her mouth with a napkin before responding. "We haven't met, but I've handled calls to him. I supervise the Vatican switchboard while also being the lead network admin here. Speaking of which, I understand you have need of a new computer system?"

Putting his fork down, Ian reached into his pocket and

withdrew a small sheet of paper, sliding it across the table to Sister Teri.

"I did have a few things in mind ...," he said, hoping there would be no pushback on his requests.

Teri feigned choking on her salad when she saw the list, at the top of which was a $30,000 price for one fully-outfitted Mac Pro alone.

"A guy needs what a guy needs to do the job," he said, winking at her.

"You've maxed out the memory?! And two Radeon Pro Vega graphic cards?! You do realize all this is coming from collection plates around the world, right?"

Dominic stepped in to allay Teri's concerns. "This all has been laid out in my budget, which already has been approved by Cardinal Wolsey at the Secretariat for the Economy. I knew we'd need this kind of equipment for the project ahead of us, so you don't have to sell anyone else on it. I already took the heat for it."

"Well, I do admit to the sin of envy looking at this," Teri said. "Mind if I play with—I mean, try it when it comes in? I've never used a Mac Pro before."

"They're awesome machines," Duffy enthused, "and a suitable fit for the demands of our new project. I can't wait to get started."

"First, you'll be getting a tour of the Archive," Dominic said, "so you know the kinds of treasures you'll be working with. The Vatican is the repository for many of mankind's most remarkable achievements in written and artistic forms. I think you'll be impressed, Ian."

"Really looking forward to it, Michael. Will Sister Teri be joining us?"

Teri looked up from her plate, thick eyebrows arched above a hopeful face.

"Can I?" she begged. "Oh, *please*? I'd love to see the Secret Archives!"

"Sure, Teri, you can come as well," Dominic said, grinning. "But prepare to be humbled."

"Check. Humility was one of my sacred vows."

CHAPTER

TWO

At Father Dominic's invitation, Sister Teri arrived at the Apostolic Archive building beneath the Tower of the Winds at three that afternoon, excited to have such a rare opportunity after her shift was over.

Historically, the Secret Archive—originally named more for privacy than for secrecy—was the pope's personal library of all documentation dealing with Church issues over the past twelve hundred years. In contrast, the Vatican Museum featured the Church's vast holdings representing many of the world's finest artistic and literary achievements.

Over those centuries, the Vatican had acquired millions of illuminated manuscripts, letters and documents from heads of state, the rarest books of all shapes and sizes, and a plethora of materials that went well beyond dealing specifically with Church issues. The Archives were a living portrait of the entire human race—

and the most exhaustive chronicle of original documents anywhere, addressing virtually every theological, political, scientific and artistic pursuit through the ages.

As the elevator descended to the cavernous underground Archives built deep beneath the sun-drenched Pigna Courtyard, Dominic explained the layout of his domain.

"When we exit, we'll be in the Gallery of the Metallic Shelves. It's been measured at around fifty-three linear miles of shelving space, not to mention wherever else materials can be stacked. We seem to be running out of space as new volumes of material join centuries of work already here. And the vast majority of it is as yet uncatalogued. That will be part of your job, Ian: helping to organize, identify, interpret and index the crushing amount of information found here. All manner of books and papers acquired since the eighth century—political and religious tracts, account ledgers, personal records and correspondence of the popes and the Curia, the Vatican's governing body—have been sitting here just waiting for you! Think about that..."

Duffy's face was aglow with anticipation. "I had no idea it was this big and so convoluted."

The elevator doors opened to reveal rows upon rows of gray galvanized steel shelving as far as the eye could see. There were no windows to cause light-polluting damage to the Archives so as they moved through the darkened aisles, sensors activated amber lighting overhead, which automatically extinguished behind them a few moments after sensing no movement.

Dominic took them into the Miscellanea section, featuring fifteen enormous *armadi*, or ancient poplar cabinets, each bearing the Borghese papal coat of arms and filled with thousands of documents which had never been seen for centuries, much less catalogued.

"I did the math once," Dominic said. "Each of these cabinets contains around ten thousand packages of papers which have never been explored. By anyone. Ever. They've just been stored here for God knows how long. To inventory just *one* package of materials would require the full-time effort of two experts over a week's time. So to record the contents of all ten thousand packages in one cabinet alone would require nearly two hundred years— and we have fifteen cabinets! That doesn't even count the miles of materials on the shelves, which are mainly just organized by year."

"And I thought my job was overwhelming," Sister Teri said, her mouth agape in astonishment. "Just think of what historic secrets any of these might hold."

Dominic sighed as they walked farther. Yes, just one such long forgotten document had led him only a year ago to revelations that could have shaken the Church to its core. Not to mention other dust-ladened texts that he and only a few others had uncovered which led to yet other secrets. Dominic now held knowledge that could never be publicly revealed, confidential historical skeletons only a precious few now shared. He glanced at the shelves heavy with history, wondering what else awaited discovery.

They had reached a far corner toward the back of the

Gallery when Duffy noticed an impressively large wooden door in the shadows.

"What's behind that?" he asked, intrigued.

"That's the Riserva. The most highly classified materials are kept in that room. I'm afraid no one is allowed entry except for the pope and me, though Cardinal Petrini, as Secretary of State, does have a key."

"Well, now that makes me want to see inside even more!" Duffy exclaimed.

"Which won't be happening," Dominic added with a sly smile. "Just forget you even heard about it." He then mentioned several specific historical documents housed in the Archives, entrancing Sister Teri and Duffy with the wealth of knowledge surrounding them.

"So where do you want me to start, Michael? It's all pretty overwhelming, to be honest."

"I've been wanting to continue getting those *armadi* in the Miscellanea cataloged for as long as I've been here. They reputedly contain some of the most intriguing of all collections in the Vatican. You're going to start with one of those."

"*Excellent!*" Duffy cheered, pumping his fist. "Do I have to wait for my new Mac Pro, or is there equipment available now?"

"We've got a complete system with scanner that you can use in the meantime. It's older, but competent."

"I'm sure we can have your new system here by next week, Ian," Teri said. "The Vatican does have priority purchasing power with our vendor, Stewart Hastings Global. I'll place the order this afternoon."

from only one time period—making it an easier first job of documentation.

He laid all papers and items out onto the table, sorting them into some logical semblance of order. In doing so, he naturally read with interest the contents of many of the papers. They seemed to be largely documents pertaining to loans and agreements between the Institute for the Works of Religion, or IOR—the formal name for the Vatican Bank—and a company called Banco Ambrosiano. Various other names were mentioned: Licio Gelli, Archbishop Paul Marcinkus, United Trading, and Roberto Calvi. And there were numerous references to something called Opus Deus.

Duffy tossed the key back into the briefcase, then took the papers and passport to his computer workstation. Launching the database software, he spent the next couple of hours scanning the materials into the system. Once he was done, he returned everything to the briefcase, closed it up, and tucked it back deep to the rear of the *armadio* where he'd found it.

Thrilled to have accomplished his first official task, he then extracted the next batch of materials for review and scanning. He was determined to have as much fun as he could understanding what his new job would entail until his new Mac Pro was delivered and his work on the new database would begin.

CHAPTER

FOUR

H aving decided to meet for dinner at Ristorante dei Musei, a trattoria just north of the Vatican wall, Ian Duffy and Milo Banducci found a table near the back wall of the restaurant.

Even before entering, from the outside Duffy had caught the aromas of freshly baked focaccia, the flat oven-baked Italian bread usually found on the table at every meal, along with scents of basil and simmering rich tomato sauces with garlic sautéed in butter. His mouth was already watering when they took their seats.

"*Due Birra Moretti, per favore*," Duffy instructed the server, ordering two beers for Banducci and himself.

"So, Milo. I've had the most amazing day! I can't thank you enough for making this possible. No other job I can think of could possibly compare to working in the Vatican Secret Archive."

Banducci, a short, prematurely balding man in his

early thirties, was unemotional in his reaction. Perhaps owing to his occupation—a banker for the Vatican—his manner was controlled and self-possessed. He ran a hand over what little blond hair remained on his head.

"No problem, Ian," he said.

"The things they have there, you wouldn't believe," Duffy continued animatedly. "Letters to the popes that go back centuries, ancient parchments penned by monastic scribes. Father Dominic even showed us documents relating to the Inquisition's 1633 trial of Galileo, who was prosecuted simply because he reasoned that the Earth and other planets revolved around the Sun at the center of our Solar System! It's crazy cool stuff!"

Banducci smirked. "I can tell you're taken with it," he said. "I'm glad you've found a place where you're happy. The Vatican can be stiflingly boring at times."

"Said the staid, unadventurous banker," Duffy laughed. "You need some joy in your life." Even in their college days together, Duffy had found Banducci's inability to let loose puzzling. And a bit sad.

"My job is my joy," Banducci said flatly. "I get a lot of gratification from it, not to mention I can go to Mass at St. Peter's virtually any time I want."

"Yes, I know that's important for you. Despite being raised Catholic, I didn't get the deeply religious gene."

"It's more than that, Ian. God has a plan for all of us. Maybe the path you're on now will show you the way."

Duffy knew better than to stay this particular course with Banducci, the most devout Catholic he knew and obsessively vocal about it. Despite his far-right views on most every topic—which was in direct opposition to everything of value in Duffy's own philosophy—he found Banducci an otherwise intelligent guy, though he wouldn't classify him as a close friend or even an engaging one. He doubted the man had any close friends at all.

"Lunch is on me today, Milo, as a thank you for introducing me to Father Michael."

Banducci didn't respond, just picked up his menu to select from the day's specials.

"Cod again," Banducci complained. "Why is there so much damned cod in Rome?"

"Have one of the pastas. Musei is known for its homemade pasta, I hear."

"Too many carbs."

Duffy silently sighed. He wouldn't be having many more lunches with Milo, that's for sure.

After ordering from their server, Duffy picked up where he had left off.

"Hey, I came across the strangest thing today. In a special section of the Archive there are these huge, and I mean huge, cabinets crafted in the Middle Ages that house items from multiple centuries. Fifteen of them, and each one is packed with documents of all sorts. Father Michael said it would take hundreds of years to catalog them all.

"Anyway, inside one of them I found a modern briefcase. Well, modern in the sense that it was from the 1980s. And inside that I came across a key on a ring and a bunch of documents relating to the Vatican Bank."

On hearing of his own institution, Banducci's ears perked up.

"What kind of documents?"

"Oh, they just seemed to be loans and agreements between the IOR and a Banco Ambrosiano. They mentioned several names, like Michele Sindona, Archbishop Paul Marcinkus and Roberto Calvi. Oh, and a passport for Calvi. And mention of something called Opus Deus."

Banducci reached for his beer and took a long draw from the glass, his eyes never leaving Duffy, who had absorbed himself in tearing off pieces of focaccia and relishing each bite.

"Did you read these papers?" he asked after setting the glass down and licking the froth from his lips.

"Some of them, yes. It's part of my job, identifying and classifying them. Why?"

Banducci was shaken but managed himself well by not showing it.

"Just curious, since it involves my bank. Where is the briefcase now?"

"I put it back in the *armadio*, where I found it."

As they continued talking, the waiter returned with their meals: a steaming bowl of pasta carbonara with aged pancetta for Duffy, and an insalata di rinforzo for Banducci—a large salad of pickled and fresh vegetables combined with cooked cauliflower, olives, capers, anchovies and parsley, over which the server drizzled vintage balsamic vinegar and Roman olive oil at the table. With his fork, Banducci picked out the cauliflower and anchovies and set them aside on a separate plate. He did not care for either.

He also did not care for the task ahead—what he now needed to tell his superiors.

But not the ones at the Vatican Bank.

CHAPTER
FIVE

Taking up most of a city block in the quiet Pinciano suburb of Rome lies the enormous Villa Tiber, a nondescript, six-story, neo-Baroque building of tan and red brick with an anonymous black door bearing a sinister, golden-beaked raptor in its center, and no signage as to the building's name or purpose.

It was the international headquarters for Opus Deus, a "personal prelature" of the Roman Catholic Church founded in the 1920s by Father Juancarlos Escobar, an especially devout Spanish priest. As a special canonical structure of the Catholic Church, a personal prelature is composed of a high ecclesiastical dignitary known as a prelate, various clergy, and lay people who undertake specific pastoral activities on behalf of the Church.

Now comprising some 95,000 members, the vast majority of them lay people with just over 2,000 priests, Opus Deus's mission was a clear one: to promote a search for holiness in ordinary living among men and women in all stations of life.

Milo Banducci was one such ordinary man, though one possessing more influence than might be expected. As he walked up to the ancient black door and punched in his personal code on the touchpad in the stone doorway, a CCTV camera looked down on him, to ensure that he was who his passcode claimed him to be. The door buzzed open.

He nodded as he greeted the receptionist, who simply said to him "*Pax*," to which Banducci provided the correct reply, "*In Aeternum.*" As he passed her, she took in the woody, aromatic fragrance of Atkinsons cologne, its ambergris and musk base notes once favored by Father Escobar himself, and now a trademark scent worn by Opus Deus members in his honor.

Banducci's meeting with Bishop Guillermo Silva, the Prelate of Opus Deus, had been scheduled for eleven, but he had arrived thirty minutes early so he could pray alone in the Santa Marta della Figli church built underground, just beneath the villa. As he descended the grand staircase, he passed a revered white, gray-veined Carrara marble statue of the Madonna and Child, framed with a jasper and gilded bronze cloisonné backing.

During his lifetime, Father Juancarlos Escobar—now St. Juancarlos, having been expeditiously canonized in 2004—was never one to quibble about the price of reverence.

Passing beneath a heraldic marble panel featuring clusters of golden angels in bas-relief, Banducci stepped into the lavishly designed nave of the church, chose just the right middle pew facing the altar, and began his devotions.

Upstairs on the fifth floor, Bishop Guillermo Silva sat in his office waiting for Banducci, curious as to the urgency of the young man's matter that required him to speak with the Prelate personally.

Silva had first met Banducci at an Opus Deus conference and, being an employee of the Vatican Bank, made sure to keep him in his intimate sphere of useful individuals. Opus had a great number of dealings with the IOR, and many more high-level transactions were planned with the bank. It was particularly convenient that Banducci worked in the commercial investments sector, since Opus Deus's mercantile property holdings were of significant value in their global holdings portfolio.

The phone buzzed. Picking up the receiver, Silva's secretary announced Banducci's arrival. "Please send him in," the bishop said.

Silva stood up and came around the desk to greet his guest.

"Milo," he said, extending his hand. "So good of you to come by. *Pax,* my friend."

"*In aeternum*, Excellency. And good morning," Banducci said, shaking the bishop's hand as he looked nervously into the man's eyes.

"Coffee?"

"No, *grazie.*"

"I'm told you were in the church. A pity you can't stay for noon Mass."

"I just wanted to pray on some issues, Excellency, one of which I bring to you with open arms, and which I believe you will find of utmost interest."

"Is that so? Tell me more."

"You are, no doubt, familiar with the Banco Ambrosiano scandal with the IOR in the 1980s?"

Bishop Silva's eyes rolled as he sighed. "Yes, I am all too familiar with it, I'm afraid." As he said this, he picked up a red and white pack of Ducados cigarettes—also a brand favored by Father Escobar—and offered one to Banducci, who declined. After lighting one for himself, he asked, "Why is it you inquire about such an old matter?" A stream of blue smoke surged from his nostrils as he exhaled.

Banducci got right to the point. "A colleague of mine works in the Apostolic Archive. Over lunch yesterday he happened to mention he had discovered an old briefcase: one filled with papers, a passport belonging to Roberto Calvi, and a key—"

Silva choked on the drag of smoke he had just inhaled and let out a couple of coughs, trying to catch his breath. He looked at Banducci with eyes wide open, eyebrows arched.

"*Calvi's briefcase has been found?!*" he sputtered. "*And in the Secret Archives?!*"

"It would appear so, Excellency. My colleague has no clue as to its significance, and I was sure you would want to be informed immediately."

Having recovered from his fit, Silva now sat in silence,

still puffing on the Spanish cigarette. Exhaling, he stroked his gray goatee as he considered this new information.

"A key as well, you say?"

"Yes. He said there was a key on a ring."

Banducci clearly saw Silva's concern from his brow, and yet there was a sense of eager anticipation in his voice. Banducci knew he had performed well.

"We have been hoping to find Calvi's briefcase for nearly forty years, Milo. From what we understood, it contained highly compromising information—names, accounts, transactions relating to, shall we say, the movement of certain funds—that cannot *ever* be made public, even after all this time. What did your colleague do with the contents? And what about the key?"

"Apparently he scanned the materials into the Archives' database, as is their routine. I expect he just left the key in the bag and returned it to its original place inside the *armadio* where he found it. Do we know the purpose of the key?"

Silva looked out the windows of his office as he recalled those early, dark days. "We believe it may open a safe deposit box holding something of profound importance. I knew Roberto Calvi well. He was a bright and extremely cautious man, and in his last week he feared for his life. Rightly so, it would appear. I expect he took great cautions with the materials entrusted to him ... materials that Opus Deus would give anything to obtain."

Silva crushed out his cigarette in a flame-red Murano glass bowl on his desk, then turned to Banducci with a penetrating gaze.

"We must acquire that briefcase at any cost, Milo. As

an Opus Deus numerary yourself, your privilege comes with certain responsibilities. You have done very well thus far. But you must find a way to obtain that briefcase without arousing suspicion. Try to see if your colleague will cooperate. If not, I must speak with Cardinal Wolsey on how to proceed."

CHAPTER

SIX

British Cardinal Alastair Wolsey sat patiently in Terminal 2 at London's Heathrow Airport, waiting for first-class passengers to be called for Alitalia's last flight of the morning to Rome. It was now just past noon, as the flight had been delayed due to mechanical issues.

The vibrating cell phone in his pocket signaled an incoming call. Taking the device out, he abruptly answered, "Wolsey."

"Your Eminence," greeted the Spaniard, "this is Bishop Silva at Villa Tiber. Do you have a moment?"

"Just, Guillermo. I'm about to board a flight to Rome any minute now. I hope so, anyway. There's some kind of mechanical delay. What is it you need?"

"Can you stop by the villa first thing on your arrival? I assure you, it is of the utmost importance ... and not something we can discuss over the phone."

"Can you give me some clue as to why I should change my itinerary?"

Pausing briefly, the bishop spoke a single word. "Calvi."

After a longer pause of his own, the cardinal quietly replied, "I will see you in three hours, provided this plane takes off. Suffice to say, you have my attention."

Baron Armand de Saint-Clair's Dassault Falcon 900 was on final approach to Rome's Leonardo da Vinci airport when Frederic, the baron's steward and bodyguard, asked the guests aboard if they wished a refill on their drinks.

"No thanks, Frederic, I'm good for now," Hana Sinclair said. She swiveled her seat to face Marco Picard sitting across from her on the starboard side. "And you, Monsieur?" she purred with a coy smile.

"I'll pass, too," Marco said, grinning back at Hana. "Why is it I can't take my eyes off you?"

"Because I'm the only woman on board?"

"Will you two behave yourselves?" Baron Saint-Clair remanded them. "Once we're at the hotel you can flirt all you want. It's unbecoming in such a confined space."

"Oh, you're so old fashioned, Grand-père. By the way, when are you meeting with His Holiness?" As a longtime member of the pope's Consulta—comprised of his closest personal advisors—the baron was often called in for his advice on a variety of Church and papal matters.

"They have just pushed the meeting back to tomorrow afternoon, Hana," he sighed, glancing at his cell phone. "We may be going on to Castel Gandolfo for a few days afterward, so we'll likely be in Rome for a while. Have you any plans while we're here?"

"Apart from seeing Michael, I have a meeting with one of my reporter colleagues at *Corriere della Sera*. She and I are working on complementary articles about EU immigration policies, particularly as they affect France and Italy, so we'll be comparing our research." As a prize-winning investigative journalist for Paris's *Le Monde* newspaper, Hana strived to establish her own independence, despite her family's fortune stemming from her grandfather's banking empire.

"As for Marco ...." She glanced at him for his own response.

"*Et moi?*" he asked. "I will be doing my job. At your side day and ..." he glanced at the baron, "well, just making sure you don't get into trouble." Marco had been hired by the baron to be his granddaughter's bodyguard after her dangerous run-in with the Italian mafia related to one of her more intensive investigations for her publisher. Since then, he'd saved her life in yet another treacherous situation and the two had become more than bodyguard and charge. "If there's time, I'd also like to visit a buddy of mine from Afghanistan, someone I served with in the *Bérets Verts*. But he's not far from the Vatican, so while you and Michael are wining and dining, I'll see if I can round up Rusty."

"*Rusty?* How does someone get that nickname?"

"In his case, he earned it," Marco replied. "He rarely cleaned his weapons when we were bivouacked in the desert, and they often jammed. The sand there was merciless. He's now an attaché here in the French embassy."

"Which means he's a spy," Hana declared to her grandfather, half-jokingly.

Saint-Clair smiled at her self-consciously. He thought back to his own missions as a spy in the *Maquis*, a shadowy arm of the French Resistance during World War II, and his tight knit band of brothers forming Team Hugo: the Vatican's current Secretary of State, Cardinal Enrico Petrini, and Pierre Valois, now the president of France.

Just then the pilot announced they were about to land and everyone should fasten their seatbelts, as there were crosswinds ahead from the *ponentino*, a cool, heavy breeze coming off the Tyrrhenian Sea.

After a bumpy landing, the jet made its way to the private Signature terminal for international arrivals, where the group quickly passed through Customs, then got into a waiting black Range Rover limousine.

"To the Rome Cavalieri hotel, please," Saint-Clair told the driver.

As the limo made its way off the tarmac and out onto the streets of Rome, Hana noticed her grandfather seemed distracted.

"What is it, Grand-père? You're not your usual energetic self today."

The baron, chairman of Switzerland's Banque Suisse de Saint-Clair and one of Europe's key bankers, paused to consider his response. "His Holiness is having some issues with the Vatican Bank, and he has requested my counsel. I won't go into details, but these problems have been around for decades. Only now is he attempting to overhaul the entire institution, which is not an easy task. He's getting major pushback from the Curia, since certain factions in the College of Cardinals oppose modernization and tighter regulations. The poor man's doing the best he can but has called on his Consulta to advise him on the matter. I have served four popes during my time on that body, but this is one of our greatest challenges. That's why you see me concerned, my dear, that's all."

"He's lucky to have your advice, Pépé. I wish you both well."

Taking an iPhone out of her bag, Hana texted Michael Dominic to let him know they had arrived. She would call him later to set up dinner arrangements for the evening.

The office of Opus Deus's Prelate had been tastefully furnished by one of Rome's preeminent interior designers, who happened to be one of the organization's elite supernumerary members.

Bishop Silva's pride and joy was his handmade, luxury Italian designer desk, a prized Pegaso from Cassoni, with half of the top and one side in matte Canaletto walnut, and the other half and side in three-quarter-inch glass. It made quite the statement to visitors, beautifully lit by the handblown Murano glass floor lamp overarching the ensemble.

Bishop Silva held court in a plush leather and walnut Arrediorg executive chair as he spoke with Cardinal Wolsey who sat opposite him in a matching guest chair.

Both men nursed a glass of Rètico, an Italian single malt whiskey.

"The significance of this find cannot be overstated, Guillermo," Wolsey said. "To have stumbled on it like this is nothing short of a miracle from heaven."

"It may take another miracle to make sure it ends up in our hands, Alastair. And that may take some doing. Nobody is permitted in the Secret Archive without special permission from the Prefect or His Holiness personally. And I doubt the pope will grant us this favor. Which means we must become better acquainted with Father Dominic."

"Yes. But I understand he is a favorite of Cardinal Petrini so we must tread carefully here. What if we were to approach him for a role in the Work? We could use his influence in the Order of the Priestly Society of the Holy Spirit. Perhaps I can convince him such an honor would be of great benefit to his career in the Church."

Silva was circumspect. "I agree we must be cautious, Alastair. But we need to know more about Dominic before approaching him with such an offer. He may already have preconceived notions about Opus, as so many do, and trying to overcome his objections may impair our chances for getting that briefcase. Moreover, he may not be a team player at all."

Wolsey took a sip of the whiskey, then lit up a Ducados. He stood to walk around the office, taking pleasure in the Spanish tobacco which, he thought, went quite well with the single malt.

"First, Guillermo, I'll get Julio Guzman, our head of Information Technology and Security, to do a background investigation on Dominic. We need to know more about him before making our move."

"Keep in mind, too, that Banducci said the Calvi materials have already been digitized and placed in the Archives' database."

"Your own IT group can make that go away; there's another job for Julio. Didn't you once tell me we have some very talented hackers in our employ?"

"Some of the best, yes," Silva confirmed.

"Well, then, one problem down. Meanwhile, perhaps you and I should invite Father Dominic to lunch one day soon."

"An excellent suggestion, Alastair. I'll have my secretary set it up."

CHAPTER
SEVEN

S itting atop a majestic saddleback hill overlooking
the Eternal City—with the brightly lit dome of
Saint Peter's Basilica dominating the breathtaking
nighttime landscape below—La Pergola, the only
Michelin three-star restaurant in the city, was abuzz with
activity.

Visitors from around the world flocked on April 21 for
the annual "birthday" celebration of Rome, said to be
founded by the mythical twins Romulus and Remus in
753 BCE. All hotels in the city were filled to capacity with
visitors eager to see the historical reenactments of chariot
races, gladiatorial battles and other sporting events at
Circus Maximus.

La Pergola seemed less a restaurant than a well-
appointed museum, with antique tapestries featuring
scenes from ancient Rome hanging on the high walls, and
rich mahogany columns supporting an intricately inlaid

suspended ceiling, offering its guests exquisite cuisine in a grand setting.

Since her grandfather maintained a permanent suite at the Cavalieri, Hana Sinclair was guaranteed a table as a resident of the hotel, in which La Pergola was also a prime draw for well-heeled visitors to the city.

In addition to Marco, Hana had invited Father Dominic and his new assistant, Ian Duffy, to join her for the reunion. It had been six months since seeing Dominic, and there was much catching up to be done. Their last adventure had involved a puzzling piece of music by Vivaldi which had uncovered a centuries-old forgery conspiracy. Between Hana's investigative skills and Dominic's knowledge of the Vatican's treasure trove of documents, they had cracked the code of this long-standing criminal pursuit.

As the waiter poured from a bottle of Brovia 2016 Garblèt Suè Barolo into waiting glasses, everyone looked over their menus.

Duffy was wide-eyed as he noted the prices. *This is unbelievable! Seventy euros just for an appetizer of marinated scampi on cucumbers?!*

He leaned over to Dominic and whispered, "Michael, I can't afford this!"

Having overheard him, Hana relieved his concern. "Ian, apparently Michael didn't tell you dinner is on me, so please don't worry about the prices: they come with the Michelin stars. Have whatever you'd like, seriously."

"It's okay, Ian," Dominic said in a low voice. "Neither of us could even afford the tip here."

Duffy gulped, then smiled weakly as he returned to the menu.

After everyone ordered, Hana turned her attention to Duffy.

"So, Ian, where do you fit into Michael's world now? What's your background?"

"Well, I majored in computer science and global history at Stanford, and Apple picked me up right out of university. I worked there on distributed computing for a few years, but really felt my passion—world history from the Middle Ages to now—was missing from my life.

"One of my buddies from college, Milo Banducci, now works at the Vatican Bank and he introduced me to Father Dominic a few months back. And now here I am. I couldn't ask for a better job, since here I can combine both interests: computers and history. The few things Michael showed me on a tour of the Archives earlier this week took my breath away. I'm pretty excited to see what else is hidden away, and the fact that I might uncover something of historical importance that has never been seen by anyone living now is just crazy to think about! The possibilities are endless."

"You're so right," Dominic agreed. "As Hana has learned over the past couple of years, treasures seemingly leap out of nowhere; the Archives are that abundant." He glanced at Hana as she returned the admiration.

"Just be careful, Ian," she said, motioning to Dominic. "This one has a tendency to find trouble when you least expect it. Discovering those treasures often comes at a price."

"I second that," Marco added. "But we have had some

great adventures, haven't we?" He looked at both Dominic and Hana as he raised his wine glass in an unspoken toast. The others joined in.

"Too bad Karl and Lukas couldn't join us," Hana said. "Have you met my cousin and his partner yet, Ian?"

Duffy looked blankly at Dominic.

"No," the priest replied for him, "we haven't had time for proper introductions yet. You'll meet them soon enough, Ian. The best Swiss Guards we have in the city, whom we count as close comrades in arms."

"As in, the combat kind of arms?" Duffy asked, a lively look on his face.

"Well, as Hana alluded to," Dominic explained, "we have had our share of capers and exploits, and some of them have required the use of force. Not that you'll find that part of your job, but when needed, it's a blessing to have such capable men on our team."

"I look forward to meeting them!" Duffy said eagerly.

Four servers then surrounded the table, each bearing hot plates for their guests.

"For Signorina Sinclair, deep-fried zucchini flower with caviar on shellfish and saffron consommé," the lead waiter announced, setting down the plate in front of Hana. "For Signor Picard, we have leg of lamb with goat cheese and broccoli florets."

"Padre Dominic, for you tonight we are proud to serve our special fillet of sea bass with Roman mint aroma, green beans and agretti. And for the young man, fillet of veal with chard. *Buon appetito tutti!*" The lead server topped off wine glasses with a fresh bottle of the Barolo, then all four stepped away from the table in unison.

Everyone looked around at the sumptuous meals, taking in the beauty of each dish. La Pergola was known for their presentations, and they did not disappoint.

As they dug into their food, Duffy avidly continued talking about his first week.

"Hey, Michael, I found a strange thing in one of the *armadi* and wondered if you'd seen it before. It was a briefcase from the 1980s, filled with all kinds of odd things. Is that typical of materials I'm likely to find?"

Dominic looked at him strangely.

"A briefcase? A *modern* briefcase? Where did you say you found it?"

"Inside one of those giant poplar cabinets, tucked way in the back behind a box of other materials."

"That's very odd. What was inside it?"

"It was packed with several things: a passport, a key, an old floppy disk, a photograph of Saint Peter's Chair with a Latin inscription, papers detailing Vatican Bank accounts and contracts with a Banco Ambrosiano, with several references to something called Opus Deus. I scanned all the papers and the photo into our system then left it all with the key and other stuff back in the briefcase and returned it to the *armadio*."

"Opus Deus?" Dominic said, surprised at hearing the name. "That's not a group one hears about very often."

"What is Opus Deus, Michael?" Marco asked.

Dominic set down his fork and took a sip of the wine.

"It's an ultra-right personal prelature of the Church, begun in 1926 by Father Escobar, a Spanish priest who has since been canonized Saint Juancarlos. Having no geographic territorial boundaries, a personal prelature simply serves people with a common goal wherever they happen to be around the world. Opus Deus is the only such prelature of its kind.

"What little I know about it is not enough for me to comment on, to be honest. I'm just surprised by a briefcase being found inside an *armadio* where only documents are usually stored. I wonder how it got there?

"Ian, let's take a look at it tomorrow. I'm curious now."

"And that's how it always starts, Ian," Hana chided, "when Michael gets curious. You've been warned!"

CHAPTER
EIGHT

Entering the Miscellanea section of the Secret Archives the next morning, Duffy walked over to the *armadio*, opened the great wooden door, removed the wooden box of other materials in front, and reached back to withdraw the briefcase he'd found a few days earlier.

"See?" he said to Dominic, removing the briefcase. "Not knowing if this was something typical of your inventory here, I didn't think much of it, other than it's not really what I expected to find."

"I'm afraid I have to agree with you, Ian. I'd never explored this *armadio* myself, but I do find this a strange thing to be here. I wonder who put it here. It had to be one of the *scrittori* before me, since no one else is permitted access."

Moving to a reading table they both sat down. Dominic turned on the table lamp, opened the case and withdrew the documents and other items, laying them out on the table. He began reading the material while Duffy inspected the passport more closely.

"This passport is for someone named Gian Roberto Calvini. But there's a similar name, Roberto Calvi, I found in those documents I scanned, the ones you're reading now. Do you suppose they're the same person? If so, I wonder why he had a passport under a different name."

"This all happened a few years before I was born, but it all looks intriguing," Dominic noted. "I do recall some scandal the Vatican Bank had with Banco Ambrosiano but paid little attention to it since it was before my time.

Across the aisle from where Dominic and Duffy were sitting, Father Pasquale Laguardia, one of the oldest *scrittori* in the Archives, was passing through the area with two other colleagues going about their normal cataloging business, each of them carrying several bundles of documents.

Seeing the briefcase sitting on the table in front of his boss, he was startled, for he had long forgotten he had placed it there four decades earlier. Should he confess the action to his superior, or not say anything? Laguardia was a good priest, with strong faith and ethical integrity. He would do the right thing.

"Father Dominic? I see you've found the briefcase. If it may be helpful, I can tell you more about it, for I put it in the *armadio* myself in 1982."

Dominic looked up, taken aback by the admission of one of his longtime *scrittori*.

"You *know* about this, Pasquale? Then yes, please do tell us more. Ian just discovered it, and we're more than perplexed by its presence here."

Laguardia took a seat next to them.

"I imagine you have already determined that it once belonged to Roberto Calvi of Banco Ambrosiano. It was at the time of his death, when I was a member of Opus Deus's Priestly Society of the Holy Spirit. I have long since broken off with the order, for reasons that don't really matter now, but I was instructed by my superiors then to look for his briefcase, which purportedly contained documents of an incriminating nature to Opus Deus and others.

"I did find the briefcase in Calvi's apartment in London, but I did not want any involvement with its contents, which I happened to look at. I was afraid of being an accomplice, or worse, that knowing what I now knew might bring harm to me. So I feigned ignorance when asked if I had found the object of their search, secretly brought it back to Rome, and hid it here in an *armadio*, where no one from Opus Deus would likely find it. And up to just now, I'd forgotten all about it."

"Well, that's quite the story, Pasquale," Dominic said, clearly relieved he now knew its provenance. "Thank you, I appreciate your candor. Now it's just a matter of understanding its contents."

"That, I'm afraid, is something which I cannot help you with," Laguardia said, still clearly fearful. "May I return to my work now, Father?"

"Sure, Pasquale, and thanks again."

"Now what?" Duffy asked. "Who might be able to help us understand the history of this, and what it contains?"

"I do know someone who might know more about

this," Dominic said. "A visiting scholar to the Archives and one of the most knowledgeable people I know, Simon Ginzberg. Maybe he can enlighten us."

Of the thousand or so requests to visit the Vatican Apostolic Archive received each year, only a select handful are officially accepted, and each of those must be approved by the pope himself after meeting rigorous guidelines and qualifications.

Dr. Simon Ginzberg—professor emeritus at nearby Teller University and a Holocaust survivor from when he was a small child—held the rare privilege of being a scholar-in-residence at the Archive. For years his work had relied heavily on intimate access to the historical records, and he was well known by the Archive's staff as a brilliant scholar, respectful of the materials provided for his review, and found in the Pio Reading Room most every day.

As Dominic and Duffy approached him with the briefcase the old man looked up, and a wide smile broke his focused concentration.

"Father Michael! What a pleasure it is to see you again. Please, do join me." He gestured at the seats opposite him. "And who is this you bring with you?"

"Simon, meet Ian Duffy, my new assistant *scrittore*. Ian, this is Dr. Simon Ginzberg." The two men shook hands. "Ian is a genius in computer programming, having worked for Apple. He'll be helping me catalogue the Vatican's profusion of documents here."

"Well, you are in for a grand journey, Ian," Ginzberg

said. "To stand amidst all the history in this building is to join hands with some of the greatest thinkers and writers through the ages. You will never tire of your job, especially if you are curious by nature."

"That I am, Dr. Ginzberg. Curious, that is."

"Please, call me Simon. How is it I might help you young men? Or are you just stopping by to say hello?"

"Actually, Simon, we have a bit of a mystery here," Dominic said, hoisting the briefcase onto the table. "Ian found this in the stacks here, and the papers inside refer to the Vatican Bank, Banco Ambrosiano and Opus Deus. May I show you?"

"Of course, you have my attention, especially with the mention of Opus Deus. And I well remember the scandal. Very bad business, that. The Vatican paid dearly to extricate itself from rather suspicious activity, not to mention the outright fraud and money laundering that took place. Let's do take a look."

As Ginzberg looked over the documents, Dominic and Duffy remained silent, giving the man time to read. After ten minutes it was clear the materials had absorbed his interest. His eyebrows shot up at various points, his head shaking at others. He emitted the occasional sigh, and his eyes narrowed in what appeared to Dominic to be a look of disbelief, even exasperation. The anticipation was unnerving, but Dominic knew better than to interrupt Simon's thought process.

"Well ..." he said with dread in his voice. Taking off his thick bifocal glasses, he rubbed his eyes. "You've got quite the provocative package here, Michael. This will not be good news to anyone, especially those in power at Opus Deus."

"Why don't we start with Opus Deus, Simon?" Dominic urged. "I don't really know that much about them, and let's assume Ian here knows nothing. What can you tell us?"

The old man sat in uneasy contemplation, twisting his glasses back and forth as he considered how to respond.

"At its roots, Opus Deus is a particularly devout order of the Catholic Church—some might even say a cult— originally established to promote sanctity among people in all sectors of society worldwide. A worthy goal, to be sure. But, as it grew—and it grew very fast, given a virtually unlimited flow of donations and properties onto its balance sheet—it became something more. Since they have come to control an international network of banks and financial institutions, with holdings said to be in several billions of dollars, many believe their goals are to gain control of Vatican finances and policies."

Ginzberg got up to walk around the otherwise empty reading room as he quietly spoke.

"There are several levels of membership in Opus Deus," he continued. "Roughly 70 percent of members, called supernumeraries, compose an elite group who are permitted to live ordinary lives, but tithe a good portion of their income to the order. Then there's an inner circle of members, about 20 percent, known as numeraries, whose lives are more or less strictly controlled by Opus. These people swear vows of chastity and poverty and usually live in monastic quarters while still operating in the secular world. Many, however, hold powerful, often high-profile positions in world politics, governments and corporations. Numeraries are allowed to keep money they earn *only* for living expenses; the rest, often as much as 75 percent of their total annual income, goes to Opus Deus.

"Then there's the clergy, roughly two percent of the membership, who belong to the Order of the Priestly Society of the Holy Spirit, an association of Catholic diocesan priests which is intrinsically united to the Prelature of Opus Deus. In fact, many of the cardinals and high-ranking bishops here in the Vatican are members, and they wield a great deal of power in policy-making and papal influence."

"I had no idea Opus was that prolific and well organized," Dominic said. "Can members of the order be trusted? I mean, like, what are their goals?"

"Well, it's not for me to speak to their trustworthiness, Michael. I would, however, be cautious in your dealings with certain members of the order—but the fact is, you may never know who they are, since their identities are usually kept secret. But their goals can be somewhat aggressive and overzealous. Besides the clergy, the numeraries are the true believers, and as you may have heard, many of them submit themselves to ritual corporal mortification: self-flagellation with short whips called disciplines, and the wearing of a barbed cilice around their thigh—both to remind them of Christ's suffering. These are medieval enactments, to be sure, and practitioners are certainly not among the majority.

"Oh, and somewhat oddly, Opus Deus are also known to be masters of technology, with substantial competence in state-of-the-art computing, and servers installed in its offices around the world running their vast business. They might give even you a run for your money in hacking skills, Ian."

Not lacking confidence, Duffy raised his eyebrows, pursed his lips, and rolled his eyes, flippantly implying *Right ... just try me.*

Ginzberg looked down again at the papers from the briefcase lying before him on the table, his thick, wire-rimmed glasses perched on his nose. He continued discussing the Banco Ambrosiano scandal and the people involved at the time, but finally returned to the materials in question.

"I must admit, the documents you have here are, how shall I put it ... provocative to say the least. But there are others here which are truly incendiary. Roberto Calvi was involved in a great many conspiracies, money laundering, and other illicit financial transactions in the hundreds of millions of dollars involving many institutions. Some say he was even intending to blackmail the Vatican. And a great light still shines upon him, even forty years after his gruesome death.

"Opus will not be pleased these have been discovered, Michael. Be very careful what you do with them. And," the old man looked solemnly at both Duffy and Dominic, "do not tell anyone else you are in possession of them."

"Don't worry, Simon," Dominic said. "We're not in the habit of disclosing Archive materials to anyone outside a small, trusted circle."

Suddenly, Duffy reddened in embarrassment, his eyes reflecting dismay.

"Are you alright, Ian?" Dominic asked, placing an assuring hand on his assistant's shoulder. "You look like you could use some air."

"No, I ... I'm fine, really," Duffy said unconvincingly. "I'm, uh, just surprised at everything Simon told us. Who would have thought my first task would have such a disturbing history attached to it?"

CHAPTER
NINE

Having just been paroled from Rome's Regina Coeli prison, Julio Guzman was enjoying his first hours as a free man. He was ready to rejoin his brothers as a supernumerary in Opus Deus, having been an elite member going on ten years now.

Guzman had been sentenced to a three-year term for creating hundreds of zombie computers by way of giant botnets—internet-connected devices infected by malware that permits hackers to control them—which he then sold to the highest bidders, who in turn used them for ransomable Denial of Service, or DoS, attacks around the world.

Just one of the many threats technology can pose in the wrong hands, DoS attacks are meant to disable one computer, or even an entire network, making them inaccessible to their users by flooding the target with traffic, or sending it information that triggers an often unrecoverable crash.

Suffice to say, Guzman was one of Opus Deus's chief architects of chaos. And he was very good at his job.

"I can't tell you how happy I am to see you again, Julio," Bishop Silva said, gesturing for Guzman to take a seat opposite the desk in his Villa Tiber office. "How are you getting on? Is there anything we can do to help you situate yourself?"

Guzman's six-foot frame resettled itself in the chair as the man considered the bishop's offer. He ran his hands over his weathered face, the heavy bags under his hazel eyes testament to the torturous boredom, brutal treatment and awful food at Rome's most infamous prison. His fingers lingered over his salt-and-pepper mustache thoughtfully as he considered what to ask for.

"A place to sleep would be a good start, Your Excellency," he said, his voice deep and raspy. At fifty, the Spaniard looked to be a much older man. But his mind was sharp as ever, and despite the conditions of his parole barring him from using computers again, he had no intention of obeying the terms of his release.

"You will, of course, stay here, Julio, for as long as you wish," Silva said with determination. "Normally our rooms are reserved only for numeraries, but your unique skillset and obvious devotion to the order compel me to make certain accommodations to you as a supernumerary. We would be pleased to have you stay here.

"And as for employment, it goes without saying those

skills can be put to excellent use here. As an extension of Vatican City, our extraterritorial status will protect you from the odious terms of your parole. No one can touch you here, you have my word."

"I am most grateful, Excellency, and appreciate your many generosities. I am anxious to get back to work however it may please God."

"Yes, I understand. But before I assign you back to our networking center, I do have a specific request. Cardinal Wolsey and I are entertaining the thought of inviting a particular cleric in the Vatican to join our ranks in the Priestly Society of the Holy Spirit. But we need to know more about this man, what his values are, his position on Opus Deus, and if he has any skeletons in the closet. In fact, we're hoping he does have a skeleton or two. I won't go into details on that just yet, but as you were once with Interpol, I'm sure you still have connections that might prove useful in that regard.

"This man is the Prefect of the Vatican Apostolic Archive. His name is Father Michael Dominic. Can you indulge us in this matter, Julio? Whatever resources we have are at your disposal."

Guzman looked thoughtful, as if recalling something familiar.

"You say this priest's name is Dominic? I wonder if it's the same one a fellow prisoner at Regina Coeli mentioned."

"Who was this prisoner, may I ask?"

"His name is Fabrizio Dante, Excellency," Guzman said. "He was a prominent cardinal at the Vatican before he was incarcerated. In fact, he was once Secretary of

State, then Archbishop of Buenos Aires, until—if I recall our conversation correctly—this Father Dominic and his associates had him imprisoned about two years ago. I rarely forget such things. I am certain it is the same priest."

"Then perhaps you can start with Cardinal Dante. Visit him. See what more he can tell you. To be candid, we are looking for some type of leverage, for Father Dominic has access to something of vital importance to us. Something we absolutely must have control of."

"I will take on this mission at once, Excellency. In the meantime, could someone show me to my room? I am in need of a hot shower, fresh clothing and a good meal. And if I may, I would like to visit Santa Marta della Figli and pray for a while."

"All of these will be provided, dear Julio. See Brother Sanchez at reception. He will get you settled in and arrange for all your needs. And our church is open for you day and night, whenever you wish to commune with Our Lord."

Originally a convent for Carmelite nuns built in 1654, Regina Coeli, or "Queen of Heaven" prison, is as far away from paradise as one can get.

As with all correctional facilities in Italy, chronic overcrowding is a common problem. Regina Coeli's capacity for 700 inmates now barely accommodated over a thousand men and women in separate buildings, with three inmates assigned to each cell in triple-stacked steel bunkbeds.

Prisoner 45789, one Fabrizio Xavier Dante, had as his cellmates two other former priests. Referred to by fellow prisoners as *i tre santi uomini*—the three holy men—Dante and his cellies attended services regularly, often officiating at Masses, and were generally regarded as untouchable by other inmates. Dante himself was a model prisoner, a trustee with special privileges, and if he was lucky, he would be up for parole consideration in a matter of months.

In the meantime, former Cardinal Dante spent his days as the prison librarian. Of higher intellect than the majority of his jailed companions, Dante was the man to know for recommending books and other suitable reading material approved by the warden.

Imprisoned by a Vatican Supreme Tribunal nearly two years earlier for conspiracy to commit murder, among other crimes, Dante was sentenced to five years of hard labor. But given his privileged status, a spotless record of good behavior, and the obviously growing problem of overcrowding, his chances for early parole candidacy were better than fifty-fifty.

And that is what he prayed for most when he attended Mass, for there were debts to be repaid, revenge to be exacted on his accusers and enactors—especially two men in particular for whom Dante had cultivated a seething hatred.

Father Michael Dominic, and Cardinal Enrico Petrini.

CHAPTER

TEN

The Tiepolo Lounge and Terrace at the Rome Cavalieri was a handsome, well-appointed room featuring tasteful Venetian art and sculptures, Renaissance oil paintings, and curved wood-paneled ceilings suspended over a dark wood-paneled floor. A polished ebony Petrof grand piano was the centerpiece of the room, at which sat the Tiepolo's star pianist playing classical jazz tunes while Hana and Dominic nursed their drinks and caught up.

"So, how are you and Marco getting along?" Dominic asked, a noticeably reticent tone in his voice.

"Well," Hana said with comparable restraint, the feelings between them still strong, while unrequited. "We've done a bit of travel lately—Barcelona, Madrid, Lisbon, and of course, Geneva, to see Grand-père. We're not living together, by the way. Each of us has our own life." She laughed nervously. "I'm not sure why I said that, it's just—"

"I understand," Dominic said quickly, smiling genuinely to reassure his friend.

Hana shifted uneasily in her seat. "My work is going well. I'm actually meeting up here with a reporter friend at *Corriere della Sera* to exchange research on the EU's immigration policies for a piece I'm doing. Not exactly the most exciting journalism, but as it's so prevalent in the news these days, there are aspects of policy that haven't been explored yet. How about you, Michael? How's life in the Vatican?"

"Well, it's great having Ian here now. He's a bright guy, and I've got great plans for him. He's a keen computer whiz, and he'll be developing a new database for the Archives, which we desperately need. Few things give me more pleasure than introducing someone of his interest and intellect to the treasures in the Vatican."

"Clearly he was excited to have found that old briefcase," Hana said. "Learned anything more about it yet?"

"Actually, he showed it to me, then we met with Simon Ginzberg yesterday and he explained a lot to us about Opus Deus, as well as the Vatican Bank scandal of the '80s. It's really just old history, nothing important."

Dominic related to Hana much of what Ian and he had learned from Ginzberg, including the unusual corporal mortification practiced by certain numerary members of Opus Deus.

"I've only heard rumors about that," she said, "but wondered if it was actually true. Curious. So, from what I recall from earlier research, the Vatican Bank scandal with Banco Ambrosiano had lasting effects on the Church's financial stability. It's probably still smarting from the affair, since things move so slowly there. But Opus Deus's involvement? That's news to me."

"It wasn't to Simon. His whole demeanor darkened when he spoke about it. He had actually met Archbishop Paul Marcinkus, then-president of the Vatican Bank, on several occasions, and said he felt there was something terribly immoral about the man. He recalled that news reports at the time were particularly harsh on Marcinkus, Roberto Calvi, the chairman of Banco Ambrosiano, and some mysterious figure named Michele Sindona, a leading member of P2, a secret Masonic organization with deep links to the Sicilian Mafia. The papers in the briefcase dealt with all these individuals. I didn't read them all myself, the briefcase was packed with them. But I expect, as Simon does, that they may hold some kind of information that is damaging to certain parties. Whether that's relevant or not today is anyone's guess.

"Simon did caution me to keep this confidential, but you know anything we talk about stays between us anyway, right?"

"Of course," Hana said, nodding her head. "So, what happened to the briefcase?"

"I told Ian to just return it to the *armadio* for now. There are too many other things needing our attention."

There was a moment of silence as each considered what Dominic had just laid out.

"Say, are you hungry?" Hana asked. "I don't want a full meal. Let's just order a couple of small plates from the bar."

"Sure, I could nibble on appetizers here all night long."

~

Though it was a cool spring evening, the fireplace in Bishop Silva's Villa Tiber office was ablaze with eucalyptus logs, releasing aromatic scents across the large room. Silva had a glass of Rètico in hand, as did his guest, while both sat around the fire talking.

"Alastair, I've asked Julio to do a background check on Dominic, so we should know soon if he has anything worth bargaining for. I still think trying to gain his trust as part of the Priestly Society might help contain him."

"Well, if that doesn't motivate him, we must consider alternatives," Cardinal Wolsey said. "Let's see what Julio finds first. That will guide our direction."

ELEVEN

Surrounded by tall stands of oak and cypress trees concealing their notorious inhabitants, the once-sacred buildings of Regina Coeli prison have sat for hundreds of years in the Rione district of Rome's Trastevere neighborhood—first as a convent in 1654, then as a prison since 1881.

In their attempts to hold the Italian government accountable for gross mismanagement of the overcrowded facility, human rights groups performed routine inspections, finding rampant cases of scabies, hepatitis C, and various STDs among the prison population; filthy, moldy open toilets situated next to small kitchen stoves in each cell, where inmates often cooked their own meals; and since there was virtually no air circulation, the stench of human waste was prevalent in the air throughout the inmates' housing structures.

The deplorable sanitary conditions of modern day were

actually a carryover from the prison's original design, conditions under which nuns were expected to live without complaint. It reminded some of the story of Galileo Galilei's daughter, Virginia, whom the famed astronomer had consigned to San Matteo Convent in Florence when he was unable to marry her off, and the convent received the dowry Galileo would have been expected to pay a husband. So even a high-born woman who could have expected to take her place in society was consigned to a life of pious submission in the confines of just such an odious setting as Regina Coeli.

As he watched a brutal game of table football being played in the tiny common room of his own wing, Fabrizio Dante yawned out of boredom, empathizing with the fate of Virginia Galilei. His loathing of his current station in life, so distant from his once regal standing as a prince of the Church, was only surpassed by his feelings for those who had put him there. But dealing with that would wait.

The PA system in his wing erupted with a scratchy announcement that Prisoner 45789 was to proceed immediately to the reception cells. Dante had a visitor.

Padding his way to reception in shoddy, white cotton slippers and the standard inmates' blue coverall, the former cardinal went through three locked and barred doors, waiting for each to be opened manually by its gatekeeper before he could pass through.

Arriving in the reception cells, he took a seat in one of the visitors' booths. Sitting across from him on the opposite side of a thick glass partition was his old prison mate Julio Guzman. Dante picked up the grimy black phone receiver from the wall to his left. Guzman followed suit.

"Tell me, Julio. What is it like now being outside looking in?"

"It was all I could do to force myself to come back here today, Fabrizio. But I am here on a mission. I actually found a job pretty quickly. Or rather, it found me. You may recall I am a supernumerary with Opus Deus?"

"Yes, I remember."

"Bishop Silva, the Prelate at Villa Tiber, assigned me to ... well, I should not mention specifics here, for obvious reasons. But I am being well taken care of there. They gave me fine accommodations, and apart from my primary assignment, I've been asked to speak with you regarding a certain priest in the Vatican: a Father Michael Dominic."

On hearing the name, Dante's face twisted into a stern mask of indignation, his pursed lips a thin line of anger. He closed his eyes for a few moments, and when he opened them, Guzman shuddered a little at what he saw in them.

"I ... I did not wish to upset you, Eminence," Guzman pleaded, referring to Dante's former honorific as a cardinal. "But it seems you do have some experience with this man. What can you tell me that might be ... well, useful to Bishop Silva's and Cardinal Wolsey's interests?"

"And what might those interests be, Julio?"

Guzman paused to consider his response, given that inmate-visitor phones were monitored.

"Apparently Father Dominic has something of utmost interest to Opus, and His Excellency wishes to have some sort of leverage ... something to induce Dominic to cooperate in handing over this ... object. As you knew him well, or so I am told, the bishop thought perhaps you might assist us."

After a moment's thought, a sneering smile crossed Dante's face, and his eyes darkened in half-lidded cruelness.

"As a matter of fact," he said, "I do have something that would serve your purposes quite effectively. But I am compelled to ask: what's in it for me? Can Silva, or even Wolsey, get me out of this hellhole? I imagine it would be a fair exchange. What I could tell you about Dominic would also rattle the highest levels of power at the Vatican." Dante leaned in closer to the glass and lowered his voice. "Have Opus use its vast influence to free me and I'll tell you exactly what you want to know. And trust me, it will be most rewarding.

"But I have one more condition. I want to be enrolled again in the clerical state, since I am still a priest under canon law. That will take the pope's personal rescript, of course, but Opus should be able to persuade His Holiness that I still have value to the Church. Make these two things happen, and I will hand over something beyond their wildest imaginations."

Guzman had expected some form of quid pro quo from Dante, but what he was asking might be impossible, even for Opus Deus.

"I will do my best on your behalf, Eminence. Please be patient as they consider your terms."

"Where else have I to go, Julio? You know where to find me."

Dante hung up the phone and padded back up to his fourth-floor cell.

"His demands are understandable," Cardinal Wolsey replied to Julio Guzman as Bishop Silva sat listening in, "but there may be complications acceding to them. I do expect we have the resources to free him. The warden is one of our supernumeraries, as is the head of the parole board. And Dante is close enough to early release anyway, especially given the overcrowding fiasco under which the state is suffering.

"But this other matter—his being reinstated in the clerical state—that, I doubt we can accommodate. Julio, did you get the feeling the information he has is of sufficient value to us?"

"Oh, yes, Eminence," Guzman said confidently. "He was quite convincing in his having knowledge of something profound on Dominic that, in his words, would 'rattle the highest levels of power at the Vatican.' I don't for a minute doubt him. The question is, is that the outcome you expect? If whatever he has is shocking enough that it could upset your current structure in play, is it worth the risk?"

Wolsey steepled his fingers under his chin as he sat in contemplation of Guzman's wisdom.

"You bring up a good point, Julio. The uncertainty of what *levels* of power he refers to is concerning. But, in the end, *we* would decide what to do with the information, whatever the risk.

"I propose we first try to induct Dominic into the Order of the Priestly Society. If that doesn't work, then we can consider Dante's more convincing proposition."

"And how do we approach Dominic with this offer? Won't he be suspicious in our attempts to get him to whistle?" Silva added, using the code word for recruiting candidates into the order.

"That, my dear Guillermo, is where your formidable gifts of persuasion come in. Make it so attractive he couldn't consider turning it down."

CHAPTER

TWELVE

A small army of aviation technicians surrounded Shepherd Two, preparing the white helicopter for the pope's brief flight to Castel Gandolfo, the papal summer residence on Lake Albano where the pontiff often held meetings away from his daily chaotic demands in the Vatican.

Armand de Saint-Clair and a few other members of the pope's Consulta were waiting in Saint John's Tower, adjacent to the papal helipad along the Leonine Wall surrounding the French-style gardens. In addition to special papal apartments used by guests of the pope, the circular 13th-century tower housed the offices of the Secretariat for the Economy.

"Will you be joining us, Alastair?" Saint-Clair asked Cardinal Wolsey as the two sat in the latter's office drinking coffee.

"Of course, Armand. As Secretary for the Economy,

any plans involving the Vatican Bank fall under my purview. I'm curious, though. Have you any idea what His Holiness wants to discuss?"

"I would have thought you'd know better than I!" Saint-Clair said, somewhat surprised. "But from what little I've gleaned, he's considering initiating a major overhaul in how international investments by the IOR are managed. Having discovered that some of the bank's mutual funds go toward munitions manufacturing and other irreligious enterprises, I'm not surprised the Holy Father has taken the matter on himself. But I imagine we will know more soon enough."

Wolsey nodded pleasantly, hiding his surprise. *How is it that Saint-Clair knows more about the Holy Father's fiscal agenda than I do? This is* my *domain!* he fumed.

A young priest knocked on the open office door.

"Excuse me, Your Eminence, but His Holiness is arriving now and Shepherd Two is prepared for liftoff. If you will both follow me ..."

The two men got up and accompanied the aide to the helipad, where the pope had just stepped out of a white golf cart while chatting with Cardinal Petrini before both boarded the helicopter. The other members of the Consulta followed him inside the craft, and a few minutes later the rotors of the AgustaWestland AW139 began spinning: slowly at first, then, once they had reached 500 rpm, the bird lifted off the pad and headed southeast toward the Alban Hills and Castel Gandolfo, some 25 kilometers distant.

~

Just south of the helipad lay the broad green grounds of the Campo Pio XI football stadium and sports complex, situated a few hundred yards from Vatican City and where the Vatican National Football Team practices and tourneys against other local soccer teams.

Hana and Marco sat in the bleachers on the bright, sunny day, watching her cousin Karl Dengler and his partner, Lukas Bischoff, train for their upcoming game with Monaco.

Hearing the blade-slapping whir of an approaching helicopter, both craned their necks skyward, shielding their eyes from the sun as Shepherd Two passed low overhead. On the field, Karl and Lukas also looked up from their positions on the pitch and saluted the pope as he flew over and waved to the players below from his window on the port side. The Holy Father was an avid fan of the game, stopping by to watch his home team train from time to time and even attending competitive tournaments when his schedule permitted.

Like his idol, the Portuguese legend Ronaldo, Karl was a striker, beloved by the team for his ability to peel off defenders to create space on the blind side of a line and receive the ball in solid goal-scoring position. Lukas was a sweeper, or defensive midfielder, whose job it was to mark free players or balls during an opponent's attack, halting any breakaways by the opponent, including any long passes towards the goal.

Their fellow Swiss Guards, Dieter Koehl and Finn Bachman, also were on the team, both midfielders, and as the late afternoon training had just ended, the six decided to catch up over beers along with Marco and Hana at Bar Gastronomia, a short walk from the stadium.

"Our game with Monaco is coming up soon, and we're hardly ready for them," Dieter said dejectedly, taking a long draw from his frosty beer.

"If they gave us more time to train," Karl added, "maybe we'd be winning more. As it is, getting out on the pitch two or three times a month hardly gives us enough practice."

Since, by its eligibility rules, the Vatican team was comprised only of Swiss Guards and Vatican Museum guards, the fact that both groups were consumed with their daily duties protecting their respective domains left little time for training. As a result, they did not win many games, causing a general gloom over the team whose passions for the sport were as strong as the pope's. But even he couldn't change the rules, nor give them more time to play.

"Don't feel too badly, boys," Hana said consolingly. "All of you are strong players, and you have the home-field advantage over Monaco. The stadium will be packed with fans supporting you. And hopefully the pope will attend, which could add a little intimidation to the Monégasques. Plus, you have God on your side!"

"Well, He must not have been watching our last game with San Marino," Lukas grumbled.

"If the rules weren't so rigid, I'd love to play with you guys," Marco enthused. "I've ripped a few to the back of the net in my day."

Karl looked at his friend and grinned. "You'd be a

great Swiss Guard, too, Marco—if you weren't so old..."
Marco laughed.

Then turning to Hana, Karl asked, "So, what brings
you to Rome this time, cousin?"

"Grand-père is with the pope at Castel Gandolfo, and
I'm meeting with a colleague at *Corriere della Sera* for a
piece we're working on together. And while we're here,
Marco is looking up an old friend he served with in
Afghanistan, some guy named Rusty." She glanced at
Marco admiringly.

Dieter appeared thoughtful for a moment, then
looked up at Marco.

"That's an uncommon name. By any chance, that
wouldn't be Rusty Brinkman, would it?" Dieter asked,
looking at the Frenchman expectantly.

Marco was shocked. "Yes! It *is* Rusty Brinkman! You
know him?"

"I do! We both practice at the same shooting range,
Tiro a Segno Nazionale, or TSN Roma. What a small
world! Rusty's a great guy. I'm a trained sniper, and even
I've learned a lot from him. So you were in Afghanistan,
too, eh? I was there for Operation Enduring Freedom in
2013."

"Yes, we were there during OEF as well, but our last
tour was in 2011. It really is a small world. Maybe the
three of us can have a beer later?"

"You bet," Dieter said. "You could also join us at the
range, if you're up for some practice."

"I'm always up for shooting. I rarely get the chance
these days. You're on."

"Well, in the meantime," Hana interrupted, getting up, "we should get going. We're having dinner with Claudia, that colleague I mentioned. See you boys later."

THIRTEEN

The next morning, Milo Banducci figured he only had one chance to try his plan. If it worked, great. Fulfilling such a task for the bishop would put him in good standing with Opus Deus, which could have future benefits.

At his desk in the Vatican Bank, Banducci picked up the telephone and dialed the operator.

"*Pronto, Vaticano,*" one of the sisters answered.

"Yes, could you connect me with Ian Duffy in the Apostolic Archive, please? I don't have his direct number."

"*Si, signore*, hold please." The nun made the connection, and the phone on Duffy's desk began to ring.

As he was scanning documents at the other end of the large office, Duffy ran through the maze of furniture to his own desk, picking up on the fourth ring.

"*Pronto*, Ian Duffy," he answered hastily.

"Hi, Ian, it's Milo."

"Hey, Milo. What's up?"

"Are you free for coffee in the next hour or two? There's something I'd like to discuss."

"Sure. I have a break coming up in about thirty minutes. Does that work?"

"It does. Let's meet at Pergamino."

"Alright. See you there."

Caffè Pergamino is a popular coffee house just a long block north of Saint Anne's Gate, the Vatican's main entrance for employees, vendors and visitors. Managed by Signora Palazzolo, an ample woman with wisps of white hair and a ready smile for every customer, the café's outside patio tables drew Vatican employees who preferred a bit of fresh air and sunshine to the rattle and clatter of the Vatican's busy canteen.

Banducci had already arrived, sitting nervously at one of the sidewalk tables with sunglasses perched on his nose while drinking a can of *Toro Rosso*, Italy's Red Bull.

He watched as Ian Duffy, dwarfed by the towering stone Vatican walls, approached the café from the southern gate. As usual, traffic was heavy and chaotic, but Duffy managed to cross the broad Viale dei Bastioni di Michelangelo without incident.

Pulling up a chair, Duffy sat down and ordered an Italian soda from the passing waiter.

"So, what's on your mind, Milo?"

"I happened to be chatting with the bank's historian the other day and I mentioned that briefcase you found. She was quite interested in it, and asked if it would be alright if we were to take a look at it for a couple days. You know, just to add to the bank's historical record. I told her I'd speak with you. Think you can manage that, Ian?"

Duffy was suddenly embarrassed, mainly by the fact that he'd said anything about it to Banducci in the first place, but now by having to turn down his colleague's request. The very man who had gotten him this job.

"To be honest, Milo, I'm afraid that won't be possible. I discovered afterward that I shouldn't even have mentioned it to you—or anyone else, frankly. There are strict rules in place, and Father Dominic takes these things pretty seriously. I'm really sorry, but nothing can leave the Archives, nor can I make copies for you of whatever's in that briefcase." Duffy drank from his soda as he waited for Milo's response.

"But surely this isn't something like handing over Galileo's trial records! It's just an old briefcase, and not even that old," Banducci said indignantly, unaccustomed to not getting his way.

"Well, I'll ask Father Dominic and explain about your historian's interest, if you'd like. Maybe he'll change his mind."

Banducci was now in a fix. The Vatican Bank didn't *have* a historian, and Dominic was likely to know that. Or quickly figure that out. His ruse wasn't working, and could take a bad turn.

"That's okay, Ian, never mind. I'll explain the rules to her, and I'm sure she'll understand. And who knows, there may already be internal ways of handling these things. I just told her I'd ask ... no big deal." He looked at his watch.

"Sorry for cutting this short, but I do need to get back.

The pope and his Consulta are meeting now about bank cutbacks, and I've got to get some information to them before day's end. It was great seeing you again, though. And I'll get this."

Banducci reached for his wallet and left a ten-euro note on the table.

"See you later." The young banker abruptly walked away from the table, then, looking both ways, gauged his run across the wide boulevard back toward Saint Anne's Gate.

What is that guy up to? Duffy wondered, watching Milo dodge speeding cars as he swiftly crossed the street.

The elegant envelope handed to Dominic by the mailroom delivery nun had the gold, embossed seal of Villa Tiber in the upper left corner. His name was flawlessly scripted on the face of the ivory-colored envelope.

Opening it, he withdrew a rich, ivory card featuring the same embossed seal of the Opus Deus headquarters, beneath which was a perfectly calligraphed invitation for Dominic to join Bishop Guillermo Silva for lunch the following day, Saturday. A car would be sent to retrieve him at the appointed hour. Curiously, he noted, there was no opportunity to RSVP, as though his presence was simply expected.

Dominic knew Bishop Silva was a very important personage in the Church hierarchy, not to mention being Prelate of the order. Intrigued by the summons, he decided he would go, if only to satisfy his curiosity. The coincidence of having so recently discussed Opus Deus didn't escape him—and added to his curiosity.

As Marco Picard walked across the Piazza della Madonna in Rome's historic Monti neighborhood, he found himself in a web of seventeenth-century ocher-colored townhouses. Long strands of ancient green ivy dangled from electric cables overhead, creating a surreal curtain between the orange buildings just minutes from the Colosseum.

Walking up the steps of the address he had been seeking, he knocked on its bright red door, raking his hair back with one hand while holding a bottle of Antinori Marchese Chianti Classico in the other.

The door creaked open wide, and Marco was greeted by a stern-faced, six-foot-two tower of muscle. The two men stared at each other impassively for a few moments, then Rusty Brinkman burst out laughing.

"*Marco, you mad dog!* Bring it in here!" Rusty grabbed his friend and folded him into a giant bearhug in the doorway, holding it for a long moment of reunion. "Come on in, amigo. Damn, it's been way too long."

"Nice crib you've got here, Rusty. And what a great neighborhood."

"Yeah, the Monti is totally the place to be, man. Awesome people, great parties, spectacular restaurants, and all the Roman history you'd want within walking distance. We love it here."

"We?! You finally settled down? Or did you just get a dog?"

Rusty laughed again, then blushed. "My single days are over, dude. I found the love of my life here and never looked back. *Cassie?*" he shouted. "Come out here, babe."

A petite and stunningly attractive blonde came out of the kitchen, drying her hands on a towel while offering her guest a warm, welcoming smile.

"Cassandra, meet my old buddy, Marco Picard."

"Rusty has told me so much about you, Marco," she said with a congenial Italian accent. "It's finally good to put a face to the name in all his war stories." She stood up on tiptoes and kissed both his cheeks, then leaned in for a long hug.

"I hope you're hungry," Cassie warned, "I've made a huge pot of bucatini all'Amatriciana."

"I'm starving," Marco replied, holding up the bottle of Chianti. "Let's bust this open, Rusty. I'm thirsty, too."

Rusty examined the bottle as he peeled off the foil cap and inserted the corkscrew. "Ooh, the riserva. This is a truly great wine. We've been to Antinori's vineyard in San Casciano, just south of Florence. Actually, although she's originally from Sicily, my Cassie here was a winery tour guide in Tuscany when we met. I was taking a tour of Super Tuscan vineyards with some friends and one day she happened to be our guide. To this day I still can't remember a word of what she told our group—I just couldn't take my eyes off her! I could tell the feeling was mutual, and, well, the rest is history."

Rusty looked at Cassie with deep affection as she pulled three Riedel Chianti glasses from a cupboard. She noted his gaze, smiled almost mechanically, then took the bottle from him and poured the wine. Despite her affability, Marco noticed some tension in their interaction.

"A toast," she said, lifting her glass. "*Cento di questi giorni*: May you have a hundred of these days."

"*Salute*," Marco said, inhaling the bouquet and taking his first sip.

"So, what brings you to the Eternal City, Marco?" Cassie asked.

"I'm here with my, uh, friend, Hana Sinclair. She's a reporter for *Le Monde* in Paris and has some business here. And since I have nothing pressing going on at the moment, I decided to join her and look up Rusty, here."

"What is it you do, when you do what you do?"

Marco paused, then glanced at Rusty.

"I'm ... well, for lack of a better word, a military contractor. I take on private assignments that various armed forces or law enforcement agencies are unable to deal with for whatever reasons."

"That sounds rather vague," Cassie noted. "Is the word you're looking for 'mercenary'?"

Marco and Rusty laughed. "*Busted!*" Rusty said, raising his glass.

"I suppose you could call it that," Marco admitted with a shy smile. "But my skills are pretty specialized. Really more about personal protection for VIPs."

Sensing his friend was reluctant to discuss it further, Rusty changed the subject.

"Tell us about Hana," he urged. "How and where did you meet?"

"In Argentina, nearly two years ago now. One of my regular clients is a prominent banker in Geneva. When needed, I'm frequently assigned as bodyguard to his granddaughter, Hana. We first met during an especially challenging operation in Bariloche, south of Buenos Aires. We met up again in Venice this past year and events took a turn toward romance. She's really an exceptional woman." Marco felt a warmth to his cheeks as he recalled special moments.

"What a lovely way to meet," Cassie said, the tip of her wine glass resting beneath her chin over folded arms. "Kind of like in a fairy tale."

"Well, trouble does have a way of finding her. It's not all champagne and roses."

They all laughed at the way Marco said it as he rolled his eyes.

"What say we eat now?" Cassie suggested, walking toward the stove. "The pasta is *perfettamente al dente*."

FOURTEEN

F ather Dominic was chatting with Karl Dengler in the guard shack at Saint Anne's Gate when a black Mercedes S550 with dark, tinted windows arrived promptly at a quarter to one.

The driver emerged from the vehicle, walked around to the passenger side and opened the rear door without saying a word. Dominic looked at Karl, raised his eyebrows, and whispered, "See you later. I hope." Karl chuckled at the quip as the priest got into the luxurious back seat of the Mercedes. The driver shut the door, returned to the driver's seat, then backed out of the gate and headed north on Via di Porta Angelica and across the river toward Villa Tiber.

On arrival fifteen minutes later, the driver once again got out to open the door for Dominic, but the priest had already emerged from the car on his own. After a moment's huff, the driver walked up to the black door of the villa's entrance and punched in a code, looking up at the CCTV camera for verification. The lock mechanism buzzed and the driver opened the door, holding it for Dominic to enter.

Waiting inside the reception foyer was a young priest. "Good afternoon, Father Dominic, and welcome to Villa Tiber. Please, follow me."

Dominic trailed the younger man up the wide, red-carpeted staircase whose high walls were lined with paintings of clergy, apparently from earlier years. The higher they got on the stairs, the older the paintings seemed to be. Dominic felt it a safe assumption that they were of some prominence to Opus Deus over time. At the very top and center of the mezzanine hung a large painting of Father Juancarlos Escobar, with fresh flower arrangements and flaming candles on either side of what was clearly a shrine to the founder.

Moving upward to the second floor, Dominic's escort led him to a set of two golden doors featuring religious themes carved in bas-relief. Swinging both doors wide open, the young priest gestured for Dominic to enter the grand office of the Prelate.

Standing in the center of the room was Bishop Guillermo Silva, resplendent in a purple cassock with matching waist sash, a purple zucchetto perched atop his balding head, and a golden pectoral cross dangling from his neck. On his right hand was a heavy, gold episcopal ring.

"Father Dominic," Silva said warmly, "welcome to Villa Tiber. It is an honor that you join us today. I rarely receive such distinguished visitors from the Vatican."

Wary of being buttered up, Dominic extended his hand.

"It is an honor meeting you, Excellency. And thank you for the kind invitation."

Silva waved it off. "Oh, think nothing of it. We have had our eye on you for some time now. You are something of a legend here, what with all the adventures we've heard about. Who knew the Secret Archives could hold such danger for a young priest?"

"Danger?" Dominic asked, clearly confused.

"Why, yes. That nasty business with the Venetian Camorra last year? And your run in with those neo-Nazis in Argentina the year before? Not to mention your remarkable discovery of that Magdalene manuscript some time ago ..." Silva let that last bombshell linger.

Dominic was stunned speechless. His jaw fell open but no words came out. *How could he possibly know these things?! Especially about the Magdalene manuscript—no one else* should *know anything about that!*

"I ... I must confess to some surprise, Excellency. My affairs on behalf of Mother Church are normally not so well known—nor publicized as far as I know."

"Never underestimate the power of Vatican gossip, Michael," he said conspiratorially. "There are eyes and ears everywhere."

Still taken aback, Dominic glanced around the large suite. An exquisite desk dominated the space, with various fine examples of small, handblown Murano glass *objets d'art* placed on the desktop. At the opposite end of the room was a sitting area with two plush, purple loveseats facing each other, a Shahrooz glass pedestal coffee table between them, and an imposing Rezzonico blue and crystal Murano chandelier suspended overhead. Clearly, Opus Deus had no budgetary constraints when it came to subsidizing management's tastes.

"Shall we have lunch now?" Silva asked, gesturing for Dominic to take a seat at a small dining table brought in for the meal. A tidy arrangement of white lilies stood in a crystal vase on a white tablecloth, with plates on either side, each covered with a silver cloche. A bottle of Prosecco was nestled in an ice bucket on a tableside stand.

Dominic took a seat as Silva removed both silver domes, revealing fresh garden salads, each topped with half moons of steamed prawns and avocado slices.

"Forgive me, Excellency, but I really must ask. What am I doing here?"

Silva smiled, expecting the question. He sat down and, after saying grace, they both began to eat.

"As I said, Michael, we've had our eye on you for some time. Regardless of what you may have heard about Opus Deus, our prelature is but a humble order of devout Catholics who help people seek holiness in their work and daily activities. To do this we employ only the finest people we can find, and though many approach us for the honor of membership, we are highly selective as to whom we permit to join.

"Your name, in fact, was brought to me for consideration by Cardinal Wolsey, Secretary for the Economy, who has the highest regard for your intellectual capacity and stellar performance in your duties with the Apostolic Archive. His Eminence would have preferred to join us today, but he is away with the pope at Castel Gandolfo.

"We would very much like to have you join us as a member of the Order of the Priestly Society of the Holy Spirit, Michael. You've made impressive progress in the Vatican, yes, but you are deserving of so much more than is available to you now. We can offer you unlimited opportunities."

And there it is, Dominic thought.

"I'm really not much of a joiner, Excellency. I actually prefer my quiet little world in the Archives and all that job entails. I'm afraid I wouldn't have much time for anything else."

Not to be so easily dissuaded, Silva pushed on.

"Well, of course you would still remain Prefect of the Vatican Archive. As a member of the Priestly Society we would impose no further commitments on your time, apart from the occasional meeting with others of like mind and aptitude. Don't rule out anything today. Please, pray on it in the meantime. God will guide you in the proper direction, of that I have no doubt."

As he continued spearing chunks of his salad, one thought kept tumbling through Dominic's mind.

They want something from me. But what?

FIFTEEN

Having returned early from the meeting at Castel Gandolfo, Cardinal Enrico Petrini reflected on what Michael Dominic had just told him about his lunch with Bishop Silva. He was perplexed and not a little concerned.

"Despite my own opinions on Opus Deus, Michael, I find it curious they hand-picked you for the Priestly Society. Not that you're not worthy of such a thing, of course, but to my understanding they rarely ever approach anyone individually. There's usually a long list of applicants seeking to join the order, and it's a protracted process, often taking months before someone is admitted. Not only is my curiosity piqued, but I'm sensing red flags as well."

"I agree, but I just don't get it. There must be some particular reason they singled me out; I can't put my finger on it."

Dominic sat in the cardinal's office looking out the window when a thought came to him.

"I wonder if it has anything to do with that briefcase?" he muttered to himself.

"Briefcase? What briefcase?"

"Oh ... well, Ian Duffy, my assistant, found an old briefcase in one of the *armadi*. It was filled with papers from the 1980s relating to the Vatican Bank and a company called Banco Ambrosiano. There were also a passport and a key in it. But nobody else knows we even have it ... unless Ian mentioned it to someone. But he knows the rules. At least I think he does. I'd better ask him."

"Who did the briefcase belong to?"

"Someone named Roberto Calvi. I discussed it with Dr. Ginzberg, who gave Ian and me some background on Calvi and Opus Deus's probable interest in the contents of the briefcase. I've been meaning to look into it more, but with the new computerization plans, I've been too busy to think much more about it."

Petrini's concern had just escalated.

"Wait ... You mean to tell me you have a briefcase containing Roberto Calvi's personal papers on the Vatican's biggest banking scandal of the century? And out of the blue you're invited to join Opus Deus?! Obviously they now know you have this briefcase, Michael. And undoubtedly they want it badly enough to get your attention. Ian *must* have told someone. This isn't good. Not at all."

Dominic now understood his mentor's concern, but still had questions.

"What more can you tell me about this scandal?" he asked.

Petrini walked over to a table with a crystal decanter of whiskey and poured out two fingers of the golden liquor in each glass. He handed one to Dominic and took a seat next to him.

"Before his untimely death, Roberto Calvi was chairman of Banco Ambrosiano, an Italian bank founded in the late nineteenth century. Because it was largely a Catholic bank, whose goals were to serve religious bodies doing pious work, it became known as the Priest's Bank.

"In the early 1970s, Calvi greatly expanded Ambrosiano's interests, creating offshore companies to transfer money out of Italy, inflate the bank's stock prices, and acquire substantial unsecured loans. Many of their investments and transactions were highly questionable, some even criminal, and the house of cards Calvi had built soon began crumbling. And since the Vatican Bank was Ambrosiano's single largest shareholder, the Church was compromised as well, having to pay some 250 million dollars to absolve itself.

"Calvi was also a member of Italy's Propaganda Due lodge, or P2, a clandestine, anti-communist Masonic order with close ties to the Mafia. Headed by a prominent but mysterious figure named Licio Gelli, P2 was implicated in an untold number of Italian crimes, including the eventual collapse of Banco Ambrosiano, the murders of journalists and politicians, and ultimately the death of Roberto Calvi himself.

"Mind you, P2 grew to become a major political force, boasting among its members many prominent journalists, members of parliaments, captains of industry, military leaders, and at least one Italian prime minister. And for some time it seemed to have operated much like Italy's shadow government.

"As Calvi's empire began to unravel, Opus Deus was about to bail out Banco Ambrosiano in exchange for something—exactly what was never made clear. Perhaps those papers may shed more light on the matter."

"Well," Dominic said, "all that certainly adds to the mystery. What do you suggest I do now?"

"First, find out if and what your Mr. Duffy may have told someone, and who that would be. As for your offer from Bishop Silva, pray on it—but don't pray too hard ...

"By the way," Petrini continued, smiling, "I have some very important news to tell you. But it will have to wait, I have back-to-back meetings today. We'll chat again soon."

Ian Duffy sat in Dominic's office, his head hung low as he confessed his blunder.

"Michael, I am *so* sorry! I didn't realize it was such a big deal until *after* I mentioned it to Milo—when we were talking to Simon Ginsberg and he threw down the caution flag. Honestly, I would never have said a thing had I known there might be trouble."

"You mean Milo Banducci? From the Vatican Bank?"

"Yes," Duffy mumbled. "And so I suppose he's a member of Opus Deus and has told them what I told him. I just feel awful about this."

Dominic sat behind his desk, hands folded beneath his chin, deep in thought. He could feel his protégé's discouragement.

"I'm not angry with you, Ian, just disappointed in the whole business."

"Well ... there's more ...."

Dominic sighed and leaned forward. "Spill it."

"Milo asked me to join him for coffee yesterday at Pergamino. When I got there he said the bank's historian wanted to 'borrow' the briefcase for a couple days to add what it contained to the bank's historical records. I told him that was out of the question, but that I'd take it up with you."

Now Dominic was angry, but not with Duffy.

"The Vatican Bank doesn't *have* a historian! That sonofabitch just wanted to get his hands on Calvi's briefcase. Obviously he'd been given orders by someone higher up, probably Bishop Silva—the one who tried recruiting me at lunch today—to use any means necessary. Now things are becoming clearer."

"Maybe we need to have someone go through these papers and tell us what's really in there. If Opus Deus wants them that badly, they must contain something important."

"But who?" Ian asked. "Who do you know that would understand how damaging those papers might be?"

Dominic considered for a long moment, then smiled.

"I know just the person ...."

SIXTEEN

With nearly one in ten Italians holding a license to own some form of firing weapon, TSNs, or National Target Shooting ranges, were popular places to practice one's pistol or rifle skills.

Behind the tawny brick façade of a castle fortress, TSN Roma hosted civilian, military, police, embassy security personnel, and others looking to master their sport or defensive competence. International tournaments frequently took place there, and the range was used often by members and visitors alike.

Rusty and Dieter were just such members, and their guest, Marco Picard, was wide-eyed at the sheer size of the range and the number of shooters currently practicing.

"How much experience do you have with weapons, Dieter?" Marco asked.

Without a hint of bragging, Dieter showed confidence in his reply.

"Well, though I am now a Swiss Guard—which has its own rigorous weapons regimen—my real training began during my years as a combat engineer in the *Kommando Spezialkräfte*, the Swiss Army Special Forces Command. As part of the counter-terrorist unit Army Reconnaissance Detachment 10, I specialized in explosive ordnance missions. I was rated one of the army's top experts in building and defusing improvised explosive devices, as well as demolition of field obstacles and enemy fortifications, all of which came in handy during my tour of OEF in Afghanistan."

Both Rusty and Marco looked at Dieter with new respect. "You never mentioned that before. ARD 10, you say? That's quite an elite unit," Rusty said with admiration, "the equivalent of U.S. Navy SEAL teams. Hats off to you, brother!" He reached out to Dieter with a fist bump.

"I'm hardly in the category Marco is, being a former Bérets Verts with the French Commandos Marine," he said humbly.

"It's not a competition, Dieter," Marco said, grinning. "You're as qualified as either Rusty or me, and that's a fact. Like he said, hats off!"

"Speaking of competition," Rusty said, "let's get some use out of this club while we're here."

Marco, Rusty, and Dieter walked past the civilian side of the range to the section reserved for law enforcement and military personnel. Dieter's position with the Swiss Guard, and his vouching for Marco and Rusty, afforded

them the opportunity to shoot on the less restrictive side
of the range. Here they could shoot from the holster and
shoot quickly, rather than being confined to slow fire from
a ready position. They could even shoot prone or from
kneeling positions.

Each man took a lane and began removing his
firearms and ammunition from their carrying cases.

Marco took the center lane and looked over to his
right as Rusty was loading six rounds into the cylinder of
his Manurhin MR73 .357 revolver.

"Seriously, Rusty? You still carrying that old wheel
gun?"

"You bet your ass, old friend. This trusty six-shooter
has seen me out of some tough spots, better than that
combat Tupperware you're sporting," Rusty replied. "I
don't know what you see in those plastic pistols."

"It's not plastic, its polymer. It's the latest thing, and
that's how I keep my edge."

"What's the youngster shooting over there?" Rusty
asked.

"SIG P220, signore," Dieter replied. "Standard issue
for Swiss Guards."

"Well, at least it's made of metal," Rusty quipped.

Marco flipped a switch on the lane divider, sending
his target carrier out to fifteen meters. The Range Master
had set them all up with standard B-27 silhouette targets
on cardboard backers.

"Okay, boys, best twelve rounds, rapid fire. Loser buys
the beers. Dieter, in deference to the limitations of Rusty's
weapon, we'll both load two mags, six rounds each, so we
all have to reload," Marco said. "Here, hand me a

magazine and I'll load it for you while you load the other. Mine are already prepped."

Once they were ready, the three stepped up to the firing line.

"Ready on the left?" Marco looked over at Dieter. "Ready on the right?" Marco checked on Rusty. "All ready on the firing line. Fire!"

Marco aimed his Glock 19 at the target, his holographic sight placing a red dot on the target as he looked through it. He cranked off six rounds in rapid succession and dropped the magazine. Taking the spare mag from his back pocket, he inserted it into the mag well and released the slide. He activated the laser aiming module locked in the Glock's accessory rail, put the projected green spot on the center of the target and fired his remaining six rounds. Eleven of the twelve rounds found their mark inside the 10-ring of the target, the other just outside.

Rusty kept pace, firing six rounds from his revolver, finishing just behind Marco. All twelve rounds were in the 10-ring.

Dieter fired his first six rounds from the SIG, dropped the mag and reloaded. *Bang. Bang. Click.* Almost without thinking, Dieter kept the gun on target, smacked the bottom of the magazine with his off hand to make sure it was properly seated, racked the slide to eject the unfired round, and resumed shooting. Four more rounds found their target.

When the line was called safe, Dieter picked up his magazine and found the dummy round Marco had slipped in it when loading Dieter's magazine.

"Here, I think you misplaced this," Dieter quipped, knowing he had passed the test.

"Yes, indeed, my young friend. A perfect failure drill. You've been well trained. Not that I had any doubts," Marco grinned.

They brought the targets back in.

"Looks like I lost," Dieter said. "I'll be buying the old men their beers tonight."

"Well, I'll let you buy me that beer, you cheeky devil, but that's some fine shooting," Marco replied as he looked at Dieter's target with ten holes in the 10-ring, closer together than either his or Rusty's targets, and two perfect eyeholes in the head.

A few more drills and Marco was sure these two had the shooting skills needed for whatever lay ahead.

CHAPTER

SEVENTEEN

After Sunday Mass, Dominic had borrowed Karl Dengler's Jeep Wrangler, drove out to Zagarolo, forty kilometers southeast of Rome, and picked up Simon Ginzberg from his office at Teller University.

Nestled on the backseat of the car was Roberto Calvi's briefcase as they headed back to the city to meet Hana at her hotel.

Parking the Jeep at the Rome Cavalieri Waldorf Astoria, just north of the Vatican, Dominic retrieved the briefcase, then he and Simon took the elevator to the seventh floor. Ringing the bell of the Palermo Suite, Hana opened the door and welcomed them in.

"So good to see you again, Simon!" Hana said warmly. "I'm glad you were able to join us to help unravel this mystery."

"Well, I'm not so sure I will be much help at all," the old man said humbly, his thick Yiddish accent always a delight to Hana's ears. "But whatever is in here that is so important to Opus Deus, perhaps we will have some luck finding it."

Dominic opened the briefcase, removed all its contents and laid everything out on the dining table, with the key catching Hana's attention. Curious, she picked it up to look at it more closely.

"Have you looked at this before, Michael?" she asked.

"Actually, no. I was more interested in the papers. Why?"

"It looks like a safe deposit box key. And it has an image on it: three layered crowns with a pair of crossed keys beneath it. Isn't that some kind of papal symbol?"

Dominic looked at the key for the first time, peering closely at the markings.

"Yes," Ginzberg said, "this is the symbol of the crossed keys of Simon Peter: the papal coat of arms. The two keys represent the power of binding and loosing—the keys to the Kingdom of Heaven. The triple crown symbolizes the three powers the pope retains as father of kings, governor of the world, and Vicar of Christ."

He looked up at both Hana and Dominic with wonder on his face. "I would imagine this could be a key to a safe deposit box in the Vatican Bank," he said candidly. "But *which* box?"

"Yes, we can't very well go through them all to see which one it fits, now, can we?" Hana said with a sly smile.

"Maybe there are clues in the papers here," she suggested. She began leafing through the pages in one unmarked folder while Dominic and Simon took other unlabeled folders. Each contained various documents, letters, and general notes about Banco Ambrosiano and the Vatican Bank, along with contracts and other official-looking papers.

"There is one curious thing here," Hana said, pulling out a small card of fine ivory stationery with an unrecognizable gold crest embossed at the top.

"Someone has written, '*pw Super Hanc Petram*' on it, followed by 'Psalm 32:7'. What do you suppose that means?"

"*Super hanc petram* is Latin for 'Upon this rock,' from Matthew 16 verse 18," Dominic quoted. "The full verse is something like, 'And I tell you that you are Peter, and upon this rock I will build my church ...'"

"But what's the context?" Ginzberg asked. "And this 'pw' part, that's not Latin. What could it mean? If it's related to Opus Deus, it could mean 'path way,' similar to the book written by Father Escobar titled *The Pathway*."

After a few moments thinking about it, Hana's face lit up.

"This may be a stretch, but it could also stand for 'password' ..."

Dominic considered this, then asked, "This may be a dumb question, but did they have computers in the 1980s?"

"Of course they did; larger computers, though. Wide use of personal computers came a bit later. I think that's something we'd have to ask Ian," Hana suggested.

"Or maybe Sister Teri knows," Dominic added.

"Sister Teri?" Hana asked, as she took a photo of the ivory card using her iPhone.

"Oh, that's right, you haven't met her yet. She's one of

the Pauline nuns who run the Vatican's computer network and switchboard. You've got to meet her, she's a remarkable young woman. And scary smart."

"What about that reference to the psalm, Michael?" Ginzberg asked. "Is that significant?"

"I don't know the passage offhand, I'd have to check. Hey, wait ... I have a Bible app on my iPhone!"

"Of course you do," Hana quipped.

Dominic grinned as he pulled the phone out of his pocket. "Let's see ..." Launching the app, he searched on the *Book of Psalms* for chapter 32, verse 7.

"Here it is: 'You are my hiding place; you will protect me from trouble and surround me with songs of deliverance.'" He looked up at the others.

"Well, *that's* not tantalizing at all!" she exclaimed. "'You are my hiding place ...'? I mean, jeez!"

Dominic took a seat and sighed. "This is all getting a bit confusing." Hana and Ginzberg sat down as well. "What say we give Ian and Sister Teri a call, see if they're up for lunch? We could use their help on this now. I know Ian's working today, despite it being Sunday. His new computer system just came in and he's probably fiddling with it. I'll try to reach Teri now."

Dominic called the Vatican switchboard. A nun answered, and confirmed that Sister Teresa was in fact working but was on another line; she would put him on hold for when her call was finished.

About a minute later she answered, "This is Sister Teresa."

"Hi Teri, it's Michael Dominic."

"Father Michael! How can I help you this fine day?"

"We're wondering if you're free for lunch now, or soon. There are some things I'm working on that require your knowledge of computers. Ian will be joining us, too, I think, along with a couple of other friends."

"I'd love to. It's ... eleven thirty now. How about twelve thirty? Where shall we meet?"

"Let's say Ristorante dei Musei, just north of the Vatican."

"I know it well. See you then, Father."

Dominic then called Duffy and made the same arrangements, though Dominic sensed Ian's reluctance in being pulled away from his shiny new Mac Pro.

The restaurant was bustling with patrons, mostly tourists —as was typical on weekends—but Dominic was able to get a table accommodating all five of them.

After introductions were made and they ordered their meals, Dominic explained what they knew about Roberto Calvi, Banco Ambrosiano, and the scandal involving the Vatican Bank in the '80s. Then he mentioned Opus Deus's involvement.

"Oh," Sister Teri cringed, then gave a mock shudder. "Not a group I'd want to go up against. They have tentacles everywhere."

"You know much about them, Teri?" Hana asked.

"Probably more than I want to," she replied. "I do find it odd they don't allow nuns in their order—not that *I'd* want to apply—but they are decidedly patriarchal by design. And though the founder, now Saint Juancarlos

Escobar, probably had the best of devotional intentions in mind when he began the order in 1928, it seems to have taken on more ominous practices along the way. And without being judgmental here, I do find that whole corporal mortification thing a strange way to honor God.

"But, technologically speaking, they truly are masters of that universe, which I find unusual for a religious order made up mostly of lay people. I know they have a powerful Tandem Nonstop computer network called *Firmamentum Sanctitatis*—Latin for Vault of Sanctity—or the FS Network for short, with Nonstop servers around the world. I expect the main host system is in their headquarters at Villa Tiber here in Rome. But why they need that kind of supercomputing power is beyond me.

"So, how is Opus Deus involved in what you're doing now?" she asked.

"Well, we're not really sure," Dominic admitted. "We do know they want whatever's in an old briefcase we found in the Archives. Simon and Hana and I spent the morning going through some of it, and among other things we discovered a passage from Matthew 16:18: *'super hanc petram'*—'upon this rock'—preceded by the letters 'pw.' No idea what the 'pw' might stand for, but Hana suggested it might mean 'password.' But isn't a password usually made up of a combination of letters, numbers and symbols?"

"Actually," Duffy spoke up, "it could be a *passphrase*, which is significantly stronger than a single password because it strengthens entropy, or the quality of a password's random nature, making it far more challenging to guess or decipher it using brute force password-cracking attacks. Ideally, a passphrase should be twenty to thirty characters or more, including spaces, such as 'vatican cross altar sacristy,' making it fairly rock-solid and largely unbreakable. So, although it's a bit on the short side, *super hanc petram* could easily be a passphrase. But to *what* is the question."

"When did this Roberto Calvi die, Michael?" Sister Teri asked.

Dominic looked at Simon, not knowing the answer.

The old man looked down at his folded hands and paused before responding. "Calvi's body was found hanging under Blackfriars Bridge in London in June 1982. I remember this because my wife died that same month." Simon's eyes teared up thinking about his wife of some thirty years, Clara.

"Well, from what I once read," Teri continued, "Opus Deus's Tandem Nonstop system was installed in 1980, a few years after Father Escobar's death. And if Calvi died two years after it was installed—and he was as involved as you say he was—he surely could have had access to the FS Network. I mean, for what else could he have used a password?"

"Passphrase," corrected Duffy.

"Whatever," Teri countered.

"Good point," Hana noted. Turning to Teri, she asked, "How might we gain access to their FS Network?"

Sister Teri and Ian Duffy looked at each other and grinned deviously.

"Father Dominic," Duffy asked, smiling, "are you sure you want to be here for the answer?"

Dominic laughed. "In for a penny, in for a pound! I

have no qualms about hacking, if that's what you're alluding to."

"That's exactly what we were thinking," Duffy said, glancing at the nun. "Right, Teri?"

Teri blushed and made the sign of the cross. "Bless me, Father, for I am about to sin ..."

"Nonsense," Dominic said, smiling confidently. "It's just research, after all. And if you have authorized access —assuming it *is* a legitimate passphrase—then I see nothing particularly wrong with it. Let's just say we'll be acting posthumously on behalf of Mr. Calvi."

"We have yet to figure out his username, though that might be somewhat easier, I hope," Duffy added. "But what if they've somehow deleted his access, or whatever he had stored on the network?"

Sister Teri considered this for a moment. "Frankly, Tandem Nonstop is a decades-old system, and though it's still in use by companies worldwide—for example, nearly every ATM today uses Nonstop technology—I doubt many changes have been made at all, since you can keep building onto those systems almost indefinitely.

"And if what you said about Opus Deus desperately wanting what's in that briefcase is true," she continued, "then chances are they want access to Calvi's protected data, too. I'd bet my pectoral cross his material is still there, intact."

"You were right, Michael. I do like her!" Hana beamed. "So now, what about that safe deposit box key?"

Dominic reached into his pocket and withdrew his keyring, laying it on the table for all to see. Teri picked it up to examine the key more closely.

"Oh, the Keys of Saint Peter," she said reverently, then, "Vatican Bank, I assume?"

"That's what we think, yes," Dominic concurred. "What else could it be?"

Hana reached into her bag and pulled out her iPhone. Flipping through the photos, she found the one she had taken of the ivory card, then passed the phone to Sister Teri.

"We also found on the same card that referenced the Matthew passage, this reference to Psalm 32:7 .... Any idea what that might relate to, apart from its scriptural meaning? What was that again, Michael?"

"'You are my hiding place; you will protect me from trouble and surround me with songs of deliverance.'"

"Wow," Teri acknowledged. "Isn't *that* tantalizing!"

"Exactly the word I used!" Hana blurted.

Teri was clearly thinking hard, and, like Hana, loved a good puzzle. "'Surround me with songs of deliverance ....' That could easily be the Vatican, what with all the choir-chanting during St. Peter's constant daily Masses. And 'hiding place' ... well, that could be anywhere—but it also could well be the safe deposit box you mentioned, couldn't it?"

Around the table, minds were working. Finally, Teri added her last thought.

"So, what if Psalm 32 verse 7 actually refers to a safe deposit box numbered 327? Simple enough to find out."

Dominic's mouth dropped open. Looking around at the others, he found similar reactions.

"Could it be that easy?" he wondered, his excitement

noticeable. "The bank is closed today, but we can give it a try tomorrow. Nice work, Teri!"

"Well, it is a long shot. But there is some clever logic to it on Mr. Calvi's part, if that is the case."

"That's also some very clever work on *your* part, Teri," Hana said, admiring the young nun.

Finally, two waiters approached the table with their meals, laying down plates in front of everyone. They began eating their food quietly, each of them pondering the unfolding mystery of Roberto Calvi's briefcase.

CHAPTER

EIGHTEEN

I t was mid-evening in London when Isabella Stewart Hastings, chairman and CEO of Stewart Hastings Global, had invited her eighteen guests to take their seats in the sumptuous dining hall of her home, Stewart Manor.

Overlooking Hyde Park in the posh Knightsbridge neighborhood, Stewart Manor was arguably among the most expensive privately owned properties in the United Kingdom—a topic commonly argued over amongst the ultra-wealthy who populated this exclusive quarter of West Central London.

With four floors and seventeen bedrooms on three acres, a palatial games room, a private cinema, spa and gym, a generous wing for the servants, and a spacious garage that held a fleet of vintage Rolls Royces, Bentleys, and armored Range Rovers, Stewart Manor was a fitting residence for one of the UK's most prominent businesswomen.

A lineal descendant in a direct line from Mary, Queen of Scots, Dame Isabella Stewart Hastings' royal blood served to open any doors she cared to pass through, including those of Buckingham Palace.

Remarkably attractive at 56—she sported shoulder-length platinum blonde hair in layers and balayage, with shiny strands in flaxen hues framing a sculpted face with high cheekbones, full lips, and vibrant dark blue, at times violet, eyes. Though decidedly attractive to the opposite sex, Isabella was determinedly single and, owing to her role as one of the most privileged numeraries of Opus Deus, avowedly celibate. Though she had an expansive wardrobe of couture fashions, she preferred black Armani Privé pantsuits, mainly to conceal the flat but inwardly-spiked cilice strapped around her thigh as a constant reminder of the pain suffered by her Lord and savior, Jesus Christ.

As the head of Deo Dicata, the gentrified fundraising arm of Opus Deus, Isabella's mission tonight was to seduce her affluent dinner guests into opening their hearts and wallets, a skill at which she was especially gifted. Understanding the power of symbology, she herself had founded the group and had chosen as its name *Deo Dicata*, from the Latin meaning "Dedicated to God," and which not coincidentally was also the historical meaning of her own name, Isabella.

As was expected of all numeraries, she donated three-quarters of her annual salary to Opus Deus, and she had no reservations that her £50 million annual tithing went to good use. As for her own lavish lifestyle, the company paid for her personal expenses, and her family's generational wealth would never leave her wanting for anything.

Isabella's dinner companion for the evening was Sir Robert "Bobby" Cavendish, executive vice president of Stewart Hastings Global and, as it happened, a close friend of Vatican Secretary of State Cardinal Enrico Petrini. The Holy See, in fact, was a major shareholder in Stewart Hastings Global, a financial conglomerate comprising numerous banks and brokerage houses worldwide as well as being a major force in supply chain management. In turn, one of SHG's subsidiaries supplied the Vatican with most of its routine operational needs, from office furniture and supplies to clerical vestments and even vehicles for the Vatican motor pool.

Isabella Stewart Hastings had been working for years to establish tight bonds with the Vatican, with one specific goal in mind. Consistent with Opus Deus's covert ambition to control the Holy See's finances and investments, Isabella had her eye on soon being named president of the Vatican Bank, a goal that would give both parties substantial influence over an institution supporting over a billion souls worldwide.

In the meantime, Isabella began her beguiling pitch to the assembled guests as her chef's servers laid out silver-rimmed plates of pheasant braised with pickled apples, leeks and hazelnuts. In exchange, her goal for the evening —as with every such successful dinner party at Stewart Manor—was £1 million, an easy achievement from the London glitterati around her table that evening.

As the white papal Mercedes S550 limousine stopped in front of his residential palazzo in Rome, Cardinal Alastair Wolsey—having returned from the meeting at Castel Gandolfo—stepped out of the car and into the light spring rain that evening, aching for a scotch.

The driver had an umbrella ready for His Eminence as he emerged, walking him to the entrance of the estate to keep the rain from soaking him.

Wolsey had phoned ahead to Bishop Silva, asking that he and Julio Guzman meet him at the palazzo at nine o'clock, a half hour from now. Meanwhile, he would change into more relaxing clothes, have one of the nuns start a fire in the library, and pour that long-awaited scotch.

Promptly at nine o'clock the doorbell rang. A nun answered it, welcoming Silva and Guzman into the foyer as she took their coats, then led them to the library where Wolsey sat in a high-backed, wraparound Queen Anne chair sipping his Rètico.

"Good evening, gentlemen," the cardinal said. "Something to drink?"

Both his guests joined him in having the whiskey, then took their seats near the fire.

"So, Julio, what have you discovered about our Father Dominic?"

"Actually, Alastair," Bishop Silva interrupted, "we should first speak about former Cardinal Dante. Though we have yet to hear from Dominic as to his decision on joining us, I thought it prudent to have Dante released from Regina Coeli in order to have his extensive knowledge and connections at our disposal. I have made arrangements with the warden and parole board for him to be released this week. He will be delivered to Villa Tiber as soon as he's free, at which time we'll get from him the information he has on Dominic, and of course he will be in our service for other missions as well."

"And have we learned what kind of information Dante might have?"

Guzman answered, "I spoke with him again just yesterday, Eminence, telling him his parole was in process, with conditions," he glanced at Silva, who nodded, "and told him we'd like at least a hint as to what he knows. All he said was it relates directly to 'Dominic's paternity.'"

Wolsey took a long draw on his scotch and stared into the blazing fire. "Interesting. And since he did imply it would shake up the highest levels of power at the Vatican, I am more than curious. Let me know when you are meeting with Dante. I want to be there."

CHAPTER
NINETEEN

A light rain was still falling across Rome on Monday morning as Dominic, his backpack slung over his shoulder, entered the round stone building known as the Institute for the Works of Religion, or more commonly, the Vatican Bank.

On the key ring in his pocket was the key to a safe deposit box, one he hoped would shed some light on Roberto Calvi's strange life, or at least whatever others, it seemed, also were trying to get to.

The inside of the bank mirrored the circular design of its exterior: a perfectly round room, on one side of which were teller windows, and on the opposite side a row of desks for managers, investment officers and other bank personnel. Dominic groaned when he saw Milo Banducci sitting at his desk. Preferring to have someone else attend to his accessing the box, he waited in line for a teller.

When his turn came, the priest walked forward to the counter where a young woman greeted him with a smile.

"*Buongiorno*, padre. How may I help you?"

"Yes, I need to get into a safe deposit box." He held up the key as if to verify the request.

"*Si.* Let me get the manager for that." She picked up the phone, dialed an extension, briefly relayed the request, then hung up.

"It will be just a moment, padre. If you could wait over there, he will be right with you." She gestured to a seating area.

Dominic had no sooner sat down than he saw Milo Banducci approaching him.

No, no! Don't let it be him!

"Father Dominic!" he exclaimed with obvious tension. "I don't think I've ever seen you in the bank before."

"Hello, Milo. Yes, I, uh, rarely have a need to come in."

"I understand you wish to get into your safe deposit box? Just follow me."

Banducci walked into the vault and up to a computer station. "What is the box number?"

"327."

Banducci looked up the account. "That's strange. You're the first person to access the box since 1981! I'm surprised it's not been considered dormant after nearly four decades. How is it you have the key?"

"Am I required to answer that kind of question, Milo?"

"Well ... no, I was just curious."

"Can we get on with it, then?"

Clearly Banducci could not prevent anyone with a legitimate key from accessing any box.

"And what is the password for the account?" he asked curtly.

Dominic instantly tensed up, not expecting the challenge. As he was thinking how he should respond, Banducci spoke again.

"Wait … Your name is not on this account. Are you sure you have the right box number?"

"Yes, that's the right number," the priest replied haltingly. Quickly thinking back to Calvi's fake passport, he decided to use that name. "I'm, uh, actually accessing the box on behalf of the Calvini family."

Banducci looked again at the account holder's name: *Gian Roberto Calvini*.

He paused. *Why was that name so familiar?* Then, grasping its significance, he straightened, and his face paled as his mind raced. *My god! This has to be Roberto Calvi's box! But how is that possible? And how did Dominic get the key?!*

Banducci looked directly into the priest's eyes. *It had to be from the briefcase!*

Dominic suddenly felt self-conscious. *He knows!* he realized, as Milo's suspicious eyes met his own. *Now what do I do?*

"And the password?" Banducci prompted again.

Disinclined to give him the only password he knew—since he was certainly aware of the man's own interest in acquiring the briefcase and that it may be the password to Opus Deus's computer network—he simply said, "Here, I'll enter it myself, thanks."

Reluctantly, Banducci moved aside, allowing Dominic access to the keyboard.

Hoping beyond hope that he had the right password, Dominic quickly entered the Latin phrase—'*Super Hanc*

Petram'—as masking stars appeared on the screen. After a momentary pause, an "Accepted" message appeared on the display. He felt a flush of triumph.

Unfortunately for Banducci, the priest's hands moved too quickly for him to see what he was typing, despite giving it his best attention as he desperately looked over his shoulder. Frustration rankled him.

"Alright," he muttered, "follow me."

He led the priest to box 327. It was the largest box the bank offered, positioned on the bottom row. Banducci bent over and inserted the bank's master key, at which point Dominic leaned down, picked out Calvi's key from others on his key ring, then inserted it into the lock while holding his breath. As he turned both keys, the bronze door opened. Dominic silently exhaled.

"I'll leave you to it, then," Banducci said, again staring at Dominic as he removed his master key. "Take whatever time you need."

The banker left the vault and closed the door behind him, giving the priest the privacy he needed.

Reaching a hand in to pull the box out of its storage cavity, Dominic discovered it didn't budge. Astonished at the sheer weight of the container, he braced his feet and pulled with both hands. He used all his might to slide the box part way out, deciding to let it remain in its receptacle rather than let it fall to the floor, much less get it up onto an inspection table.

Dominic pulled back the clasp and lifted the lid, which was, thankfully, hinged in the middle. He was stunned at what he found.

The box was filled with gold bullion.

He counted sixteen brilliant trapezoidal gold ingots with various impact and scribe markings on the face of each one.

No wonder it was so heavy! Dominic mused.

But on top of the gold bars sat a large, purple velvet bag tied at the top.

He picked up the bag, feeling the heavy weight of it. Whatever was inside moved around easily as he felt the hidden contents with his hands.

Opening the cord tie at the top, he spread the enclosure open.

The bag was filled with diamonds. A lot of them.

Moving to the inspection table, Dominic poured the gems out onto the stainless steel surface, the sound of the stones scattering on the table echoing off the walls. By his rough count, he figured there must be about five hundred of them—large, beautifully cut square diamonds, glittering under the brilliant, overhead LED lights.

The scene took his breath away. He had no idea as to their value, but suspected Hana might know better. Gathering them up, he replaced the gems in the velvet bag, then dropped it into his backpack.

He also took out one gold ingot to show the others and dropped that into his pack as well.

As for the rest, obviously he was unprepared to do anything with it, so decided to let it be for now. He took a photo of it using his iPhone, then closed the box, shoved it back into the receptacle, and locked it.

• • •

Sitting back at his desk now, Banducci was dumbfounded at finding what he assumed was Roberto Calvi's account in his own bank, and under a different, though closely resembling, name, for that matter. *If it was Calvi's, why hadn't this account been deemed dormant? The man died in 1982! But the account holder's name wasn't Calvi, it was* Gian Roberto Calvini, he fretted. *Could they actually be one and the same?*

Then he looked at the account balance under the same name: roughly twenty million euros! And earning healthy interest for over four decades.

Looking at the account's transactions, Banducci discovered a list of regular, identical transactions going back all the way to 1982 and beyond—and continuing to this day. Relatively small, routine, automated quarterly money transfers to a Swiss bank, which would explain why the bank's systems had not deemed Calvi's account dormant, since there was constant activity on it. But he also noticed there had been no other deposit or withdrawal transactions, and no beneficiaries or other allowed names on the account, since 1982.

It had to be Calvi's!

And since all high-balance VIP accounts came with a free safe deposit box, no one had ever questioned why it had never been visited.

He wondered what was in the safe deposit box Dominic was now accessing. The suspense was torturing him. Unfortunately, there was no way the bank alone could open the box without the key Dominic was holding. He had to report this activity to Bishop Silva.

Finally, Dominic emerged from the safe deposit vault, and simply waved to Banducci as he headed toward the exit.

As he watched the priest exit the bank, Banducci picked up the phone.

CHAPTER
TWENTY

Ian Duffy was entranced by the power of his new Mac Pro, the finest piece of computing equipment he had ever worked with; and as a seasoned Apple alum, that was saying something.

It was lunch hour, and sitting next to him in his office in the Archives was Sister Teri, who was similarly amazed at what this machine could do, and how fast it did it. Both were self-confessed geeks of the first order.

"You should see my collection of old Apple computers, Teri," Duffy suggested. "I've even got an Apple II GS from 1986, which was state-of-the-art in its day. It's my pride and joy, and worth a small fortune now."

"Wow. I've never even seen one of those. I can't imagine it next to this behemoth. By the way, how do you plan on approaching development of your Archives database?" she asked.

"I'll start by laying out the schema for data input based on what the old system, here, took in," he replied, "then build in remote networking capabilities for broader internet access so that scholars worldwide can access whichever files the Archives Council permits to be made public."

"Cool," Teri enthused. "I'd love to see some of your code when you're deeper into it."

"Sure, we can arrange that."

Hearing someone enter the door, they both turned to see Father Dominic, breathless after running from the Vatican Bank back to his office.

"You won't believe what just happened," he announced, clearly excited.

"What?!" Duffy and Teri asked at the same time.

"I went to the bank to see if I could get into the safe deposit box. The key worked! It *was* box 327! The account was under the name Gian Roberto Calvini, like we found on Calvi's fake passport, and the password he wrote down was the right one!"

Teri and Duffy were both wide-eyed as Dominic's words fell out of him.

"So what did you *find*?" Teri asked urgently. "What was in the box?!"

Dominic set his backpack down on Duffy's desk and removed the gold ingot, setting it on the desktop.

Having never seen a gold bar before in person, both Duffy and Teri's mouths hung open.

"Oh. My. God," Teri uttered, reaching out to touch the inscribed markings on the ingot. Duffy lifted it up to feel the weight of it.

"Good grief! This must be thirty pounds or so."

"And there are fifteen more just like it still in the safe

deposit box," Dominic said. "But that's not all ..." He pulled out the purple velvet bag, pushed everything else on the desk mat aside, opened the bag and let the diamonds cascade out onto the mat.

Teri and Duffy were speechless, taking in this new measure of Roberto Calvi's strange life.

"I have never seen anything like this before in my life," Teri said with amazement.

"Well, who does it all belong to now?" Duffy asked.

"I have no idea," Dominic reckoned. "But since it's obviously been sitting there for nearly forty years, maybe more, I imagine no one will ever claim it."

He left the obvious thought hanging in the air.

Meanwhile Teri silently calculated the value of the gold, referencing statistics found using the internet on her phone. *Figuring sixteen bars with a standard bar weighing 12.4 kilograms, or 400 troy ounces, and gold is valued at, what is it today ... $1800 per ounce, that's ...*

"*Jesus wept*! That gold is worth way over *ten million dollars*!"

"Seriously?" Dominic asked.

"That can go to a lot of good causes," she added. "Just sayin'. As for the diamonds, that'll take someone more familiar with gemology. But I'd guess they're worth a lot more."

"Yeah, I was thinking this might be more Hana's expertise. She travels in those circles," Dominic said, smiling knowingly. "Well, for now, we should try accessing Opus Deus's network. Milo asked for the password to access the safe deposit box, but—"

"*Milo*?!" Duffy exclaimed.

"Yes, he was the one who escorted me to the vault. It required a password as well as the key, but I didn't want to tell him what it was so I entered it myself on their system. So now we should try it on the order's network to see if Calvi used it there, too. It may be a long shot, but we'll never know unless we try."

"We don't want our IP address to be seen or tracked by them," Teri cautioned, "so be sure to use a VPN."

"Good point," Duffy said, turning to face his computer. Then, using Terminal on his Mac, he got into Opus Deus's Tandem network using the old TELNET protocol.

On the command line he was prompted for a username.

"It's asking for a username first, Michael. What should we try for that?"

The three of them considered the obvious options, writing them down on a piece of paper.

RobertoCalvi
RCalvi
RobertoC
GianRobertoCalvini
GRCalvini

"We'll just take them one at a time. It may not even be a name; it could be anything," Duffy said with frustration. "And what was that password?"

"'*Super Hanc Petram*,'" Dominic said. "Try it case-sensitive, with spaces, as it was written and which worked at the bank."

Duffy entered the first name, *RobertoCalvi*, then the password. It was rejected.

He went down the list, manually entering each contrived username and the same password every time.

None of them worked.

He tried alternate variations, with the same result.

Dominic thought of other options. Then he remembered Simon Ginzberg telling him Calvi was a member of P2, which might have some relationship. *What did Simon say they called themselves ...? Black Friars?*

"Ian, try the username, BlackFriars."

Again, the entry was rejected.

Dominic thought a bit longer this time. "Try it in Italian," he urged, *FratiNeri.*"

Duffy entered *FratiNeri* followed by the password. The system briefly displayed a sequence of progressing dots, then a new page appeared, labeled 'Members Only.'

"It worked! We're in," Duffy said jubilantly. "Brilliant thinking, Michael. This is the simplest hacking job I've ever done."

Dominic took a deep breath. "Spare me the details of your hacking exploits, Ian. I don't need to add that to my confession this week."

"Okay, let's see what mischief we can get into here," Duffy said, focused on his mission. "Now *there's* something you can add to your confession," he quipped, looking at the priest.

"Point taken," Dominic admitted, properly chagrined. He pulled up a chair next to Duffy and Teri and peered at the screen while the young technician's hands flew over the keyboard.

"I wonder," Sister Teri posed. "Is hacking a sin?"

She looked at Dominic for an answer. He simply shrugged his shoulders. "Moses didn't have a computer, so I'd have to say no." They all laughed.

"I can't believe how antiquated this system is," Duffy said. "I'm surprised it's so widely used even today."

"So, first," the young tech guru explained, "I'm checking to see if Calvi had admin access, so we can establish a back door user account in case they discover this one and close it down."

Navigating to the Users database, he checked Calvi's privileges.

"Awesome! He *was* an admin on the system, a lower level one, but we can still create another account. He must have been some big deal with P2."

"He was so prominent in the financial world at the time that he was known as 'God's Banker,'" Dominic said. "I'd say that's a big deal, and Opus Deus must have thought so, too."

"What username do you want to give us?" Duffy looked at Dominic.

After thinking a few moments, Dominic said, "Use '*JEscobar*.' That's the name of Opus Deus's founder. Anyone seeing that might be less inclined to mess with it."

Duffy created a new user record as directed while devising an ironclad password, then started poking around the network.

"I assume we're looking for any files stored under Calvi's user folder," Duffy said. "Got anything else in mind?" He looked at Dominic for suggestions.

"If you can find it, a member directory of the order."

"Good idea." Duffy worked his way to the User File section, retrieving several folders attributed to Calvi. In another administrative section he found a database of all members and downloaded that as well.

Dominic looked at his watch. "I've got a meeting with Cardinal Petrini now. Why don't you just download everything you can find and store it on your system here? We can review them later."

"Exactly what I was thinking," Duffy said. "What about the, um, gold and diamonds?"

"Don't worry, I'm putting them in the safe in my office. I'll see you both later."

Julio Guzman had been sitting at his computer workstation probing the Vatican's firewalls when he suddenly noticed an open communications port that had been previously invisible. He immediately launched a program that would enter through the open port and establish a permanent connection that would be nearly undetectable to the network admins at the other end. He began searching the directory for files related to Roberto Calvi and was instantly rewarded with a master file containing all the banker's digitized documents. He quickly downloaded them to an external drive and then, using a disk utility program, he erased the sub files and performed a seven-time overwrite of the affected memory sectors to prevent the files from being recovered, while leaving the master file and the file names so it looked as if the data were still intact.

Duffy was downloading the Calvi files from the Opus Deus computer when a window popped up from his antivirus program. While Macs were notably resistant to viruses, it never hurt to be careful, especially with so much highly sensitive data to protect. Duffy had written some additional code into the open-source program to detect particularly stealthy breaches of the firewall and other intrusions—but somebody had just established a connection through one of the ports he had been testing for external access.

"Teri, quick, give me a hand," he said urgently. "We have an intrusion. Get on that other terminal and launch a program called 'Counter Strike.'"

Sister Teri rushed to an older computer nearby, quickly scanned the applications folder, then launched the desired app.

"I've got all the Calvi files from Opus Deus here," Duffy noted, "so I'm getting out now and closing that port."

Launching his system monitoring suite, he surveyed the ports for activity and determined that the intruder was modifying files.

"Whoever's at the other end is messing with the Calvi files from the briefcase. *Oh, for god's sake!* They must have been watching our activity while we were watching theirs! But they probably haven't seen us since we had an actual login. I'm shutting down all the external ports.

"Okay, let's see what he did here ... *no* ... *No!!* The file names are all there but the data is gone!"

"Oh, Ian," Teri moaned, "all that time spent scanning the docs. All gone. At least we still have the briefcase."

"Yeah, well, only that copy of the files is gone. I keep periodic off-site backups both in the cloud and locally. He might have gotten the local copy, but not every one. Did you get Counter Strike launched?"

"Yes, I did. What is it going to do?"

"It's a Trojan program. It looks for any data copied from the computer it came from and deletes it. He may have tried to erase our data, but he's just lost all the files he got from us. I used to have it erase everything, wipe a drive clean, but I didn't think Father Michael would approve, so I pulled some of its teeth, so to speak. Now to make sure he can't get back in...."

Guzman went to check the contents of the files he had just downloaded, but when he tried to open them, he discovered they had deleted themselves and were now gone. *The network admin at the Vatican must have more skills than I thought,* he seethed.

He ran an anti-virus scan, discovered the trojan and deleted it. But the lost data couldn't be recovered. That made getting the actual briefcase all the more important.

He wasn't looking forward to explaining his failure to Bishop Silva.

CHAPTER
TWENTY-ONE

The earlier spring rain had freshened the papal gardens as Dominic walked through the lush grounds on his way to the Government Palace. Fresh scents of rosemary, honeysuckle and cedar permeated the air. As he walked over the ancient pathways, he was reminded of the legend of Saint Helena having brought an ox cart of earth from Golgotha to where the Vatican now stood, symbolically uniting the blood of Christ with the home of His Vicar on Earth, on land used exclusively for gardens and a small seven-acre forest. Dating back to medieval times, the Vatican Gardens also featured ancient orchards and even vineyards extending across fifty-seven acres north of the Apostolic Palace. Comprising half of the total Vatican acreage itself, it was truly its own extraordinary ecological habitat.

As Dominic reached Petrini's office the cardinal's secretary, Father Nick Bannon, gestured for the young priest to go on in, as the Secretary of State had been expecting him.

"Good afternoon, Eminence," Dominic said, beaming. "I have some interesting news."

"There's a coincidence," Petrini replied. "I have news for you as well. But you first."

"I paid a visit to the Vatican Bank using the key we found in Roberto Calvi's briefcase. Sparing you the details of how, we eventually discovered it was assigned to safe deposit box 327. Once I got into the vault, alone, I opened the box to discover it contained *sixteen bars of gold*—some four hundred pounds of it! And that wasn't all."

Reaching into his pocket, he withdrew a single large, square diamond, placing it in front of the cardinal.

"There was a velvet bag containing around five hundred of these."

Petrini's eyes opened wide upon seeing the sparkling stone.

"Well. You certainly have been busy, Michael. All this from Calvi's safe deposit box?"

"Yes. I took one of the bars and the entire bag of diamonds for safekeeping in my office. This stuff had to have been sitting there for at least forty years, and I'm certain no one else knows about it. The question is, what to do with it all?"

Petrini did some quick calculations in his head. "My god, Michael! That's almost ten million euros' worth for the gold alone! I'm shocked no one has claimed all this by now."

"But how could they if they didn't have the key? I'm certain Calvi was the only one who knew about the treasure, since he obviously must have put it there himself, a bar or two at a time."

Both men were silent, consumed in thought. Petrini stood and walked over to the window, watching a cluster of nuns in their black and white habits strolling through the papal gardens below. He always smiled at the sight, fondly recalling that the children of Rome called them *bagarozzi*, or black beetles.

"You say there were documents in the briefcase as well? I think they should be reviewed, to be certain this wealth wasn't snatched from some unsuspecting source, as we discovered a couple years ago with that Nazi treasure stolen from Jewish families. Barring anything of that sort, I will also check with our attorneys, but I see no reason why we couldn't then simply take this unclaimed largesse and move it into the Holy Father's Peter's Pence fund."

"I was thinking the same thing, Eminence. There are so many charitable uses that I know our Holy Father already funds from Peter's Pence—it would certainly help a great many. And most likely it had to be ill-gotten gains from some nefarious operation, don't you think?"

"That would seem to be the most likely scenario, yes. I wouldn't put it past Calvi to have obtained both the gold and diamonds by some shady means or other.

"Alright, after I speak with our legal team, we'll take action then. But given Opus Deus's interest in you, and our assumption that they want that briefcase, is there some way you could identify the gold if it came to our needing to?"

Dominic mulled this over for a moment. "I think so,

yes. I have an idea. Let me see if it works and I'll explain later.

"So," he continued, "you said you had some news to share, as well?"

Petrini walked over to his son and embraced him for a long moment.

"Well, Michael," Petrini began, a humble tone to his voice, "it appears there's a chance you may be looking at the next pope."

Dominic stood there, stunned at the news. "How could you possibly know this?"

"His Holiness took me aside at Castel Gandolfo during our meetings there. We walked through the gardens, just chatting, you know, about the difficulties of the bank and other matters, when he turned to me and said, 'Enrico, you have been my most loyal aide and closest friend for years, and certainly among the more accomplished secretaries of state the Church has had. I want you to know that I am planning on retiring, very soon now, and I have put you at the top of the list of *papabile* as my personal choice to be my successor—and of course, should the College of Cardinals be so guided by God during the conclave.'"

Dominic broke out in a huge smile and pulled Petrini in for another warm embrace.

"That is truly amazing news! I'm surprised His Holiness is retiring, but it isn't as if it's the first time a pope has done so. I won't jinx it by congratulating you now, but I have no doubt you'll be a superb pontiff."

"As I said, it's just a chance. But it is a most humbling prospect, and I must admit I was taken by surprise when the Holy Father told me I have his exclusive support. It's not something I had ever given a moment's thought to."

"And that's why you'll make a great leader: your natural humility and big heart."

"But you must tell no one about this, Michael. No one yet knows about his plans."

"That goes without saying, of course."

"There is but one potential problem—and I trust you know what that may be."

Dominic needed no further hint, for having learned only a year ago that Petrini was his biological father, he knew that could indeed present problems for his papacy if it were ever made public.

"Apart from Armand de Saint-Clair, whom I've told and trust with my life, my fear rests with the only other person who knows about our, well, delicate situation. Fabrizio Dante. As far as I know, he has yet to reveal it. But a man like that can never be trusted, and I expect my possible elevation to pope might cause him to rethink his leverage. As you know, I have told His Holiness about the matter, and I do have his absolution and blessing. Others, however, may not be so accommodating, especially those with papal ambitions themselves."

Michael reassured him. "Well, with Dante in prison, I doubt you have much to worry about. The man has been terribly disgraced."

"All the more reason for him to carry revenge in his darkest of hearts," Petrini said, concern furrowing his brow.

"For now," Dominic said in an upbeat tone, "let's just

celebrate the honor you've been given by the Holy Father's deep trust in you."

"You're right, Michael, of course," Petrini said, now smiling again. "We'll just put that behind us for the moment. I just had to tell you, because ..." Petrini paused, emotion clouding his face.

"Yes, I know," Dominic said, his own eyes tearing up in pride for the father he never knew, yet the man he had been closest to in his entire life.

After Dominic returned to his office, he began rifling through drawers and cabinets to find the implement he determined would be the perfect tool for what he had in mind—a MicroScribe, a tungsten carbide punch scriber that simply imprinted his name, "**M DOMINIC,**" in microscopic letters no more than one-half millimeter deep and two millimeters long. It literally took a microscope or a high-powered magnifier to read the impression left after punching most any desired object— soft materials such as wood and wax, or even steel, brass, platinum, silver ... and gold—but was otherwise invisible to the naked eye.

Dominic had used it in the past for marking textbooks in college, and even his bike for riding around campus, just in case it ever got stolen so he could identify it later.

Where did I put that thing? I know it's here somewhere ...

Hidden in the back of the top drawer of his desk, he found the small box in which the scriber was encased in foam. On one end was a round, black plastic knob for gripping the punch; at the other was a small point, inconceivably small enough to contain his name.

Grabbing his key ring with the key to the safe deposit box on it, he left his office and headed back to the Vatican Bank, a mere 500 meters from his own building, intent on leaving his mark on the gold in the event Banducci and his cohorts got any ideas to abscond with it.

Entering the bank, Dominic was relieved to find that Milo Banducci was not at his desk. Approaching a teller, he requested access to the safe deposit vault, which—he was happy to find—another assistant manager would help him with.

Once inside the vault, he opened the safe deposit box, knelt down to take each 27-pound bar out and set it on the floor to mark it. The gold was soft enough that it didn't require much effort—simply a firm press down on the MicroScribe handle—and his name was now stamped between the bar's standard impact markings, practically invisible to anyone looking directly at it.

Replacing each bar back inside the safe deposit box, he closed the door, locked it up, then left the vault, waved goodbye to the assistant manager, and returned to his office.

CHAPTER
TWENTY-TWO

The gleaming navy blue and white Gulfstream G700 soared through clear skies on its way from London to Rome. With capacity for thirteen passengers in four separate living areas, the G700 was the most luxurious private jet on the market, and Isabella Stewart Hastings would have nothing less.

Apart from the two pilots, accompanying her on the flight was her company's executive vice president, Sir Robert Cavendish, her personal assistant, two bodyguards, the chef and a flight attendant.

"Bobby," Isabella asked, "you'll be visiting Cardinal Petrini while we're in Rome, yes?"

"Indeed, I will be, Isabella. Why do you ask?"

"I'd like you to arrange a meeting for me with the cardinal and the Holy Father—together, if possible. Tell him the subject will be a substantial donation I'm considering making to Peter's Pence. That should ensure an audience."

Peter's Pence was, for lack of a better word, the pope's personal slush fund. One day each year Catholics worldwide made their contributions to the special plate, which the pope could use in any way he desired, without accountability.

"I'd be happy to, of course," Cavendish replied, making notes in the leather Moleskine pad he always carried. "Shall I allude to a general figure you might have in mind?"

"Tell him ..." she paused a moment, "*if* he asks, tell him it could be in the range of five million pounds. I want to get his attention."

"That should certainly do it. You know I'll handle it properly. *If* he asks."

The flight attendant, a handsome, muscular young man who Isabella enjoyed flirting with—though she had no interest at all in pursuing either sex or a relationship—approached her from the galley.

"May I get you anything more before we land, Ms. Hastings?" he asked in a low, husky voice, flashing a bright smile, his eyes penetrating hers seductively.

Isabella smiled teasingly, her hand reaching up to brush the man's bicep, then purred, "Not at the moment, Oliver. But thank you." As he turned to walk away, his eyes held hers for another moment, then he disappeared in the secluded galley in the aft section, taking his seat there. Isabella repositioned herself in her own luxurious seat as the cilice dug into the flesh of her thigh, a constant reminder of her self-imposed restraint.

Though steadfast in her vow of celibacy, Isabella Stewart Hastings enjoyed the power she possessed over controlling men's sexual drives, denying them the privilege of getting anything more from her apart from the pleasure of a brief, coyly intimate encounter.

The G700 was on final approach to Fiumicino Airport in Rome when the secure satellite phone on the console next to her seat softly hummed. Lifting it from its cradle, she simply answered, "Yes?"

"Good afternoon, Dame Isabella," the familiar baritone voice greeted her, "this is Cardinal Wolsey. I understand you will be arriving soon, and just wanted to confirm that our limousine will be picking you up at the private Signature terminal."

"Thank you, Eminence, that is most kind of you. I expect we will be proceeding directly to your offices at Villa Tiber, then?"

"Yes, that's right. You'll be meeting with Bishop Silva, Milo Banducci, our man at the IOR, and me. We could arrange for a late lunch if you'd like."

"That won't be necessary, Alastair," she replied. "I'm meeting someone for an early supper this evening. So, we will see you shortly, then. Goodbye." She placed the receiver back into its cradle.

Turning to her assistant across the aisle, she asked, "Alexis, would you hand me the Vatican Bank's financial report that Bishop Silva emailed to us?"

"Yes, it's right here ... somewhere." The young woman scrambled through her briefcase for the requested documents. Finding them, she reached across and handed the bound packet to Isabella. She began reading the executive summary:

"Key financial data for the Institute are the following: €5.0 billion of client assets of which €3.3 billion are assets managed for third parties or under custody; €36.4 million, as a net result illustrating the risk-based and faith-consistent investment process applied to manage IOR proprietary and entrusted assets; €645.9 million of net equity after distribution of profit and considering the allocation to the equity reserve decided by the Commission of Cardinals."

Very nice net equity figures, she considered. *IOR management is doing a fine job.* Further reviewing the summary, her eye was drawn to one notation in particular:

"During the past year, the IOR has continued to strengthen its senior management team and increased its investments in IT including a comprehensive development program launched in order to raise the resiliency of the IT infrastructure and reduce IT risks with increased cyber security."

Interesting, she mused, *and about time.* For a glacial bureaucracy often accused of still operating under a medieval mindset, Isabella was pleased to see the Vatican focus more on the bank's Information Technology systems—all of which, of course, had been purchased from a subsidiary of Stewart Hastings Global.

She was most impressed with the IOR's goal of strengthening its senior management team, which was the primary agenda prompting her visit. As president of the Vatican Bank, she would have to move to Rome, naturally. But such a vaunted position would also open up new doors of influence: doors that will then also be open to Opus Deus.

Having departed from the jet at the Signature terminal, the armored black Mercedes-Benz Sprinter limousine van accommodating Isabella Stewart Hastings' entourage of five, sped through the chaotic traffic of the city on its way to Villa Tiber. Tapping his influence with the *Carabinieri*, Bishop Silva had also arranged for a police escort to help clear the roads for his VIP guests.

On arrival, the two bodyguards checked the area for potential threats before permitting Isabella to emerge from the van while the driver punched in his passcode on the entrance panel, opening the black door for his party to enter.

Cardinal Wolsey, Bishop Silva and Milo Banducci were waiting inside the reception foyer. After introductions were made, Silva led them up the wide, red-carpeted stairs past the Escobar shrine on the mezzanine and up to his office on the second floor. Flinging open the golden doors, he welcomed Dame Isabella and Sir Robert inside the well-appointed office. Alexis and the two bodyguards were invited to wait in the guest lounge.

After some initial small talk, Wolsey got to the point of their meeting.

"Isabella, as you know, our goal is to see you installed as the IOR's next president. Your generosity to our order and to the Church has been greatly valued, of course, but your own expertise in the areas of international finance and investments is what will matter to the advisory board who report to a committee of cardinals and the pope himself, and they will make the decision in that regard. Our objective is to properly influence them to make the right choice. And that would be you."

Isabella turned to Bobby Cavendish expectantly.

"Um, yes," Cavendish began haltingly, "I, uh, will be meeting with my good friend Cardinal Petrini, and we expect he will arrange a meeting for Isabella with His Holiness while we are here. Ms. Hastings plans to donate a significant sum to Peter's Pence, one that will surely earn the pope's attention. We believe this, together with her impeccable credentials, would be a prudent start. As the IOR's own former president Paul Marcinkus once said, 'You can't run the Church on Hail Marys.'"

"Well," Cardinal Wolsey noted with pride, "we have already been laying discreet groundwork with our people at the Vatican and the IOR. As it happens, for some time I have been in possession of certain documents that will not only embarrass the president but immediately force his resignation. As chairman of the bank's advisory board, I have the power to effect such changes. At that point we will be poised to make our move, articulating the truth to our best advantage."

Isabella shifted in her seat, the constant pain of the cilice now causing her patience to be tested. "I would rather not be aware of specifics, gentlemen, as you might well understand," she said curtly. "Do what must be done, but kindly leave me out of it."

"Of course, Isabella, we all understand that," Wolsey confirmed.

"I think our business here is concluded for the moment, then," Isabella said, standing. "We're staying at the St. Regis should you need to reach me. I have a supper engagement this evening, but you can contact Alexis any time at my number. If that's everything, I'll say goodbye for now."

Wolsey and the others stood to see Isabella and Cavendish out, then he, Silva and Banducci returned to the Prelate's office.

"That woman is a force to be reckoned with, Guillermo," Wolsey cautioned, a faraway look in his eyes. "I know her better than anyone. She may not appear overbearing, but she does have a habit of making suggestions without options. Her power could very well exceed our own. We must keep her in check."

CHAPTER
TWENTY-THREE

O n a towering hilltop overlooking the softly undulating hills of the Tuscan commune of Arezzo lay the luxurious estate known as Villa Rosso, named not so much for the house itself being red, or "*rosso*"—though it was a dark shade of ocher befitting its historic masonry—but for the lush red wines its vineyards produced, wines rated among the finest in all of Tuscany.

Once owned by an Italian financier named Licio Gelli, Villa Rosso was secretly known to its members as the headquarters for the clandestine masonic lodge Propaganda Due, and Gelli had been grandmaster of the lodge until his death in 2015.

Founded in 1877 to defend the Catholic Church against the expected Antichrist, Gelli's later revisionist goal for P2 was to form a new political and economic elite to steer Italy away from the perils of communism by means of an authoritarian form of democracy. The covert objectives of this ultra-secret society became more ambitious than simply seeking the reinstatement of a fascist form of government in Italy. It sought the establishment of extreme right-wing governments throughout the world, doing away with the timid inefficiencies of conventional democracies.

Though the lodge's Masonic charter had been withdrawn in 1976, P2 still operated clandestinely, in contravention of Article 18 of the Italian constitution that banned secret associations. With lodge branches established in Italy, France, Portugal, Germany, England, several South American countries, and even the United States, P2 counted among its members prominent judges, legislators, ministers and cabinet members, police and military leaders, industrialists, bank presidents, journalists, and several Mafia families, as well as leading religious figures who were members of Opus Deus. In other words, P2 was highly influential in all walks of life.

By no small coincidence, Villa Rosso's present owner, Silvio Pollastri, served as current grandmaster of Propaganda Due, a role he assumed on the death of Gelli, its former venerable master, along with the property he acquired in the transition.

As he rode his horse through the tilled clay paths of Merlot vines on his beloved estate, his trademark orange sunglasses perched on his nose, Pollastri stopped from time to time to pluck a cluster of the dark blue–colored grapes to sample their plummy texture. Distinct from table grapes, wine grapes were smaller, with sweeter flesh but chewier, thicker skins, leaving a bitter taste impression. And like any seasoned winemaker, Pollastri chewed on each one for a moment, then spat it out. Not quite ready for harvest yet, he determined.

His riding partner for the afternoon was Julio Guzman, head of IT and security for Opus Deus and also a P2 member. But he was not an equestrian, and his horse sensed the rider's anxiety, reacting with a slower, unstable gait and lowered head carriage.

"Can't you tell this horse to calm down, Silvio?" Guzman asked.

"It doesn't work like that, Julio. He can smell your fear. Don't be hesitant, be assertive. And be mindful of your posture and where you place your legs, not on his flanks like you're doing now. Would you rather walk back to the house?" Pollastri smiled at his companion, then remounted his own horse.

"Let's head back, then."

Guzman was clearly in favor of that. As they ambled back to the ranch house, Pollastri continued their earlier discussion.

"As for this Calvi briefcase you mentioned ... Can't you just storm the Vatican and take it? You must have the ways and means of getting inside."

"It's not that simple. Security there is too heavy, especially getting access to the Secret Archive. We are trying one or two ways, though it's doubtful they will work. That's why I'm hoping you have insiders placed there."

"We do, but only in the Government Palace, where it matters most for our purposes. A number of cardinals and bishops are P2 members, yes, but I doubt they'll have much success getting in, either.

"This damned Banco Ambrosiano business still follows us, after all these years, Julio. If what you say is true, then I agree, we must get the briefcase and relieve ourselves of whatever pending disasters it may hold. Calvi protected himself wisely, and the names on his papers alone could bring us great harm, even today. Have you brought Isabella into this yet?"

"Yes," Guzman confirmed, "Wolsey and Silva met with her yesterday to lay the groundwork for her taking over the IOR, but the briefcase was not part of their discussion. Oh, but something else: Banducci discovered that Calvi, under a different name, still has an active account with the bank—one containing twenty million euros! He also has a safe deposit box to which the prefect of the Vatican Archive has the key. We don't know what's inside it, but this Father Dominic accessed the box a couple of days ago. We assume the key was found in the briefcase."

Pollastri was silent for a moment as he considered the safe deposit box.

"Are you familiar with my predecessor's activities at all, Julio?"

Though Guzman was nearly sixty, he knew little about Licio Gelli other than he had headed P2. "Assume I know nothing. What can you tell me?"

Pollastri stroked his horse's mane as he spoke. "Gelli was a brilliant financier and had established an extraordinary network of associates in the banking world and other international financial institutions going back to pre-World War II days. During the 1930s he was one of Mussolini's fascist Black Shirts, eventually becoming liaison between Italy and the Third Reich, dealing personally with Hermann Göring, commander in chief of the Luftwaffe.

"In 1942, Gelli was implicated in the plundering of Yugoslavia's treasury, including escorting a sham Red Cross-marked train secretly transporting fifty-five tons of gold, some of which had gone missing before reaching its destination. After the war, Gelli collaborated with Britain's MI-5 and the American CIA in orchestrating the infamous ratlines during which hundreds of Nazis escaped to South America and elsewhere under the code name, 'Operation Paperclip.' The Nazis paid for this service exceedingly well—in gold, diamonds, property and other assets—from which Gelli demanded a forty percent commission.

"In the 1960s, P2 had only a dozen or so members, and he was asked by current leadership at the time to restructure the lodge and increase its membership with the 'correct people.' By the 1980s, he had expanded its ranks to well over a thousand members of some prominence—all very secretively, since such associations were banned by law. Roberto Calvi was one such member.

"As for that gold I spoke of?" Pollastri pointed to his flowerbeds as their horses approached the villa. "Police raided this very house in 1998 and found two million dollars' worth of gold ingots buried in the geranium and begonia pots! Not nearly as much as Gelli was expected to have, by the way, which makes me wonder—could some of the rest be in Calvi's safe deposit box?"

He looked darkly at Guzman, the seeds of a plan forming in his mind.

TWENTY-FOUR

H ana's planned visit with Claudia, her colleague at Italy's *Corriere della Sera* newspaper, had gone well as the two of them worked on a joint article covering European Union immigration policies, to be published simultaneously with France's *Le Monde*. Now free for the afternoon, Hana called Michael to see if he'd like to have lunch.

"I would!" Dominic said. "And there's much to tell you, too. There's a little trattoria across from Saint Anne's Gate called Paisano; let's meet there in half an hour."

As he led Hana through the exercise of his getting into the bank's safe deposit box vault with Milo, Dominic ended with the denouement.

"And it was packed with bars of gold!" he said excitedly. "And a huge bag of these ...." He reached into his pocket and placed a single square diamond in front of her.

Her eyes took on the seasoned look of one who had seen many such stones in her life. Though impressed, Hana assessed the stone academically.

"Well … This is quite the find—an octagonal Asscher cut stone. And a fabulous specimen. I'd say this is about 10 carats. You say you found *five hundred* of these?! All the same size?"

"Yes, I'd say it was around that number. All in a rich, purple velvet bag with a gold drawstring."

"Michael," she whispered in the crowded café, "that bag is worth a fortune, and I mean that literally—*a fortune*! This stone alone is probably in the range of two hundred thousand dollars or more. So, if you have around five hundred, well, that's … *one hundred million dollars*! At least!"

Dominic paled on hearing the breathtaking figure. He just stared at Hana, blinking in shock.

"What are your plans for all this? " Hana asked, intrigued with her friend's dilemma.

Regaining his composure, Dominic replied, "Well, I've already discussed that with Cardinal Petrini. He feels it would be appropriate to move it all into the pope's Peter's Pence fund, where it can go to good use. Each pope has pet charities and causes they support during their time in office. The fund helps support humanitarian initiatives and social promotion projects."

"There may be legal implications in all this," Hana cautioned. "He should discuss it with the Vatican's attorneys before doing anything."

"Yes, he's intending to do that," Dominic said, then, "Listen, not to change the subject too abruptly, but why don't you join Ian, Teri and me after lunch? We're going to look over the Calvi documents we found on Opus Deus's computer."

"*Found*?!" Hana said, surprised. "Why, Father Dominic ... Have you been complicit in computer hacking?"

Dominic's face reddened as he held up his hands in surrender. "Not really. It was, um, Ian controlling the computer the entire time. I merely watched."

"I'd love to," Hana said with a sly smirk. "Do you realize this will be my first visit to your office? I've never even seen your so-called Secret Archives."

"Well, we'll change that. You'll get the rare VIP tour."

Hana was more than impressed at seeing firsthand the treasures her friend personally oversaw as prefect of the Apostolic Archive. Dominic introduced her to some of the Vatican's finest pieces: the extensive record of Galileo's trial for heresy during the Inquisition of 1633. The failed petition of seventy-five English lords formally requesting the pope's annulment of the marriage between Henry VIII and Catherine of Aragon, a massive parchment with eighty-five red wax seals dangling from thin hemp cords attached to it. He showed her the extensive collections on John Calvin and Martin Luther, documenting the formation of their own Protestant theologies after breaking with the Catholic Church.

Recognizing how truly rare an opportunity this was, Hana's eyes glistened with emotion. She had been through so much with this man over the last couple of years, and had taken his work for granted, as some ethereal occupation she hadn't really considered too deeply. Now she knew just how important his vocation was, not simply as a priest, but as one of the world's most significant custodians of history.

Standing next to her, Dominic looked into her eyes, grasping the visceral reaction of what she was experiencing.

"So you do have a day job, after all," she said as she poked him in the ribs.

"Well, I do like to stay busy in between our adventures," he responded.

"Pretty overwhelming, isn't it?" he asked gently as she struggled to take it all in.

Hana opened her mouth to say something, but the words wouldn't come. She sat down on a nearby wooden bench in the spacious gallery, looking down one aisle as far as the eye could see.

"It's much more than overwhelming, Michael. I honestly had no idea how important your work was. These are one-of-a-kind objects, irreplaceable, and so vital to the human experience. It's a pity so few actually get to see any of it. Thank you for sharing this with me."

"I suppose I do take it for granted now, having been here for awhile, something I swore I'd never allow myself to do. It wasn't that long ago I felt the same emotions you have now. I find it breathtaking again, just sharing it with you."

Hana nodded as she stood up, looked deep into Michael's brown eyes, then reflexively gave him a long, warm embrace.

As Dominic held her, he felt the pull of conflicting

emotions, of an unexpected lust. They were completely alone and no one would ever know what might have transpired. He drew her into his body more forcefully now and shut his eyes, if only to hold his impulses in check and not act on them. It was a galvanizing moment. Before he knew it, he found himself kissing her passionately, their lips finally joined after years of longing, and it felt exquisite. He never wanted the moment to end.

Hana leaned into him, accepting the mutual compulsion to have each other, at least for this moment.

As he opened his eyes, Dominic realized he had just taken a forbidden journey. He tried to swallow, but his throat was suddenly tight. He looked at Hana longingly. Then, over her shoulder, he glimpsed a large golden crucifix hanging on the wall behind her. Instantly, his body stiffened, and he slowly pulled away, placing his hands on her shoulders as he gently pushed her back, his head lowered.

"I … oh, my," she murmured, clearly taken aback. There was nothing more to say that wouldn't complicate an already awkward moment, one she thoroughly enjoyed but, she realized, had implications.

"It's … um, kind of intense down here, isn't it?" Hana quipped. "No wonder you limit the public's access."

Dominic grasped the chance to lighten the mood. "No kidding! It's easy to get carried away. Let's, um, go upstairs and join Ian and Sister Teri," he suggested, a chill suddenly making him shiver.

Hana laughed self-consciously. "Yes, please, anything to … yeah, that sounds good."

As they walked upstairs and into Dominic's outer office, Ian Duffy was, as usual of late, deeply engrossed in his new computer. Sister Teri sat beside him in her blue and white habit, assisting him on the new schema for the Archives database. Both of them were in their element.

"Alright, you two, break up the fan club," Dominic said, still struggling to recover himself. "We have work to do. Ian, could you get that briefcase? It's time to do some deeper digging into what we have here."

While Duffy went to fetch the briefcase, Hana looked around the office, her thoughts drifting back to earlier moments as Teri showed Dominic the progress they had made on the software project.

Several minutes later Duffy returned, briefcase in hand. They all moved to an open table, where Dominic again spread out the materials, assigning packets of documents to each of them for closer inspection.

"We're looking for any kind of incriminating evidence that might link Opus Deus with Propaganda Due, or what may just be shown as P2. Suspicious bank transfers. Unusual contracts. Any mention of gold or diamonds. Hana, since you have a mnemonic gift for names and companies, you take Opus Deus's membership roster and see if any names jump out," Dominic proposed. "I'll take half to help out."

Opening the directory, Hana noticed it was organized alphabetically by name, then by rank: supernumeraries, numeraries, numerary assistants and associates, Clergy of the Opus Deus Prelature, the Priestly Society of the Holy Spirit, and a smattering of other, lesser-ranked members and affiliated non-members. She handed the top half to Dominic.

As they went about their tasks, the room was quiet but for the turning of pages and the hum of air conditioning. From time to time another member of the prefect's staff would approach Dominic with some question or other, and after resolving it Dominic returned to his work reviewing the members roster.

"Well," he said, as he explored the B section of numerary names. "I suppose I shouldn't be surprised, but Milo Banducci's name appears here. That's one confirmation out of the way, and which accounts for his peculiar behavior."

Duffy looked sideways at Michael, guilt still weighing on him for having started this whole business by his blabbing.

Hana had been making notes on a separate legal pad as she flipped through her pages. "I recognize several prominent journalists here, as well as industrialists and bankers, many of whom I believe are close associates of my grandfather. Wait until he hears this."

"For now, let's keep our findings to ourselves," Dominic cautioned. "See what we have when we're finished, then decide what to do with it."

Hana's stack of papers also included reference to assets for use in P2's activities.

"Calvi does mention the gold and diamonds here, on a list of properties and other assets controlled by P2, confirming they are held in the Vatican Bank. He doesn't indicate values, but I imagine that might have changed depending on whether he made or removed deposits over time. Not to mention their values change with time anyway."

Continuing review of his own documents, Dominic came across a vaguely familiar name. "Hey," he said suddenly, "why does the name Isabella Stewart Hastings ring a bell? Anyone know who she is?"

Sister Teri spoke up without hesitation. "You bet I do. She's the CEO of Stewart Hastings Global, a major supply chain company from whom the Vatican gets nearly everything it needs. She's also one of the world's richest women. *She's* on the list?!"

"She is. Given her presumed assets, then, she must be a whale for Opus Deus in terms of donations and connections."

"Wait," Duffy interrupted, only half paying attention to the others, "you said Isabella Stewart Hastings? I found a document here earlier and I think her name was on it. Let me check ..." He flipped through papers he had already gone through until he found the recalled page.

"Yep, here it is. Looks like her birth certificate, with a coat of arms at the top. Born 12 April 1965. Her mother was Victoria Hastings, of the Royal House of Stewart, and it shows her father as Alastair Wolsey."

"*Alastair Wolsey*?!" Dominic exclaimed. "Could that possibly be the same *Cardinal* Alastair Wolsey, current Vatican Secretary of the Economy?!"

Sister Teri gasped. "Cardinal Wolsey has a *child*?!"

On a hunch, Hana flipped ahead to the Ws in the roster.

"You won't believe this," she said with some satisfaction, her instinct paying off, "but Wolsey is also a member of Opus Deus! He's shown here as being in the Order of the Priestly Society of the Holy Spirit. It also has 'P2' appended to his name."

Again, Sister Teri, fast becoming the team's historian, provided clarification. "Well, that's even more unsettling ... Father Michael probably already knows this, but P2 is code for Propaganda Due, a pseudo-Masonic organization that supposedly was shut down in 1976, banned in Italy as a secret lodge. But rumors have been floating for years that it's still very active, clandestinely moving to overthrow left-leaning democracies. And their reach is extensive, currently operating in many countries. I could go on, but I just wanted to point that out ..." She smiled humbly as she folded her hands in her lap.

"This gets weirder by the minute," Dominic said, perplexed. "Good catches, everyone. Now we just have to figure out what it all means."

"What about this 3.5-inch floppy disk?" Ian asked. "Do we even have a machine here capable of reading one?"

"Not that I'm aware of," Dominic replied. "I've never even used one, myself."

"As it happens, I do have a vintage Apple II GS equipped with a disk reader back at my apartment. Like I told Teri, I collect old Apple computers."

"You're such a geek, Ian," Teri chided. "What are those good for these days?"

"Well, Sister Smartypants, at the moment it's the only thing we have that can read this disk."

"Hmm," Teri murmured. "Point taken."

"I'll take this with me when I leave tonight and see what's on it. Who knows ... maybe it's gold of a different nature."

"Michael," Hana said, "Calvi has a strange note here that I don't quite understand. It simply reads 'The Dictum Covenant lays over the chair.'"

"Dictum Covenant?" Teri asked. "What do you suppose that refers to? It sounds kind of ominous."

Ever the puzzler, Hana's interest was piqued. "'... lays over the chair'? What chair?"

Duffy rummaged about the papers on his desk and pulled out the color photograph of the Chair of Saint Peter.

"I'd bet my new Mac Pro he meant *this* chair. It's the only photo among his papers—and it happens to be a chair! And a rather significant one."

Everyone turned toward Duffy, looking at the image he held above him. He brought it over to the table the others were working at and laid it down. Each of them peered closely at an image most were familiar with.

"I don't see anything that stands out," Hana said. "How could it be 'laying over a chair?'"

"That's what I intend to find out," Duffy said assertively. "Maybe the answer is on this disk."

In his apartment that night, Ian Duffy booted up his old Apple II GS and inserted the floppy into the disk drive. After a few minutes of grinding and clicking sounds typical of the old machines, several folders eventually appeared on the small display monitor. One of the folders was labeled "Key–Part A."

Key? Duffy wondered. *Key to what?*

Opening the file, he found a series of statistics identifying what appeared to be coded pixel locations, the kind used to carry encoded messages in an arcane cryptography practice known as steganography—the hiding of discreet information within other visible information. There was also an odd reference to something Calvi called his "Plutus Vault," with notations next to it reading, "Account BSSC Box 148625." This was getting more complex by the minute.

But where was the "visible information" these statistics referred to? It has to be the photo of the chair!

Duffy loved this type of enigma. His mind was built for problem solving, and it began racing to put pieces together without having the full picture yet.

He was fairly certain now that the "visible information" was that photograph of the Chair of Saint Peter. It was the only photo in Calvi's briefcase, oddly so, and he did make reference to something that "lays over the chair." He looked closely at it again, this time with a magnifying glass. Nothing was visible to his eye beyond what appeared on the photo.

But, it could very well be that its pixels were marginally offset from their proper registration. Or maybe there was an overlay of a secondary image, the one containing the steganographic statistics. But to "see" those he would need one or more keys to decrypt the underlying data.

In the meantime, he faced the daunting challenge of getting files off the floppy disk and onto something more modern. He had long bemoaned the fact that his eighteenth-century apartment building in Rome had no broadband, forcing him to use a landline for internet connections, but as he did most of his work at the office that was normally of little concern.

For once, though, he wasn't troubled by the disadvantage, for he could use an old Hayes 9600-baud modem he had to access the Apple II GS's dialup capabilities. But that would require some form of account that still used dialup ... a problem he hadn't foreseen.

Then he remembered—AOL still uses dialup! And though it was relatively ancient technology, nearly two million people still use the service today. Signing up for a new temporary account, his modem made the handshake connection with his vintage machine and, though it seemed to take forever, uploaded the files into his new account in the cloud. Then it would simply be a matter of connecting with his Mac Pro in the office to retrieve them. He grinned at the workaround, grateful to the dedicated legion of AOL members for keeping the old service alive. The important thing was that he managed to acquire and store the material off the old floppy disk.

He knew he was on to something now and was certain it held the key to important information, especially since Calvi went to so much trouble encoding it.

But there were always two keys to solving such a code.

The second key, which he presumed would be identified as "Key–Part B," would have the statistical characters that are assigned to the various color values of the photograph. Only by having all three parts, including the original image, could the message be recreated.

But where would they find this second key?

TWENTY-FIVE

A white Mercedes limousine had just pulled up to Saint Anne's Gate when Sergeant Karl Dengler approached the driver's window.

"Welcome to the Vatican," the Swiss Guard said. "Do you have an appointment?"

The back window rolled down and a dapper man in his 80s answered the guard.

"Yes, Sir Robert Cavendish to see Cardinal Enrico Petrini. Our appointment is for ten o'clock."

Dengler checked the authorized guest list, then signaled for another guard to raise the boom barrier.

Addressing the driver now, Dengler said, "You can park in any available space on your right," gesturing to the commercial area of the grounds. "Here are your passes, one for your dashboard, and the other for Signor Cavendish."

Then, turning to the passenger, "Sir Robert, a guard

will meet you at your car and you will be escorted to the cardinal's office in the Government Palace."

The limousine pulled forward onto Via di Belvedere, then turned right, parking in front of the central post office. One of the Swiss Guards met the vehicle and escorted Cavendish to the palace while the driver waited in the car.

"Bobby! What a great pleasure it is to see you again," Petrini said warmly, extending his hand to his British friend of many years.

"And you as well, Rico," Cavendish replied. "We have so much to catch up on and yet, so little time."

Petrini gestured for the man to take a seat in the cozy sitting area by a window looking out at St. Peter's Basilica. The cardinal's assistant, Father Bannon, brought in a silver tea set, poured two steaming cups of Earl Grey, then left the office, gently closing the door behind him.

Cavendish spoke first. "Since neither of us can abide small talk, Rico, I'll come right to the point. Isabella wishes to make a substantial contribution to the Holy Father, to Peter's Pence, of course. She appreciates the fine work he is doing with the fund—at least that which has been made public, anyway—and she is aware of the diminishing contributions made by the world's Catholic faithful in these uncertain times. Do you feel His Holiness would be of a mind to accept such an offer?"

Petrini knew his friend well, and assumed there were provisions attached, as there usually are with such offers

—especially from someone as powerful as Isabella Stewart Hastings.

"Bobby, I can assure you the pope would be most grateful for any contributions that benefit those we serve. But—and this will come as no surprise—may I ask what it is Dame Isabella might be expecting in return?"

"Simply an audience with His Holiness, that is all. I would imagine a donation in the range of, oh, say, five million pounds sterling would certainly merit such a privilege." Cavendish raised the cup of tea to his mouth and took a confident sip.

Though he withheld any visible reaction, Petrini was stunned at the amount. That figure was around the same amount the Vatican spent on the city's materials and supplies each year, most of which were purchased through Stewart Hastings Global.

"Have you any idea what she plans to discuss with His Holiness, Bobby? I imagine there must be some purpose she has in mind."

Cavendish paused before speaking, glancing up at the gold and white dome of St. Peter's as he took another sip of the Earl Grey.

"Word has it that the president of the Vatican Bank may be retiring soon, Rico. As CEO of one of the world's foremost financial management institutions, Isabella feels she would be a prime candidate for the post, should such a vacancy arise."

"I admit to some surprise hearing this, Bobby ... I have heard no such rumors! But I will certainly look into it. As for addressing such an issue with the pope, that may be premature. May I take this up with him first?"

"Of course, as you wish," Cavendish affirmed. "But she is in Rome as we speak, and only came here with that goal in mind. I do realize this may seem impertinent, but might we have your response by tomorrow morning?"

Petrini mentally checked the pope's calendar between now and the next day. He did have a meeting scheduled with the Holy Father at the end of today, and he could take the matter up with him then. But he was oddly discomfited by Isabella's aspiration.

"Bobby, I'm intensely curious why Isabella would even want to be—for lack of a better word, stuck—in such a comparatively low-level position, given her standing in the global financial community, not to mention her broader business involvements. Is that something you could address?"

"Unfortunately, I'm afraid I can't. I suppose she considers it a greater privilege to serve the Church in this way, lending the IOR her highly regarded credibility and pristine reputation in leadership. Do give it careful consideration, Rico. I'm certain Isabella would be most grateful."

"I will, yes. You'll hear from me this evening after my meeting with the pope. Given such a generous donation, I'm almost certain he would be pleased to meet with Isabella, though naturally no conditions can be attached to such a gift. I'm sure you understand."

"Yes, of course. It was so good seeing you again, my friend. Until later, then."

The two men stood and shook hands, then Petrini walked his guest to the door, outside of which a Swiss

Guard had been posted to escort Cavendish back to his car.

Returning to his desk, Petrini picked up his telephone and dialed the Vatican Bank.

"Bishop Wolaschka, please. Cardinal Petrini calling."

A moment later the German president of the IOR picked up the receiver.

"Klaus, this is Enrico. Am I to understand you are planning to retire soon?"

Wolaschka was as surprised as Petrini was on hearing the news. "Why, no such thing has even crossed my mind, Eminence! Why would you ask?"

"Hmm. Just a rumor I heard."

"You say there is a rumor going around to that effect? Who would say such a thing?"

Petrini was momentarily silent as he considered Wolaschka's response.

"Never mind, Klaus. As I said, it was just a rumor, apparently unfounded. Thank you for taking my call." He hung up.

There's something else going on here, Petrini pondered. *But what?*

TWENTY-SIX

A squad of eight Swiss Guards in full gala uniform, sharp-bladed halberds in hand, encircled Isabella Stewart Hastings and Sir Robert Cavendish as they escorted the honored guests in a procession from their limousine in St. Peter's Square and into the Apostolic Palace for their private audience with the pope.

Having been briefed on what to wear, Isabella donned her preferred black Armani Privé pantsuit and modest low-heeled, closed-toe pumps, with a black French lace mantilla veil covering her platinum hair styled in a low tendril twist. She was the epitome of a respectful yet fashionable Catholic devotee.

Entering the palace, the heavy-booted sounds of the guards' synchronized marching echoed through the marble halls, making the experience all the more regal for Isabella and Cavendish. Such intimate papal audiences are rare, but Isabella had banked on her international standing—not to mention her sizable donation—to get the pope's personal attention, and the gambit had, at least up to now, paid off.

As the procession led them through special rooms known as the Sala dei Sediari and the Sala di Sant'Ambrogio, they were joined by the Prefect of the Papal Household and two Gentlemen of His Holiness, lay dignitaries of the Papal Household who are summoned to receive and accompany guests of the pope. The entourage then proceeded through a small passage leading to the pope's private library, where the audience would take place.

Two assistants from the Prefecture of the Papal Household greeted them to explain final protocol for the audience, while half of the squad of Swiss Guards took their ceremonial positions in the library for the pope's protection.

As instructed, Isabella and Cavendish, himself wearing formal morning attire, were standing when the pope entered the library. Eschewing the kissing of the Ring of the Fisherman, the pope gave both of them handshakes, then hugs, and invited them to be seated in two white brocaded chairs set in front of his large, wooden desk, behind which the pope sat in his own matching chair.

"Your Holiness, it is a great honor that you receive Sir Robert and me today," Isabella began, "and we are grateful for your time."

"It is *my* privilege meeting you, signora, and you, signore. And I wish to thank you for your most generous donation to the Obolo di San Pietro, or what you may know as Peter's Pence. It will go to most worthy causes, I can assure you."

The pope then offered small talk to make them more comfortable, asking about their impressions of the Vatican, if they had been to St. Peter's Basilica yet, if they followed his beloved San Silvestro football team ... Then, a few minutes later, he got to the presumed point of the visit.

"Now, Cardinal Petrini informs me there may be something we might possibly do for you, yes?"

Taken by surprise at his sudden and straightforward candor, Isabella steeled herself for the moment.

"Your Holiness, as you have likely been advised, my background in international financial management can be of tremendous value to the Vatican Bank. I did not intend for this to be a job interview, but if you can find it in your graces to consider me for a leadership position at the IOR, I believe I could be of significant benefit."

The pope leaned back in his chair, rubbed his hands together thoughtfully, then leaned forward, folding his arms on the desk as he looked Isabella in the eyes. As he came forward, however, he pressed a hidden button beneath his desk.

"From what I am told, signora, yes, your qualifications are unrivaled by most. When that time comes, we shall certainly consider your kind offer."

A few moments later, the two wide doors of the library opened, and in came the same contingent of aides, prefects, the Gentlemen of His Holiness, and the four additional Swiss Guards.

The brief audience was clearly over.

The pope stood to shake their hands, then gave them his personal blessing as they bowed their heads. A photographer was on hand to take official pictures of the three together. Then, bidding them goodbye, the pope passed through the library door and into the Sala del Tronetto, returning to his office.

The same procession that had brought them into the papal library took place again, this time in reverse, taking them back through all the lavishly appointed rooms and outside to their limousine parked next to Bernini's columns in St. Peter's Square, where two Swiss Guards had been posted for security during their visit.

Now alone in the limo, Isabella and Cavendish looked at each other silently.

"Well, that happened," she said flippantly. "Is that all five million pounds gets one these days?"

"Now, Isabella, have patience. You couldn't have expected much more from the man, if you think about it. You got your audience, he is now personally aware of your ambitions, and we did not have to go through underlings to achieve it. As you are well aware, Opus Deus can exert its own influence in the matter—as the pope said, when the time comes. And whatever Wolsey has planned, that time may come sooner than later."

"You're right, Bobby, as usual. Would you have Alexis prepare a thank you note to Cardinal Petrini for his hand in this? It wouldn't hurt to keep the line of communications open with him.

"Let's have lunch back at the St. Regis, after which I'll give Wolsey and Silva a call to update them on our meeting. Then we'll head back to London this afternoon."

Celebrating midday Mass at Santa Maria della Pietà—just one of fifteen churches, chapels and oratories inside Vatican City—Father Michael Dominic raised the sacred host high in the air as he performed the Consecration. Acquitting himself in the rituals of the Mass gave him a stronger sense of self, of deeper connectedness to the faithful whom he served. And with all that was going on, he needed the service as much as the multitude sitting in the pews.

Extending the invitation to Communion to those attending—and even midday Masses at the Vatican were well patronized—Dominic dispensed the consecrated Eucharistic Sacrament to those who approached the Communion rail, some thirty souls at today's service.

Giving his final blessing and dismissal, Dominic concluded the Mass and returned to the sacristy, changing into his street clothes to meet Hana for a late lunch across the street at Paisano Trattoria.

"So, how much longer are you staying in town?" he asked her as they sat down at their table.

"My grandfather just left, returning to Geneva, so I'm here for the duration. I can work on my story with Claudia as needed, then take a flight back to Paris when we're done. I'm in no hurry."

"Good. I like having you here. Where's Marco, by the way?"

"He and Rusty are off doing whatever it is men do together. Probably at the shooting range or working out."

Dominic's phone buzzed in his pocket. Taking it out, he saw it was Bishop Silva calling.

"Let me take this, I'll only be a minute." He got up and went outside the trattoria while answering the call.

"Good afternoon, Father Dominic," Silva greeted him. "Have you given further thought to our proposal inviting you to join us?"

Dominic took a moment to gather the right words.

"Your Excellency, while I am deeply honored, I'm afraid I must remove myself from consideration."

Silva paused before replying. "Are you absolutely certain that's the right decision, Michael? You would be much better off with us than not …"

Dominic was instantly alert. "I'm not sure I agree, Excellency, but why do I get the feeling that sounds like an ultimatum?"

"Not at all, Father," Silva said, his tone terse and unconvincing. "I should think you would find such an offer in your best interests, that's all."

"I think I would know better what's in my best interests, Bishop Silva. But thank you for the invitation, and for the call." Dominic tapped the red End button.

Returning inside to their table, Dominic sat down in a huff.

"That bastard Silva really irritates me," he told Hana. "He as much as threatened me for not being willing to accept his offer to join the Priestly Society."

"I wouldn't worry about him, Michael," Hana soothed, then thought again, as if recalling a memory.

"But, the last time I said that we were subsequently chased by neo-Nazis in Argentina. Okay, maybe it is time to worry a little ..." She let out a nervous laugh.

Guillermo Silva looked at the man sitting across from him as he hung up the phone.

"Unfortunately, Julio, Dominic has chosen to take the less cooperative path. It appears we'll have to take matters into our own hands now.

"Do what you must to get both the briefcase *and* that key to the safe deposit box. We're running out of time."

TWENTY-SEVEN

E arlier that morning, prisoner number 45789 at Regina Coeli Penitentiary had been up since five o'clock gathering what few personal items he had accrued during his nearly two years of confinement, and now sat on his dingy cot waiting to be summoned.

As he sat there looking out the small filthy window of his cell, the dome of St. Peter's Basilica taunting him in the distance, his only thoughts were those of revenge.

Hearing his number called over the scratchy PA system, former cardinal and Vatican Secretary of State Fabrizio Dante stood up, took a final look around his lockup cubicle, then passed through its open door for the last time and headed down four flights of stairs toward the out-processing center and his path to freedom.

Once there, he signed several forms, was told of his parole conditions, recovered his stored personal effects, and received a debit card containing his leftover prison earnings plus unspent commissary funds. A guard escorted him through a long series of barred doors and dank passageways of the four-hundred-year-old building, manually unlocking and relocking each door until they reached the exit, where the guard simply held the door open for the now ex-con.

Dante stepped out into the morning light, a free man by the graces of Opus Deus, and took a deep breath.

Across the street a white Audi A8 luxury sedan was waiting for him, its chauffeur standing by the driver's door smoking a cigarette. Seeing his passenger step out of the prison exit, he raised his hand signaling to Dante that he was here for him.

The former cardinal crossed the street. As he approached the car, the driver held open the back door for him, took his bag of personal effects to put in the trunk, and then removed the cigarette from his lips and tossed it on the ground.

"Good morning, Signore," said the chauffeur as wisps of smoke drifted out his nostrils. "Cardinal Wolsey and Bishop Silva are waiting for you at Villa Tiber. Arrangements have been made for your accommodations, to stay there for as long as you wish."

Saying nothing, Dante looked at the man blankly then stepped inside the vehicle, leaning his head back for the brief ride to Opus Deus headquarters.

"What do you mean, you can't have me reinstated into the clerical state? That was part of our deal."

Dante sat impassively in Silva's office, adjacent to Cardinal Wolsey's chair and across from the bishop, who sat behind his desk. Sunlight streamed into the room through sheer white curtain panels draped over open, tall arched windows, a slight breeze causing them to ripple and flow.

"Fabrizio," Wolsey began, "surely you of all people must know such reinstatement must be approved by the Holy Father himself. And I doubt he is of a mind to do so, given your punishment. We will continue to petition his office, of course, but this will take time.

"Meanwhile, there is the matter of Father Dominic's paternity you promised us. Could you give us details on that now, please?"

"Yes, there is that," Dante mumbled. He struggled to find any other recourse, for once he had given up the most precious information he knew they sought, his immediate value to them would be diminished.

"Gentlemen, could we not do this later, once I've settled—"

"No, we cannot!" Silva interrupted him. "Time is of the essence here, Dante. Many things are in motion of which you are not aware, and we must have that leverage now. If, as you say, this knowledge would 'rattle the highest levels of power,' then please accommodate us in exchange for the freedom you now enjoy."

Out of options, there was nothing Dante could do now to delay the inevitable. He sighed.

"Cardinal Petrini is Michael Dominic's biological father."

Both Silva and Wolsey looked at Dante as if he were mad, their mouths hanging open in astonishment.

"And you ... you have proof of this?" Wolsey asked.

Dante fidgeted in his seat, clearly uncomfortable by the reply he was about to give.

"Well ... yes ... proof exists. However, it was confiscated by the Carabinieri when I was arrested. I do not know where it is now."

"What kind of proof?"

"I had DNA samples analyzed for both men and the heredity was a perfect match. I had my suspicions for some time but needed proof, so I had covert samples collected from both Petrini and Dominic and sent them to a lab here in Rome. The analysis came back positive."

"Might the lab still have results on file?"

"No, I made sure the samples and original diagnostic reports were destroyed. The only evidence now lies somewhere in the state's repository."

Silva considered this for a moment. "Does Petrini know you're aware of this?"

"Oh, yes. I made it quite clear to him the lengths to which I had gone to obtain such damning information. I have no doubt my incarceration was in part his act of revenge for that.

"Perhaps you could use your influence with the Carabinieri to retrieve the diagnostic report I retained."

Wolsey looked at Silva for some kind of confirmation of such a possibility, but the bishop shook his head.

"There is a chance," Silva offered, "that we might simply use the knowledge of it to intimidate Dominic, motivating him to hand over the key and briefcase to maintain our silence. His allegiance to Petrini is widely known, and that alone may cause him to act."

Dante looked up. "'Key and briefcase?'"

"Yes, we discovered Dominic found Robert Calvi's briefcase—the one that went missing after his death under Blackfriars Bridge—which contained, among what we must assume are highly incriminating papers, a key to a safe deposit box in the Vatican Bank. Our man there, Milo Banducci, watched as Dominic entered the vault, spending some time there looking at whatever was in it."

"And where is this briefcase now?" Dante asked.

"That's one of our problems," Silva continued, glancing at Wolsey. "We understand they now have digital copies of the briefcase's contents, but our efforts to obtain copies electronically were unsuccessful. We are told the briefcase is in one of the *armadi* in the Apostolic Archive. There's no way we can get to that, unfortunately."

Dante allowed a grim smile on hearing this. "I wouldn't be too sure about that. Remember, I was once Secretary of State and I know the Archives well. There are fifteen of those *armadi*, and I still have a particularly capable mole in the Vatican, Father Bruno Vannucci, who might be able to get what you need. It will take some careful planning, though."

Silva cocked his head as an eyebrow curved upward, encouraged to hear this.

"How might you go about this, Eminence?" he asked, appealing to Dante's ego using his former honorific.

"I haven't been addressed as such for two years now, Guillermo. Thank you. I will speak with Bruno, see what he can do. He has a gift for stealth that has come in very handy in the past. In exchange, I will ask again: please put more effort into restoring my clerical state. I have much more to offer you. Getting the briefcase is your last gratis accommodation from me."

"Thank you, Fabrizio," Wolsey said. "As always, your wisdom and connections are invaluable. And of course, I shall personally petition the Holy Father on your behalf. On that you have my word."

TWENTY-EIGHT

T heir lunch over, Hana and Dominic stepped out of Paisano's and into the bright sunlight along the Via della Conciliazione. Turning right toward the Vatican, Caligula's Obelisk loomed in the near distance, in the very center of St. Peter's Square, as they ambled on the sidewalk chatting.

Watching them from behind the tinted windows of a stolen black Fiat Talento van parked in front of the trattoria, Julio Guzman sat quietly smoking a cigarette. His two companions, one driving and one squatting down in the back, also watched and waited.

Sitting in the front passenger's seat, Guzman cracked the window to let the smoke out.

"How's this going down?" the man behind him asked.

Guzman paused a moment before answering, gauging

the situation. "Banducci told me the priest carries the key on his key ring, so we have to assume he has it on him.

"Enzo, turn onto Via Rusticucci just up ahead as they approach the curb, then you jump out and restrain the girl. Make sure she doesn't scream while Gino and I pull Dominic into the van. Then jump back in and get us out of here, fast.

"Gino, then you hold Dominic down while I get the key from his pockets. Deal with him if he doesn't comply, just keep him alive. We'll dump him out when we have what we came for. And keep your masks on. Our paths may cross again."

As Enzo slowly pulled the van out into the light traffic, the other two men put ski masks over their heads. When Dominic and Hana were about ten meters from the curb, Enzo turned onto the side street, stopped the van, then put on his own mask. There were no other pedestrians in sight.

As the two approached the van, still chatting, Enzo got out and came around the front, while Guzman and Gino opened their doors and leapt toward Dominic. Enzo grabbed Hana, holding his hand over her mouth as she started to protest, pulling her against the brick wall of the adjacent building to keep her out of sight from the main boulevard. She tried struggling fiercely to shake him off, but the man's hold on her was too secure.

Gino thrust his arm around Dominic's neck in a vice grip that stifled his ability to shout, dragged him into the back of the van where Guzman lifted his legs and tossed him inside, then slammed the van door shut. Enzo pushed Hana away, and as she fell onto the sidewalk he ran around to the driver's side. She screamed for help in Italian, "*Aiuto! AIUTO!*" as the van screeched away from her and drove off in the distance.

Hana pulled out her phone and with trembling hands dialed 113 for the *Polizia di Stato*. She took note of the van's details as she watched it recede.

In the back of the van, Dominic struggled to free himself, kicking Guzman in the face with all the force he could muster while Gino's grip on his neck squeezed tighter, threatening to force the consciousness out of him. Guzman's fist came down hard, landing a heavy punch on Dominic's abdomen, knocking the wind out of him as he doubled up in pain. Easier to hold down now, the Spaniard reached into Dominic's right jeans pocket and withdrew the key ring he found there, pocketing it himself. The priest slumped over, unconscious, Gino's choke hold having taken effect.

Breathing heavily, Guzman sat up, took his mask off and wiped the blood off his forehead from the cut Dominic's boot had inflicted, then lit another cigarette. "Enzo, next alley you find, pull into it," he barked.

Seeing a narrow, ancient alley just ahead, Enzo turned into it and brought the van to an abrupt halt. Gino opened the van's rear door and pushed Dominic's body out onto the cobblestones. With one final look, Guzman tossed his cigarette into Dominic's face as he lay there, slowly coming to.

The door slammed shut, and the van took off down the alley.

. . .

As he lay there, Dominic opened his eyes, the painfully bright sunlight adding to the killer headache he now felt from the lack of oxygen. The first thing he saw was a smoldering cigarette laying in the cobblestone grout a couple of inches from his nose. The band around the filter read "Ducados."

Pulling his arms up, he slowly raised himself into a sitting position.

Who the hell were those guys?! Why me? And where's Hana?

He looked up and down the alley, seeing no one else in sight. He felt around in his pockets. Phone? *Check*. Wallet? *Check*. Keys? *Missing*.

Pulling out his phone, he called Hana.

"Michael?!! Where are you? Are you okay?! Who were those men?"

"I'm in some alley."

"Stay where you are," she said. "The police are here and we'll come to you. Which alley?"

Dominic looked up at the corners of the buildings around him, hoping to find one of the plaques that commonly identify alley names in the older sections of Rome.

"I'm on Vicolo Pilati, just off Via del Mascherino. I'll be waiting here."

Hana passed the details to the female officer who had responded to her call, and the two of them took off in her blue-and-white Alfa Romeo Giulia, lights and siren blazing.

Dominic was now standing on the corner of the alley and the main street when Hana and the police car pulled up. Leaping out of the car, Hana rushed into his arms, tears flowing. Dominic embraced her back, but held one arm up and away from her—for in that hand was the cigarette his attacker had thrown out of the van.

"You may want to put this in an evidence bag, Officer. One of the men, a Spaniard by his accent, tossed it at me before they drove off."

"Grazie, signore," she said, taking it with a gloved hand. "May I see your identification? And can you describe these men and their vehicle?"

After presenting their IDs, both Dominic and Hana offered what descriptions they could of the three assailants and the van while answering the officer's other questions. Dominic told her they had only taken his key ring, nothing else. When they were finished, she offered them a ride back to the Vatican, which they gratefully accepted.

Back in Dominic's office, Hana was perplexed.

"Why did they take you? And why just take your keys?"

"I've been thinking about that, and the only answer I keep coming up with is the most logical one: for the key to the safe deposit box. Someone from Opus Deus wanted whatever they think is in it badly enough to rough me up. And I imagine it could have gone worse. But I did get in a solid kick in the face of one guy, the one who seemed to be the leader. Even with that ski mask on, it must have hurt him pretty badly. But I got as good as I gave. He landed a pretty nasty gut punch in return." Dominic unconsciously rubbed his abdomen as he spoke, wincing at the memory, the pain still smarting. *That's gonna leave a bruise*, he thought.

"Hopefully the police can find a fingerprint or get DNA off that cigarette," Hana said. "Those guys have to pay for what they've done."

"I doubt the police will take time for a DNA scrub. It's expensive, too, especially for a minor assault. But a fingerprint would be good. I've never seen Ducados cigarettes before, but then I'm not a smoker so I wouldn't know the world of tobacco brands." He smiled weakly.

"When Marco finds out about this he'll be pissed. You know how defensive he gets about my safety."

"At this point there's nothing he could do either— except, as you say, get pissed about it."

At his desk in the office, Ian Duffy was now certain there was a registration overprint on the photo of Peter's Chair. That had to be the image containing the steganographic information he suspected had been discreetly overlaid.

He downloaded Calvi's old floppy disk files from AOL to have available for when, and if, they ever found Key-Part B.

Meanwhile, Sister Teri had taken her lunch hour to continue poring over the documents in Roberto Calvi's briefcase and his files on Opus Deus's computer network, confident she could make more sense of it all on her own.

The one thing that had caught her attention before—that veiled reference to P2—was of particular interest. Through her own studies she knew that the secret Masonic lodge could be of particular danger to her beloved Church, one of the few things that could anger the otherwise even-tempered nun.

As she paged through the two-inch stack of papers that had yet to be reviewed by anyone—those enclosed in an "Unread" folder she had previously prepared, being a hyper-organized sort—she came across what appeared to be a planning summary document in someone's handwriting, presumably Calvi's. On it were various notations of the outstanding debts of Banco Ambrosiano, notes on how to get the IOR to assist in resolving those debts—and the mention of gold and diamonds in the safe deposit box in the Vatican Bank.

The notes went on to discuss someone by the name of Silvio Pollastri, and his taking over as Grand Master of P2 on Licio Gelli's death. Other loose notations on the page indicated "Villa Rosso, Arezzo / P2 GHQ," which she took as a reference to general headquarters.

Interesting. P2's headquarters is in Tuscany?

This new revelation excited her. Could this Pollastri be the current P2 leader?

She kept reading through the materials until she came upon an unsent letter to the Vatican Secretary of State:

Your Eminence,

This letter is to inform you of a nefarious plot by Opus Deus and Propaganda Due. Their goal is to install a pope of

their own choosing, in order to promote their dual agendas.
They have dedicated a substantial amount of gold and
diamonds to this effort, to be used to sway the College of
Cardinals at the appropriate time, those who are not
already members in their organizations, which are many. I
have hidden this treasure from them in hope of stalling, if
not preventing, this horrible scheme, and now I fear for my
life. Funds are now being amassed from various sources
and are being held in accounts at various banks, including
an account and safe deposit box in the Vatican Bank under
my pseudonym, Gian Roberto Calvini. I have hidden a copy
of the Dictum they have mutually signed in the photo of the
Chair and locked away the keys to decode it. Should I be
eliminated, you will have to bring this terrible crime to
light. May God grant you strength.

Roberto Calvi

Sister Teri sat bolt upright in her chair, shocked at
what she had just read.

"Ian ..." she quavered, then gulped. "Ian, you have to
see this."

"Wait, I'm pretty deep into something here ..."

"Ian!" she protested. "This is more important than
scribbling code right now!"

Duffy turned to look at her, annoyed at being
interrupted. "Jeez, don't get your habit in a twist. What
is it?"

First, Teri explained to him more of what she knew
about P2's background and overarching goals: the
downfall of democracies and installation of far right

governments, not much different than Hitler's invasion of Poland in 1939, she pointed out, ultimately leading to the Third Reich's blitzkrieg and fascist takeover of other countries. Only in this case P2 would use religion as the instigating force, in alliance with well-placed political leaders who favor their cause. And what better, more easily accessible target than the Vatican and its influence over a billion Catholics worldwide?

Then she showed Duffy what she had just read. A student of history himself, he quickly grasped the vision she presented.

"Holy smoke, you're right. Calvi was covering his backside by writing and holding onto this in case he was caught, but it explains exactly what that Dictum is. Michael needs to know about this!"

"And pronto," Teri added. "We also have to learn more about this Silvio Pollastri. Let's see what more we can find online."

Launching a browser, Teri searched on the man's name and location. A huge list of results returned, at the top of which was Villa Rosso Vineyards in Tuscany. Clicking on the website, she navigated to the About page.

"That's got to be it!" Teri exclaimed. "The villa is in Arezzo, and is owned by Silvio Pollastri. This must be his cover pastime while he runs his evil empire."

"Aren't you being a bit overly dramatic?" Duffy asked with a smirk.

"I've studied this group for awhile now, Ian. They do have a history akin to truly wicked deeds: high-profile crimes including casual murders and planned assassinations, corruption, bribery, collaboration in juntas of foreign governments, not to mention their close ties to the Mafia. Licio Gelli was the last Grand Master, and while searching his villa—that would be the same Villa Rosso, by the way—among the gold and other things police found a document titled *Plan for Democratic Rebirth*, which called for a consolidation of the media, suppression of the power of trade unions, and revision of the Italian Constitution to suit their goals. According to these papers, Italy was just the start. Never underestimate the power and reach of Propaganda Due.

"Licio Gelli died in 2015, which means it's now Pollastri who's leading the organization. If P2 *is* planning for their own man to be the next pope, they're probably laying the groundwork already. That's clearly what Calvi had in mind for that gold bullion and the diamonds, probably all of which had to come from illegal money transfers, fraudulent loans, and the Mafia. It's all here in writing! But we *must* find that Dictum Covenant to prove there was an executed memorandum.

"Meanwhile, whom do you suppose they're choosing as pope?"

"Well, I'm hardly the one to ask about that. Father Michael may have a better idea. Meanwhile, let's keep going through what we have here. There are likely to be other important details we'll find.

"Plus," Duffy added, "I've just discovered something really intriguing. We may be close to finding that elusive Dictum Covenant."

CHAPTER
TWENTY-NINE

B esides holding the post of Vatican Secretary for the Economy, Cardinal Alastair Wolsey also served as chairman of the advisory board governing the IOR. In that role, all bank personnel ultimately worked under his direction, including its president, Bishop Klaus Wolaschka.

A German national working in the Vatican Bank since 1960, Wolaschka had been recommended for the job by a prominent Franciscan cardinal he knew well at the time, one who happened to be a fellow conspirator in implementing the Argentinian segment of the ODESSA network, the abhorrent ratlines tasked with secreting Nazis fleeing out of Germany and down to South America with the cooperation of the Catholic Franciscan order. While in his early teens by the end of the war, Wolaschka had helped over three hundred Nazis find their way to Argentina with support from President Juan Perón after he came to power in 1946. Included among them were many high-value targets sought by Israeli Mossad: Dr. Josef Mengele, Adolf Eichmann, Josef Schwammberger, and Erich Priebke, among others.

In the intervening years, no one had ever accused Wolaschka of his complicity in such war crimes and he had convinced himself that no one ever would.

But he was wrong.

Being British, Alastair Wolsey never much cared for Klaus Wolaschka, for as a child he clearly remembered the devastation caused by the Blitz of London, a tenacious German bombing campaign against the United Kingdom in 1940 and 1941. His family home had been destroyed and his father killed in combat: the kinds of memories a child would not soon forget.

In his earlier years as an assistant scrittore in the Vatican Secret Archive, decades before Michael Dominic's arrival, Wolsey had discovered sensitive Franciscan records identifying Klaus Wolaschka as an agent for ODESSA. Furious at first, intending to expose the German and have him ousted from the Vatican Bank, Wolsey's political instincts held him back, cautioning him to hold onto the records until the time came when they might prove more useful.

And, as he had earlier alluded to with regard to Isabella Stewart Hastings, that time had come.

Having been summoned to Cardinal Wolsey's office in Saint John's Tower, Bishop Wolaschka glanced at his watch again, irritated that he had already been waiting thirty minutes to find out why the cardinal had sent for him. He never did care for his boss, and the feeling was mutual.

The door to Wolsey's office finally opened and an assistant emerged.

"Cardinal Wolsey will see you now, Excellency. Please, do come in."

"It's about time," the bishop muttered under his breath. His stout body swept into the office, his flush face taking on the amaranth red of his pellegrina cape.

"What is it this time, Alastair?" he asked, not bothering to mask his irritation.

"In this office you shall address me as Eminence, Bishop Wolaschka. Please, have a seat."

"Yes, *Your Eminence*," he snapped churlishly.

"I'll get right to the point. The time has come for you to step down. Your services are no longer required at the IOR."

Wolaschka's face turned crimson, anger now displacing impatience, his eyes wild with fury.

"What on earth do you mean, *step down*?! I shall do no such thing! On whose authority?"

"On my own, of course," Wolsey said. "As chair of the advisory board, I am authorized to take such action on my own merits. However, you may want to take a look at this before making a complete fool of yourself." Wolsey handed him copies of what clearly were aged war-era documents.

Wolaschka accepted the pages, then leaned back in

his chair to read them. As he read, his face drained of color. Feeling faint, he held on tightly to the arm of the chair.

"Where ... where did you get these papers?" he stammered. "None of it is true!"

"I'm afraid it is, Klaus. All of it. Irrefutable proof of your collaboration with the Nazis. Not something the Holy Father would look kindly upon, not to mention the world's financial community. Your reputation would be ruined if this were to be made public. I suggest we avoid all that by your making the logical move to retire. Besides, you're an old man now. Isn't it time you stepped down for your own sake?"

Wolaschka was speechless. He felt his whole body sink in on itself, as if all the air had been released from a balloon. He was doomed. Tears began streaming down his fat cheeks.

"But ... I was just a boy then ... and ... and I—" he faltered.

Wolsey looked at his calendar. "I suggest you hand in your formal resignation to me effective in two weeks' time. And do be careful what you do in the meantime, Klaus, else this may not go as discreetly as one might hope.

"One more thing. When you meet with Cardinal Petrini, and others whom you will obviously encounter during this transition, I want you to formally and wholeheartedly endorse Isabella Stewart Hastings as your successor. She has already been vetted and is fully capable of taking over. Do I make myself clear?"

Wolaschka couldn't feel his legs as he tried to stand, but eventually made it to the door. Turning to look back at Wolsey, the bishop opened his mouth as if to say something, then stopped, simply nodded, and stumbled out of Saint John's Tower and into the papal gardens.

CHAPTER

THIRTY

S itting at an intimate table on the quaint cobblestone alley outside La Pasticciera, Hana Sinclair and Marco Picard took in their morning ritual of caffè and bombe alla crema, one of Rome's most iconic pastries, with the heady honey perfume of nearby cabbage roses adding to the comfy aromas of the café's freshly baked pastries and roasted coffee beans.

"I'm just glad you're okay," Marco said after Hana told him of Dominic's and her encounter with their attackers. "But how's Michael doing?"

"He took the worst of it," she said, sipping her espresso with a faraway look in her eyes. "I hate it when any harm comes to him. He's such a good man with a kind soul."

Hana's clear affection for the priest was not lost on the French commando. He had long realized there was competition for Hana's affections, though Dominic's was a situation that in itself could pose no rivalry for his own feelings. Still, he was burdened with a stubborn tinge of jealousy he couldn't shake.

The phone in Hana's bag rang. She pulled it out to answer. Seeing it was Dominic calling, her face lit up.

"We were just talking about you. How are you feeling today?" she asked.

"Better, just a few scrapes from being thrown on the cobblestones like a sack of potatoes. I won't be running for a few days, but I'll live.

"Hey," he added, "could you and Marco come to my office now, or soon? Sister Teri and Ian have something important to share, and I'd like you and Marco to be here."

"Sure, we should be able to get there in thirty minutes or so. Saint Anne's Gate entrance?"

"Yeah, Karl's on gate duty this morning, he'll give you passes."

"What we found is a strong and compelling indictment against P2," Teri said, looking around at the others gathered in the conference room.

"Roberto Calvi's documents unequivocally show their goal as being the installment of their own pope. It appears they want to control the Vatican and—through the IOR and Vatican City's own economic institutions— its financial ways and means.

"These papers name the current Grand Master of P2 as being Silvio Pollastri, a well-respected man with a large vineyard and ranch in the Tuscan town of Arezzo, about seventy-five kilometers southeast of Florence."

Teri further elaborated on the historical background

of police raids on Villa Rosso, the gold discovered there during Licio Gelli's tenure as Grand Master, and the probability that Pollastri is now running things here in Rome from his estate in Tuscany.

"I wouldn't be surprised if P2 and Opus Deus were jointly collaborating on some kind of operation here. Their goals are not mutually exclusive. They could even be behind the attack on you, Father Michael. P2 has been known to control governments, and their people are embedded everywhere. It's quite likely each of you know many of them, just not their secret affiliation with the organization. And it *is* highly organized and fiercely clandestine."

"Speaking of clandestine," Duffy added, "I've discovered something on that floppy disk we found in Calvi's briefcase."

He went on to explain how he used AOL as the coordinating medium to get the files onto his Mac Pro, and his discovery of half of the key to unlock the image containing the steganographic information.

"In steganography, messages can be embedded into digital images using methods that are imperceptible to the human eye, but such distortions can fundamentally alter the underlying arithmetic elements of an image, known as statistics. In order to detect the presence of hidden information in Calvi's image of Peter's Chair here, I'll use a process known as Linear Discriminant Analysis, a widely employed method for pattern recognition. This model contains higher-order statistics that capture certain information on the images, which is substantially modified when a secret message is embedded in an image. As a result, we're able to detect at least the presence of whatever steganographic message Calvi has overlaid in the image. Now we just need to find the second key to unlock it. *That* is where I believe we'll find the official Dictum Covenant, the proof we need to expose their operation. Unless we have that, the rest is merely hearsay from Calvi."

"And where might that second key be?" Dominic asked.

"Calvi did mention something called his 'Plutus Vault' in what information I was able to decrypt, but I don't know what that means, or even where such a vault might be."

"Plutus," Teri said, her hand shooting up anxiously as if she were in class, "was the Greek god of wealth. Not surprising Calvi would use him, given the treasure we've found so far."

"Maybe there's more in this Plutus Vault, then. Or better yet, that may be the location of Key-Part B. By the way, Calvi also made mention of..." Duffy referred to his own notes, then continued, "'BSSC Account Box 148625.' So it must be a safe deposit box, but who knows where?"

"Wait!" Hana said suddenly. "BSSC could refer to my grandfather's bank, Banque Suisse de Saint-Clair. It does have a branch here in Rome, maybe that's where the box is! I'll call him and ask if he's ever heard of such a thing as a Plutus Vault, and if it's somehow related to his bank. If anyone would know, I imagine he would."

"That's great, Hana, thanks. So, let's get back to P2's papal ambitions," Dominic said. "Any ideas on *who* their candidate might be, Teri?"

The young nun glanced at Duffy before she spoke. "From what we can glean from Calvi's notes, combined with the identities we found on Opus Deus's member roster, Ian and I think Cardinal Alastair Wolsey stands the greatest chance of being their pick. But if word of Isabella Stewart Hastings being his daughter gets out, his candidacy carries some pretty ruinous baggage with it."

"Since no one else knows you have proof of that," Marco observed, "you may be able to circumvent Wolsey's even being considered in the future."

After carefully considering the situation, Dominic decided the others needed to know at least part of the privileged information Petrini had shared with him, in order to better evaluate how to proceed.

"Listen ... I can't say more now—and promise me that what I do say here doesn't leave this room—but there's a good chance we're looking at a new papal conclave soon."

Gasps from Teri and Hana echoed off the walls of the small, bare conference room.

"How do you even *know* this, Michael?!" Hana asked. Sister Teri's hand covered her mouth in astonishment.

"As I mentioned, I can't reveal anything more. I was held to secrecy, but in light of these new circumstances with P2, the situation has changed. The point is, there will be candidates lining up as papabile. I believe Cardinal Petrini would be the pope's personal choice; that's fairly obvious even to casual observers. But if Wolsey emerges as a contender, we must act accordingly. P2 *cannot* gain control of the Apostolic Throne. And at the moment, the outcome of that prospect could well be in our hands."

Her lunch hour over, Sister Teri returned to the Vatican switchboard, while Hana and Marco took a taxi back to her hotel. Dominic had promised Cardinal Petrini an update on the Archives database development soon, so he and Duffy spent the next hour finalizing their report.

Dominic's desk phone rang. He answered it.

"Father Dominic? This is Father Bannon from Cardinal Petrini's office. Could you and your assistant meet with the cardinal now?"

"Hi Nick," Dominic said, then, with concern, "You got a cold or something? Your voice sounds off."

"Yes, sorry," the muffled voice acknowledged, "it's just the change of seasons, I suppose. Will we see you shortly … Michael?"

"Sure. We should be there in about twenty minutes. See you then." He hung up the phone.

Finishing up their preliminary report, Dominic and Duffy gathered up their papers, then left the office for the long walk through the many-acred papal gardens to the Government Palace.

Taking the old elevator to the fourth floor, they greeted Father Bannon, their report in hand.

"Hey, Nick. Feeling pretty badly, eh?" Dominic asked.

Bannon turned around in his chair. In a perfectly healthy voice with clear eyes, he replied, "Actually, I'm feeling great, Michael. How about you?"

Confused, Dominic's face screwed up. "But you had a nasty cold just minutes ago when you called me!"

"I didn't call you …"

"Cardinal Petrini didn't ask for us to meet him?!"

"No, the cardinal is in a meeting with the Holy Father. Why?"

Dominic turned to Duffy, a look of dawning suspicion on his face, then one of alarm. "Ian, where did you leave the briefcase?"

"On the floor next to my desk," the young Irishman said apprehensively. "You don't think—"

"Yes, I do. Sorry, Nick, we've been duped. Later."

Slamming open the door to the stairs, taking the steps two at a time with Duffy close behind, Dominic ran down the four flights and sped back through the gardens to his office, a good five-minute run at best.

But they were too late. The briefcase and all the Calvi papers previously laid out on Duffy's desk were gone.

THIRTY-ONE

Minutes earlier, Father Bruno Vannucci had walked out of the Archives building, casually but confidently, as if he belonged there, an old brown leather briefcase dangling from his hand stuffed with the papers he had gathered from Ian Duffy's desk. He was proud of himself for masking his natural lisp and emulating the deeper voice of a sick Nick Bannon. *Old sick Nick,* he giggled to himself.

Hailing a taxi just off St. Peter's Square, he told the driver to take him across the river to Villa Tiber in the upscale Pinciano suburb. As the cab followed the road encircling the historic Villa Borghese and its two hundred acres of fabled gardens, Vannucci wondered how his old boss, former Cardinal Dante, was faring. He had yet to see the man since he had gotten out of prison, having only received a phone call asking for this risky favor. It was a miracle he had been paroled early, but Vannucci was well aware of Opus Deus's powerful influence, for which Dante's release must have been responsible.

Arriving at Villa Tiber, Vannucci paid the driver and approached the black door. He rang the bell, and a few moments later he heard a buzzing sound as the lock released. The priest turned the bronze handle and entered.

He told the receptionist he was here at the request of Fabrizio Dante.

"Yes," the man at the desk said, "Signor Dante has been expecting you. Please, have a seat." The man gestured to a seating area next to a statue of the Virgin Mary.

Vannucci had never been inside the headquarters of Opus Deus before and was impressed at the opulence of the building's art and furnishings. Looking up to the mezzanine, he noticed the burning candles and freshly cut flowers adorning the shrine to Saint Juancarlos, in whose honor a great many people served, he recalled from prior reading.

"Bruno ... So good to see you again, old friend."

Fabrizio Dante, in a smart, dark-blue Ferragamo suit with a white Zegna double-cuffed shirt and striped red tie, held out his hand to Father Vannucci, who stood looking at his former boss in awe.

"It is good to see you looking so well, Eminence, and a great honor to shake your hand," Vannucci lisped, his high-pitched voice always an irritation to Dante.

"Come, let us go to my office and ... discuss things." Dante led the way down a long hall to a suite of offices with windows facing the outside gardens.

Once inside the spacious room, Dante closed the door and drew the blinds on the windows.

"I must apologize for being a little short on time today, Bruno. They have me involved in many projects here, to which I have acceded as part of my gratitude for their help in getting me out of that hellhole, Regina Coeli. I cannot even mention its name without shuddering.

"Now, let's see what you've brought me here." Dante looked as ravenous as a wolf when his eyes fastened on the briefcase. He wanted a good look at its contents before anyone else at Opus Deus, in the event there may be something in it he might use for his own calculated purposes. As he reached for the briefcase, the door to his office suddenly opened. Backlit by the bright, outdoor windows behind him, Julio Guzman's dark silhouette stood in the doorway.

"Ah. I heard we had a special visitor," he said in a rather accusing manner. "And has he brought what we were expecting, Fabrizio?"

Surprised and upset by the interruption, Dante tried to buy time.

"Can you not give us a few minutes to catch up as old friends do, Julio?" he said in a tersely threatening tone. "We can get to our business afterwards."

"I don't mind at all. Just give me the briefcase now so I can have the first look at Calvi's papers. There is work to be done, after all."

Silently burning with fury, his plan for isolated review thwarted, Dante reluctantly picked up the briefcase and handed it to Guzman.

Without a word, the Spaniard took the briefcase, then

turned and headed for the door. Stopping, he looking back at Vannucci.

"Enjoy your visit, Father," he said, a smirk distorting his bearded chin. "And thank you for your help in bringing this to us. May we call on you again if needed?"

Vannucci first glanced at Dante, as if seeking permission. Absent a nod or any type of affirmation, Vannucci simply turned back to Guzman, nodded meekly and said, "Yes, as you wish."

"You can leave the door open, Julio. Father Vannucci was just leaving," Dante muttered. Then, "I must get back to work, Bruno. Can you see yourself out?"

The priest was startled at his former mentor's abruptness. Where was the "catching up" he had mentioned? "Of course, Eminence. And if you require anything more, I—"

"Yes, thank you," Dante interrupted brusquely. "Goodbye for now."

Back in their office, Dominic and Duffy were dejected over being so easily manipulated by someone they assumed must have been an operative for either Opus Deus or P2. Their only reason for optimism was that Duffy had already scanned everything into their system, so at least they had high-resolution copies of all relevant documents, and the floppy disk was still at Duffy's apartment.

"Hey!" Duffy exclaimed. "They didn't get the photo of

Peter's Chair! It's over here on our working table. That's a blessing. We need that to interpret what's on it."

"Why is the photograph itself so important? We have copies, right?"

"Copies won't show anything more than what our eyes pick up. Only the original has the digitization encoding on it. I'm guessing that the Key-Part B is what we need to use to decrypt the code. Meaning the Plutus Vault is likely a computer program. Then we could scan the image back into the originating Plutus Vault program to interpret the coding.

"We just need access to this so-called Plutus Vault. That's the hitch. So, for now we wait to hear what Baron Saint-Clair has to say about all this," Dominic said. "Hopefully Hana hears from him soon."

As he stood at the windows in his office, Armand de Saint-Clair dictated a letter to his secretary while absently looking out over the tree-lined Quai du Mont-Blanc at the magnificent yachts docked in the Lake Geneva marina, adjacent to the headquarters of Banque Suisse de Saint-Clair.

The thoughtful flow of dictation was interrupted by a ringing phone, which his secretary answered.

"It is your granddaughter, Monsieur," she said to her boss. "Would you prefer to take it in private?"

Saint-Clair smiled broadly. "*Oui*, Paulette, *merci*." Then, taking hold of the receiver as his secretary left the office, he greeted Hana warmly. "*Mon bébé*! What a pleasant surprise. What can I do for you?"

"Have you ever heard of something called a Plutus Vault?"

Saint-Clair stood stock still as he looked out the window over the lake, stunned to hear Hana say the words.

"Wherever did you hear such a thing, my dear?"

Without going into extraneous detail, Hana gave him a review of their recent activities involving P2, its agenda, and the Plutus Vault being named by Calvi as the repository for a special key they were seeking to solve a vexing puzzle.

"Calvi also made a note that read 'Account BSSC Box 148625,' and I assumed that might have something to do with your bank. Does that sound familiar at all?"

Saint-Clair paused, weighing his legal Swiss fiduciary responsibilities with the desire to help his granddaughter with anything she needed. But after all, he reasoned, it *was* his bank.

"Hana," he began, "the Plutus Vault was a creation of mine in the 1980s, when such technology was just starting to take hold of the banking world. No one else had it at the time, and to my knowledge we still have several active Plutus account holders, despite other, more modern means of depository these days. You say this account holder has been dead for some time now?"

"Yes, Grand-père, Roberto Calvi passed away—he was murdered, actually—in 1982. Does that help or hinder things?"

"Well, both, in a manner of speaking. Let me ask

François, our director-general, to check into things, and I'll get back to you shortly."

~

"Marco, I'm heading back to the Vatican to wait for my grandfather's call there," Hana said as she adjusted her makeup in the mirror. "Would you like to join me, or do you have other plans?"

"I have no intentions of letting you out of my sight until this situation with Opus Deus and others involved is resolved. I won't have you dragged off the street again." He hugged her from behind. As Hana leaned into his embrace she looked at him in the mirror, but her thoughts went back to that moment with Michael in the Archives a few days earlier. Again, she found her emotions torn.

The taxi having delivered Marco and her to Saint Anne's Gate, Hana collected visitor passes from the Swiss Guard and walked up the Belvedere to Dominic's office, where they joined the others. As it was now the end of her shift, Sister Teri was back as well, keen to continue their work on the Calvi documents.

Half an hour later, Hana's phone lit up, showing her grandfather's image on the screen.

"Find anything, pépé?" she asked.

"Actually, yes. Quite a bit," Saint-Clair replied. "Monsieur Calvi does have a Plutus Vault account here. But he left no beneficiary or other authorized names on the account, so we must presume it has been abandoned.

We will, of course, take measures here to deal with that. But frankly—and this accommodation must stay between us, Hana—I see no reason why I cannot give you access to Plutus, if what you told me about this P2 brotherhood and their scheme against the Vatican is what's at stake."

"Thank you so much, Grand-père! So, how do we get access to the safe deposit box?"

"Well, it is not a safe deposit box in the traditional sense, my dear, though in this case one does accompany the account. The Plutus Vault itself is a digital safe deposit box, the first of its kind those many years ago. I can give you access to it here in Geneva. But you must have the password to the account, plus the original image and both keys to unlock the data. Do you have all that?"

Hana's exuberance flatlined. Ian didn't mention a password. "Pépé, would you hold for a moment?"

Turning to Duffy, she asked, "Was there some kind of password Calvi mentioned? He says we need one to access the vault, in addition to the original image and both keys."

"No. I found nothing like that anywhere," Duffy said despairingly. "Plus we still need Key-Part B. Now what?"

Sister Teri sighed, then spoke up. "Do I have to do *all* the work around here? Just try the only password we know that worked before: 'Super Hanc Petram.'"

"Pass*phrase*," Duffy said, laughing at her antics, then, nodding to Hana, "It's worth a shot."

Picking up the phone again, Hana relayed the passphrase to her grandfather. A few moments later he responded.

"François tells me that appears to work, Hana. But

you'll need to come here, and bring with you the original image scanned by the Plutus Vault program as well as the decryption keys."

"We have everything except the second key. Pépé, would it be possible to check the actual safe deposit box connected to that account? There's a good chance the second key might be there."

"Not having the owner's key, I'm afraid we would have to drill to open that box, something we wouldn't do without the boxholder's permission. Or that of the heir."

"But Cavi is dead, Grand-père. And you said there are no other signers on that account. Nor heirs according to anything we've discovered."

"Hmm. Well, this will take several minutes while we find the personnel and equipment. Why don't I call you back once we've accomplished that? It shouldn't take too long."

"*Merci*, Grand-père. We'll be here waiting for your call."

Thirty minutes later Hana's cell phone hummed. Seeing it was her grandfather, her hand leapt to the Slide to Answer button.

"*Oui*, Grand-père?"

"You are in luck, Hana. There *is* a diskette in Monsieur Calvi's box, and I would wager it contains the second key you seek. I shall leave it with François."

Hana was overjoyed at the news, giving a thumbs up to the others.

"Alright, pépé. We'll make plans to come to Geneva right away."

"And just remember, Hana, we never had this discussion ..."

"Of course, our lips are sealed. Thank you, Grand-père. I'll let you know when we'll arrive." She pressed the End button on her phone.

Hana looked at the others and smiled.

"Who's up for a trip to Geneva?"

CHAPTER

THIRTY-TWO

J ulio Guzman set the briefcase on the floor next to
his desk in Villa Tiber and withdrew the first
manageable stack of Calvi's papers to review. He
expected to be here awhile.

Much of what he read was already known to him—
the scandals at Banco Ambrosiano and the IOR, Calvi's
legal problems, the valid suspicion of his early demise.
But there was new information here he found both
encouraging and disturbing.

First, he discovered a list of assets to be used in
support of P2's agenda, including an unspecified amount
of gold and diamonds, plus whatever funds Calvi had on
deposit at the Vatican Bank. Once they got Isabella
appointed as IOR's president, they would take possession
of these needed resources in order to better position
Cardinal Wolsey as their papal candidate, according to
plan.

Then he found the birth certificate for Isabella

Stewart Hastings—which named Wolsey as the father! He slapped his forehead out of frustration.

Then he was surprised to find that Silvio Pollastri's name had been identified as the proposed P2 Grand Master following Licio Gelli's death, and Villa Rosso revealed as P2's headquarters. That might present problems, too. *Pollastri will not be pleased.*

But reading the underlined memorandum Calvi had noted was the real eye opener, especially the final clause:

The Dictum Covenant, officially executed by both parties, is safely hidden in the photo of the Chair of Saint Peter and on the disk.

What photo? What disk? Guzman quickly searched the briefcase and through all the papers for either of the items, with no luck. *Dammit! Dominic and his people must still have those.*

And what's this about a "Dictum Covenant," and some strange reference to a "Plutus Vault"? There was more to Calvi's legacy here than met the eye, of that Guzman was convinced. And the facts that Dominic and his colleagues have already seen all this, and may even be acting on it now, were of profound concern.

He had to get to Villa Rosso. Immediately.

The Roma Tiburtina, the next train leaving for Arezzo, departed the Rome Termini station at eleven o'clock. Guzman would reach Arezzo by two, which should give him enough time to finish reviewing the other documents in Calvi's briefcase—which he brought with him—before giving Pollastri the mixed news.

He had yet to hand over to Banducci the key he'd taken off Dominic to recover the gold and diamonds from the safe deposit box at the Vatican Bank. That will surely come in useful for their now-accelerated plans. He had already heard through Wolsey and Silva the rumors floating that the pope might retire soon, and Wolsey himself was already posturing for the occasion, furtively lining up a cabal of supportive cardinals to vote in his favor, in exchange for all manner of potential indulgences. Calvi's loot from the bank would come in handy for achieving that. *Vatican City is a small world, where everyone can be bought and nothing is sacred*, he mused, snickering at the profane thought.

Having rented a car at the Arezzo railway station, Guzman drove through the vibrant rising and falling hills in the heart of Tuscany. In the distance and in every direction, tiny towns perched on the peaks of steep hills. He passed stone farmhouses set back off the main roads whose driveways were invariably lined with tall cypress trees waving in the slight breeze: features common to the Tuscan countryside. One day he would settle down here, where the pace of life is more sensible than the frenzy of Rome. And he would be done with all this darker business. Maybe he would even have a vineyard, like Silvio Pollastri.

Turning onto the long drive leading to Villa Rosso, its own towering cypress trees lining both sides of the driveway for nearly a quarter of a mile, Guzman finally reached the house and stables. Hopefully he wouldn't be expected to ride another damned horse again.

Two men he had seen before, both dressed in jeans, cowboy boots and Stetson hats but undoubtedly well-armed beneath their duster coats, met him as he parked the car next to the barn.

"Don Silvio is expecting you, signore," one of them said, pointing. "He is in his private office. You know the way."

Guzman simply nodded in acknowledgment as he pulled the briefcase out of the back seat and made his way to the Grand Master's office.

"Buongiorno, Julio," Pollastri greeted his associate. "And how are things in Roma these days? You bring me news, I hope."

"*Si*, Silvio, I bring you much news, most of it great, some ... well, you decide."

Guzman set the briefcase on a large, wooden table in the office and withdrew all its contents, laying it out in some orderly fashion.

"I can spare you having to read all this, but wanted you to see Roberto Calvi's infamous briefcase, the one everybody had been looking for over the past forty years. Turns out it was discovered by that priest we spoke of, Father Dominic, buried in the Vatican Secret Archives for God knows how long.

"Obviously Dominic and his people have already seen

it, and we must presume they've read everything as well. There was also a key in it, one to a safe deposit box at the Vatican Bank, which I now have in my possession. Though I have yet to access it, these papers reveal that the box contains a fortune in gold and diamonds, which will go a long way toward supporting Wolsey's papal candidacy and fund our additional missions. Once we have achieved that, everything will be in place to control the Vatican as Propaganda Due has long intended. Licio Gelli's plan was genius. Finally, we'll have a dedicated P2 leader with the ecclesiastical power of Opus Deus behind him.

"But there are a few things here which I do not understand, Silvio. Perhaps you might be able to shed light on them."

"Such as?" Pollastri asked.

"Calvi makes mention of a 'Dictum Covenant,' a 'Plutus Vault,' and a 'disk,' none of which I found in these papers. He also mentions an important photo of the Chair of Saint Peter, which also is missing. I have to assume Dominic has these items, and we must get them back from him somehow. This 'Dictum' seems to be connected to them. Are any of these familiar to you?"

Pollastri stood up from his chair, looking thoughtfully out the window at his horses in the pasture. Then he turned back to Guzman, the veins in his neck and face now throbbing with anger.

"The Dictum Covenant is a secret reciprocal document signed by our predecessors that officially united both P2 and Opus Deus in this endeavor. It can *never* be seen by anyone outside either organization, Julio, for if made public it could destroy everything we have waited decades to achieve! Do you understand?"

Guzman trembled in the shadow of his boss' anger. He offered, "Yes, yes, I understand. Calvi's notes say that the document is 'safely hidden in the photo of the Chair of Saint Peter and on the disk.' From what I read, I take it that Calvi used some form of encryption on the photo, and most likely the disk has the keys to decrypt it. I've had some experience with this, Silvio, when I was with Interpol. I found neither of these, but I pledge to you I will get those materials back."

Pollastri sighed and sat back down. "That's all I wanted to hear, my friend. I know you will take care of things accordingly. Go, do what you must. Take your materials, here, too. I have no interest in reading them."

As he drove away from Villa Rosso, Guzman cursed in a torrent of Spanish expletives. Though he would see this last operation through, he was sick of it all. He had just gotten out of prison himself! *Why did I even mention that damned key?! I could easily have taken the gold and diamonds for my own and nobody would have been the wiser. Then I, too, would have my own villa and vineyard. With no fucking horses.*

THIRTY-THREE

T he china teacup in his hands rattled nervously on its saucer as Bishop Klaus Wolaschka sat outside the office of the Vatican Secretary of State, waiting for His Eminence to finish a phone call.

This would be a most difficult moment for him, but his hands were tied. His reputation would be ruined if Wolsey's blackmail threats came to pass. *Perhaps Petrini would still have use of me elsewhere.*

The great doors to the secretary's office opened wide, and Cardinal Petrini held out both his arms, inviting the bishop to come in.

"*Buona sera*, Klaus. How might I be of service to you?"

The two men settled themselves in the plush seating area next to the windows overlooking St. Peter's Basilica.

"Your Eminence ..." Wolaschka began, then tears came to his eyes.

"My apologies, Eminence. But ... I regret I must inform you that I am stepping down as president of the IOR. At my age the job has just gotten to be much too overwhelming, especially given the Holy Father's forthcoming institutional changes. I no longer have the fortitude of youth to bear such responsibilities."

Petrini was surprised, especially given that the man was clearly fighting emotional distress in the telling of it, something he wouldn't have expected from one so determined.

"And this is your own decision, Klaus? You are not being coerced by anyone? If so, I can surely help you in that regard. I well know how the politics work around here."

Emotions again clouded the stout bishop's face as he fought for self-control, his bulky frame shifting on the scarlet damask sofa as he struggled for a more steadfast response.

"I think it is time for new and perhaps younger management to succeed me, Eminence. In fact, I am told Dame Isabella Stewart Hastings has a strong interest, and certainly the seasoned capability required, in succeeding me. She is the one person whom I would most heartily endorse."

"Yes, Signora Hastings has already met with His Holiness and myself on the matter. I must confess I have some apprehensions on the timing of all this, however. But if this is your heart's desire, Klaus, I shall take it up with the Holy Father at once.

"Does this mean you wish to retire? Or would you consider reassignment to some less-demanding post?"

Wolaschka's face brightened. "*Si*, Your Eminence,

another posting here would be entirely welcomed. I only wish to serve the Church until my final days."

"Then we will find you something more suitable, though it may take some time. Until then, after your departure from the bank, why don't you take a sabbatical, get some rest? It will be good for you."

"*Grazie mille*, Eminence, I am most humble and so grateful for your accommodating me. We will speak again soon, I am sure."

By Monday, three days later, Petrini and the pope had agreed on Isabella Stewart Hastings as the most logical replacement for Bishop Wolaschka to head the IOR. There was little time for a long succession of interviews, as they wanted someone up-and-running before they began any of the changes the pope hoped to instigate. And both men concurred that her credentials were more than sufficient for the heavy burdens that lay ahead in reforming the Vatican Bank.

At Wolsey's urging, Wolaschka had consented to stepping down earlier so that the new president could get a more expeditious start on her new job.

Meanwhile, Isabella had wasted no time in leasing one of the most fashionable villas in the Tridente neighborhood of Rome, home to the Trevi Fountain, the Spanish Steps and the magnificent churches of the Piazza del Popolo. Many of the city's most glamorous hotels and fashion brands were situated in the Tridente, among them Fendi, Gucci and Valentino. She would be quite at home here.

But for now, there was work to be done.

Having secretly met with Cardinal Wolsey, Bishop Silva, Julio Guzman and her newly named general manager of the bank, Milo Banducci, Isabella had received her initial marching orders. Orders from Opus Deus, not the Vatican.

Dealing with the quietly classified dormant account of Roberto Calvi, she had instructed that the twenty million euros be transferred into a shell account under the joint control of Opus Deus and P2. Thus the bank's deposits would still be in high balance and not show a massive withdrawal. At least not yet.

Then there was the safe deposit box to deal with.

As arranged, Julio Guzman was expected at the bank momentarily to open box 327, as he had the only key.

Banducci and Isabella were in her office discussing personnel changes when Guzman walked in the door.

"Ready to see the legacy Calvi left us?" the Spaniard said, smiling as he dangled the key next to his head.

The three of them eagerly walked into the vault, then closed the door behind them. Banducci pulled out the bank's master key and inserted it into the left lock, then Guzman inserted his key into the right lock. Turning them both, the bronze door swung open.

Guzman knelt down to pull open the steel drawer.

"It's incredibly heavy," he noted, pulling on it with all his might. He brought it out just enough for the top to clear the upper ledge, allowing the lid to be raised. And then he lifted it.

Marveling at the many bars of gleaming gold, Guzman lifted one out, handing it to Banducci. While he and Isabella admired it, Guzman looked for the bag of diamonds Calvi mentioned.

But they were gone.

"The diamonds are missing!" Then he counted the ingots.

"And there are only fifteen bars here!" Looking up at the others, a fierce look on his face, he seethed, "Obviously, Dominic took the diamonds and one of the gold bars for himself. Or worse yet, to show to Petrini. This presents more problems than we're prepared to deal with. By Calvi's own estimate, those diamonds alone were worth a fortune—and that was forty years ago. Their value today has increased exponentially. We have to get them back!"

"Milo," Isabella said emphatically, "move this gold into our main vault. Make sure it's concealed in some kind of container so staff doesn't see it. Julio, make plans to retrieve the diamonds from Father Dominic, whatever that takes. Just ensure that no trace of complicity leads back to us. Best to use outside resources to handle this."

She looked at Guzman with a firm resolve. He nodded knowingly.

"There is one way we can try that should get Dominic's cooperation," he said. "But if that doesn't work, I have just the man in mind for something more ... compelling."

CHAPTER
THIRTY-FOUR

Early the next day, Michael Dominic's run took him across the broad Via dei Fori Imperiali and through the Suburra, the most ancient inhabited area of Rome away from the most touristed parts of the city. The early morning air was thick with scents of Chilean jasmine, honeysuckle, and petrol fumes as he jogged through the semi-industrial working-class neighborhood, one that so reminded him of Queens, New York, where he grew up.

Slowing to a cool-down pace as he crossed the Sant'Angelo bridge spanning the Tiber River, he turned left up Via della Conciliazione as the massive dome of St. Peter's Basilica loomed ahead. A block or so before reaching Saint Anne's Gate, he stopped at Caffè Pergamino on the Piazza del Risorgimento, where sleepy-eyed patrons nibbled on small, sticky cakes washed down with a demitasse of thick, sweet espresso before heading into work, most of them Dominic recognized as being Vatican employees.

After changing into the black cassock awaiting him during his runs, the young priest emerged from the restroom refreshed and energized, ready for his own cup of coffee while he read the morning paper before heading into the office.

As he sat restfully at a sidewalk table in the warm morning sun, he looked down the long boulevard to the ancient, circular stone façade of the Vatican Bank, just inside the city's gate. With all that had been going on, he'd forgotten about the gold sitting in that safe deposit box. He should probably attend to that soon; maybe have Karl and Lukas give him a hand retrieving it, especially since Isabella Stewart Hastings—named an Opus Deus member on their roster—was now in charge.

As he opened the morning edition of *Il Tempo* to catch up on the latest news, a shadow fell across him, blocking the sun. When it didn't move, Dominic looked up to find a man standing there, staring at him. Because the man was backlit, Dominic couldn't make out his face.

"May I join you, Father Dominic?" the man asked.

Dominic held his hand up, shielding his eyes from the sun's outline of the figure. There was something familiar about his voice.

"And who might you be?" he asked cautiously.

"You can call me Julio," the man said as he presumptuously took a seat anyway. "It seems we have in common some unfinished business that needs to be resolved."

The Spaniard! The one who attacked me! Dominic now

saw the slight scar on the man's face where he had given him a rough kick inside the van when he had been abducted the previous week. He sat up straight and tossed the newspaper onto the chair next to him.

"*You!*" Dominic exclaimed angrily. "You've got some nerve. What makes you think I won't kick the shit out of you right now?"

"Really, padre," Guzman said amicably, "do you think that would be sensible? A priest attacking an unarmed man here in broad daylight? I am only here to talk business, that is all. I mean you no harm."

Dominic stared at him with hostility, his peaceful morning now turned contentious.

"What possible business could I have with a thug like you?"

"I do apologize for my rude behavior last week, padre. I was only doing my job, it was nothing personal. I work for an organization whose interests, to some degree, overlap with your own, though I am afraid it must remain nameless."

"I already have a pretty good idea of who that might be, *Julio*. But please, get to the point. What is it you want?"

"It seems you have taken something that does not belong to you, from a safe deposit box in the Vatican Bank. A large quantity of diamonds, in particular. Oh, and one gold ingot. Those rightfully belong to the organization I represent, and we want them back."

"And I assume you can show me proof of such ownership?" Dominic asked assertively.

Guzman looked hard at the priest, their eyes held fast

together. Then the Spaniard smiled coldly.

"I am told you had a close familiarity with a former cardinal named Fabrizio Dante, if I am not mistaken."

Dominic nearly shuddered at hearing the name. But he was perplexed. "What has Dante got to do with all this?"

"Well, you may not know that he has just been paroled from Regina Coeli, and now works for us. And he told me the most fascinating story about your father. That *is* Cardinal Petrini we are talking about, is it not?"

Dominic froze. *No ... No! It can't be!*

"Cardinal ... I mean, *ex*-cardinal Dante is not a man to be trusted," Dominic scoffed. "He is a proven liar and a traitor to the Church. What he's told you is utterly preposterous. Where is his *proof* of such a baseless claim?"

Guzman had not expected the priest to demand proof —proof which they did not have. His only choice now was to keep bluffing.

"Oh, proof exists, I can assure you. Something about genetic testing from your combined DNA analyses?"

Maintaining an unflustered posture but inwardly terrified of what he had just heard, Dominic stood up. "You've wasted your time this morning, signore. I should have you arrested for kidnapping, and now blackmail. In fact ..." He took out this phone and dialed 113 for the *Polizia di Stato.*

Guzman also stood, hostility now replacing his controlled demeanor. "I *will* get those diamonds, padre, and the gold, one way or another. If you don't give them up within forty-eight hours there will be a higher price to pay. You will hear from me again tomorrow."

The Spaniard quickly walked away from the table, turned into the alley behind Pergamino, and disappeared. Dominic ended the call, pocketing the phone.

He sat down again, rattled by the encounter and potential exposure. *Dante? Out of prison?! That sonofabitch is no end of problems for us!*

"This is a terrible situation I've placed you in, Eminence," Dominic confessed, after informing him of the encounter with Guzman. "I'm so terribly sorry."

"Nonsense, my boy," said Cardinal Petrini, unperturbed. "I know for a fact that the *Gendarmerie* had confiscated all of Dante's files, including that accursed DNA evidence. I have a trusted confidant at the department, and he has personally assured me that documentation had been destroyed. We should have no fear of that scurrilous bastard now. It's his word—as an ex-con and felon, mind you—against ours. And since the Holy Father already knows, my standing as papabile remains unblemished."

"Well, that makes me feel so much better. You do have a wide net of confederates in Rome, don't you?" Dominic said, smiling knowingly.

"Power does have its privileges, Michael, when used sensibly. One learns early here to keep Roman bureaucrats, in particular, tractable and close at hand. As for this Julio person, let me do some digging. If he's at all associated with Opus Deus we'll know, and deal with him appropriately for the harms he's caused."

CHAPTER

THIRTY-FIVE

"I'm so excited to see Geneva," Duffy said to Dominic as the two continued working on fleshing out the schema for the Archives database. "I've never been to Switzerland."

"There's a lot to like there, Ian," Dominic explained, putting his pencil down. "Though it's now largely Catholic, it was once known as the 'Protestant Rome,' and John Calvin, the proponent of Calvinism, was its spiritual leader, kind of like our pope. That was in the sixteenth century. Then France stepped in two hundred years later and cultivated the city as its own, bringing Roman Catholicism with it.

"You'll really like Hana's grandfather, too. Baron Armand de Saint-Clair is quite an important figure in Geneva. His centuries-old bank is on the Quai du Mont-Blanc, just across the harbor from the heart of the city's Old Town and the Temple de Saint-Pierre, the site of the old Roman forum. Loads of history there, which I know you're really into."

"You bet, I am. Hopefully I'll have time for a bit of sightseeing. So we're still on for leaving tomorrow morning?"

"Yep. The train leaves at six ten. The trip is ten hours or so, and really, it's a wonderful journey through the Alps. Bring your laptop with you if you want to keep working.

"Oh, Karl Dengler will be joining us, along with Hana and Marco. Cardinal Petrini insists we have protection with us, given the credible threats by Opus Deus and possibly P2. That Julio character yesterday alluded to a certain warning, and His Eminence wants us to take no chances."

Early the following morning at Rome's Central Station, the team boarded the Frecciargento high-speed train destined for Milan, where they would transfer to the Bernina line and travel on into Switzerland, bound for Geneva.

This particular route took them through countless tiny towns in Italy and Switzerland, where the train stopped to pick up and drop off passengers, giving the team a true sense of engaging with the people and the surrounding landscapes.

Hana had booked first class passage for all of them, for a quieter and roomier journey. She and Marco sat in one row toward the back of the car, as did Karl behind them, where he could keep an eye on everyone ahead of them. Dominic and Duffy sat together chatting up front while Duffy accessed the onboard WiFi via a VPN as he worked on his database. The Peter's Chair photo and floppy disk taken from Calvi's briefcase containing the keys to the Dictum Covenant were safely tucked away in his backpack, on which all eyes were frequently focused.

As they passed into the French Aosta Valley and on through Chamonix, the awe-inspiring summit of Mont Blanc towered above them. Crossing the Swiss border, they took in the spectacular glaciers and Alpine meadows unique to the Swiss countryside, with abundant waterfalls and snow-capped peaks viewable from both sides of the car. At certain points the train dropped down with breathtaking drama from soaring mountain terrain into lower, stunningly lush valleys filled with wildflowers and meandering rivers and streams. Though Hana was born in Switzerland and usually traveled by plane, even she was moved by the natural spectacles that only train travel afforded.

As the red locomotive nosed into the Gare de Genève train station, Dominic and his friends gathered their gear and luggage and prepared to disembark.

Hana's grandfather had told her he would arrange for a limousine van to pick them up in front of the station by the newspaper kiosk, a common area for taxis and cars waiting for arriving passengers.

But after twenty minutes without any sign of the van,

she called her grandfather at his estate to check on its status. Frederic, the baron's butler and bodyguard, answered the phone.

"*Bonjour, mon petit* Hana," he greeted her, his voice slightly apprehensive. "I am afraid the baron drove away in his Maserati last evening, and not only has he not returned, I have not yet heard from him, which is quite unusual. He told me he was going into the office and that I was not needed, but when I called there this morning they said they have not seen him. I must confess, I am quite worried."

"That's odd. He assured me a van would be picking us up at the train station thirty minutes ago, Frederic, but it hasn't shown up yet. Did you make those arrangements for him?"

"I did not, Mademoiselle, and I surely would have been tasked with that. He did mention you were planning to come soon but had not yet given me details. Shall I send a car for you now?"

"No, we'll take one of the taxi vans. There are five of us, Frederic, so we'll need five bedrooms prepared, if you don't mind."

"Of course, Mademoiselle, I shall have the staff attend to that at once. But what are we to do about the baron?"

Deeply concerned, Hana wasn't sure how to respond. "Let's wait until we arrive, and we'll handle things then. See you soon, Frederic." She disengaged the call.

Looking up at Dominic and Marco with a worried look, she explained. "My grandfather is missing. At least he hasn't phoned Frederic, with whom he stays in constant touch, since last night when he drove himself to the office. And he never arrived at the office either. Something is definitely wrong, I can feel it."

Marco reached out and put his arm around her. "Don't worry, we'll find him. There's got to be some logical explanation."

Twenty minutes later, the taxi van dropped them all off at La Maison des Arbres, the baron's magnificent waterfront château on the shore of Lake Geneva. Nestled on four acres, the property boasted a three-story manor house with twelve bedrooms, a converted barn with separate apartment and pool, and an unspoiled view of Mont Blanc.

Frederic and several of the house staff met the group outside the main entrance, managing their luggage and escorting them to their assigned bedrooms: Dominic, Duffy, Karl, and Marco each to their own, with Hana shown to one of the master suites. Marco looked at her with obvious longing.

"While we're under my grandfather's roof," she cautioned out of respect, "we should have our own rooms. But that doesn't mean you and I can't be together at night." She winked at him, then told him she needed to freshen up. After unpacking, Marco joined the others downstairs in the great room.

"Frederic," Marco asked the butler frankly, "has the baron often disappeared like this before? Are there any places you think he might have gone? Perhaps he has a mistress, or ...?"

"Oh, *mais non*, Monsieur!" Frederic said, furrowing his

bushy eyebrows defensively. "The baron does not have a mistress, at least not now, as I would surely know this. And also, *non*, he has not behaved like this before. He does often take his personal car, the Maserati Quattroporte, out for the occasional amusement, but never has he stayed out all night without first telling me of his plans. That is why I am most concerned. This is not the pattern of a man for whom I have now served nearly thirty years. I know him well, Monsieur."

As Frederic fetched beer, wine or cocktails for each of them, Hana sat on the curved leather sofa next to the fireplace, her eyebrows knitted in concern.

Just then her phone rang. Looking at it, her grandfather's image appeared on the screen. Her heart leapt.

"*Grand-père!* Where *are* you?!" she pleaded.

At first, there was silence. Then a man's voice spoke, calmly but firmly. Though it was muffled, Hana sensed a vaguely American accent. She quickly put the call on speaker so the others could listen in.

"Hello, Miss Sinclair. First, I want you to know that your grandfather is in good hands and, for the moment, safe. We understand you and your colleagues are now in Geneva. That is good. I trust Father Dominic is with you and that he has brought the floppy disk to the Plutus Vault with him. As for the diamonds, it's unlikely you would have traveled with those, but they will be part of the terms I will explain in a moment."

Listening carefully, Marco had a faint suspicion he knew that voice, but he couldn't place it. It was in the patterns of speech. He turned to Dominic and whispered into his ear, "Does that voice sound familiar to you?" Thinking hard, Dominic shook his head. Looking around the room at the others, each also shook their head in turn.

"Who *are* you?" Hana asked, desperate to know more. "And what has my grandfather to do with this?"

"He is simply a pawn on the board, but a most valuable one—to you, anyway. First, those diamonds are of considerable value to us, and you must have them brought to Geneva immediately. Once they have arrived, I ask that you urge Father Dominic to comply with our request to deliver both the diamonds and the disk at the place and time of our choosing. And don't bother calling the *Polizia cantonale* either. Such a foolish move won't end well for the baron. I will be back in touch tomorrow evening. Have the diamonds here by then." The call was disconnected.

Dominic was first to speak. "He said *Polizia Cantonale*, which is *Italian* for the Cantonal Police here in Geneva. Since French is the local language, why would he have said it in Italian? His accent sounded more American to me, but something was off about it, besides his voice obviously being somehow masked or muffled."

Karl nodded. "Michael, if we do need those diamonds," he proposed, "we should have Lukas get them and bring them up on the morning train tomorrow. He can certainly handle himself in getting them here safely. Can you ask Cardinal Petrini to have him excused from duty, if you think that's a good idea?"

"Absolutely I do, and yes, he'll understand. I put the diamonds in my safe in the office, but I'll give Lukas the combination. I don't give a damn about them if it means saving Armand from these bastards.

"As for that disk and the Plutus Vault—Ian, we have some quick work to do. There's no way I'm losing access to whatever's in that Dictum Covenant. That's the proof we need for everything that's at stake now.

"So, here's what I have in mind ..."

After calling Petrini and telling him of their plans, Dominic called Lukas Bischoff. He explained the situation about the baron being kidnapped and the need for the diamonds, gave him the combination to the safe, and told him to ask for Father Laguardia, one of the assistant scrittori in the Secret Archives, for access to his office. Then to take the first morning train to Geneva, making sure the diamonds remained discreet and secure. He should also bring his pistol, just in case.

Lukas was only too happy to oblige, for he yearned to be back home in Switzerland to see his family.

After Lukas advised Father Laguardia of Dominic's request, the priest unlocked the office, allowing the Swiss Guard access to the safe. Opening it, he retrieved the purple velvet bag of diamonds—which were much heavier than he'd expected—and dropped them into his pack.

All he had to do now was make reservations for the morning train.

THIRTY-SIX

I n the shadow of Mount Pellegrino, the sacred hill overlooking the bay of Palermo, Sicily, lies the Church of San Cataldo in the town's central Piazza Bellini. Built in 1154, when Sicily flourished under Norman rule, the church was revered as a notable example of Arab-Norman architecture: a rare style unique to the region.

The bells in the piazza's clock tower had just struck noon, and Don Alfredo Costello, the *capofamiglia* of Sicily's Cosa Nostra crime family, sat praying quietly in the pews between towering gold Byzantine arches bordering both sides of the nave. Surrounding him at discreet distances were several hulking mafiosi in dark suits, not praying so much as standing guard over the boss.

The tall wooden doors at the entrance of the church creaked open loudly, echoing throughout the great and silent hall. The sound of footsteps approached Don

Alfredo from up the main aisle, and since no one had stopped whoever it was, the boss assumed it was his longtime consigliere, Santo Petrucci, the only one allowed unrestricted access to the *padrino* at any time.

The man took a seat next to the boss, waiting in silence until he was permitted to speak. After making the sign of the cross, Costello leaned back from his kneeling position and sat down on the wooden bench. A simple hand gesture encouraged his consigliere to proceed.

"Don Alfredo," Petrucci said in a reverential whisper, "there has been a development in Rome which requires your attention. You will, of course, recall the cache of diamonds you loaned to Roberto Calvi in that effort to save Banco Ambrosiano? Well, they have resurfaced."

Costello allowed a subtle jerk of recognition on hearing this, his head leaning slightly closer to Petrucci as he continued speaking.

"This information comes from our man inside Propaganda Due, and I believe it to be legitimate. It appears that our friends at P2 and Opus Deus are up to something—a kidnapping I am told. The diamonds have not only been discovered—apparently in Calvi's safe deposit box at the Vatican Bank, after all these years—but they are being used among the ransom demands by P2.

"The diamonds are presently in the hands of a Vatican priest, a Father Michael Dominic, who was told to arrange for a courier to bring the diamonds from the Vatican to Switzerland. I am told this courier will most likely be on tomorrow morning's train from Rome to Geneva.

"As your humble advisor, Don Alfredo, may I suggest that you order the diamonds be recovered on behalf of *la famiglia?* That treasure belongs to us, not P2 *or* Opus Deus. On your order, I am prepared to dispatch our man in Rome to acquire the stones—which, if it is even close to the same bag we handed Calvi, are now valued at around eighty-five million euros."

Looking up at the golden crucifix hanging over the altar, Costello weighed the potential consequences—mainly, would there be war?

Satisfied with his decision, he turned to his consigliere. "You have done well, Santo. Make it so. Bring the diamonds back home."

Italy's *Guardia di Finanza*, a law enforcement agency under the authority of the Minister of Economy and Finance, is essentially responsible for dealing with financial crimes and smuggling inside the country's borders. Later that afternoon, the GdF's Intelligence Division had intercepted a series of telephone calls between Sicily and Rome, the tapping being an ongoing practice of the division as they constantly monitored all Mafia communications traffic throughout Italy.

Lieutenant Emilio Russo, the Officer in Charge, was handed a transcription of the intercepted calls by an aide, and as he read it his eyebrows wobbled between interest and confusion.

Vatican diamonds ... Propaganda Due and Opus Deus ... Father Michael Dominic ... tomorrow's train from Rome to Geneva ... and a kidnapping?!

All the makings of something big going down—but

what? He would be wise to call the Vatican Secretary of
State and inform him of this, just in case it meant
something to him.

Having worked with Cardinal Petrini many times
before, Russo's call was put through immediately. He read
the transcriptions to Petrini word for word.

"Emilio, I cannot thank you enough for passing this
on to me," Petrini said, an urgency to his voice. "I know
what this refers to and it's something we can handle
internally, I assure you. Nothing for your department to
be concerned about."

"I thought as much, Your Eminence," Russo replied,
"and happy to oblige. Good luck with whatever it is."

After hanging up, Petrini was now even more worried.
Lukas may be in grave danger en route to Geneva.

"*Nick!*" he called out to his secretary. Father Bannon
appeared at his door a few moments later. "Call Corporal
Lukas Bischoff and get him up here immediately."

"Handle it however best you feel it necessary, Corporal,
but do not take any needless risks!" Petrini said forcefully
but caringly. "These are not the kind of people you want
on your back. They are ruthless and they mean business. I
cannot afford to send additional men with you, I'm afraid.
We will need every available Swiss Guard here in the next
several days. I cannot explain why yet, so forgive me. Just
take extraordinary precautions, whatever you choose to
do, and get back here soon."

"Thank you, Eminence, I will," Lukas said with

determination. "And I appreciate the heads-up. I'm sure Father Michael will keep you updated as things progress."

Leaving the cardinal's office, Lukas headed directly to the canteen, since he hadn't eaten yet. He could think out his strategy better on a full stomach.

As he sat at his table enjoying a spicy lasagna and simple salad, Sister Teri came over to join him, her own tray of food in hand.

"Hi, Lukas. May I join you?"

"Sure, Sister Teri, have a seat."

As she cleared her tray, transferring the plates to the table, she noticed Lukas appeared to be absorbed or distracted.

"A penny for your thoughts," she prompted.

Looking around to check if anyone was nearby, Lukas decided to confide in her.

"You're aware of everything that's going on, aren't you? I mean with the baron's kidnapping and Father Michael and the others in Geneva?"

"You bet, I am," she said, turning serious. "Ian has been keeping me updated by text and email. How are things going?"

He leaned in toward the nun, keeping his voice low. "Well, it's a long story, but in a nutshell ... Michael has asked me to bring him a bag of diamonds on tomorrow's train to Geneva to pay the ransom demand. Somehow the Sicilian Mafia found out and they're sending their goons to try to find whoever has the diamonds and steal them—

that would be *me!* So I'm alone in a quandary here, wondering how best to handle things."

"Are they expecting a Swiss Guard, or you specifically, or ...?"

"Who knows how much they know?! I don't even understand where they're getting their information. They must have informants everywhere, I'm sure of it. Hey, *you're* not one, are you?" He smiled as he said it, then took a bite of his salad.

"Yes, Lukas, I confess. I'm Mother Superior of the Pauline Mafia." They both laughed.

"Seriously, though," Teri prodded, "what *are* you going to do?"

"I've no idea yet. Any suggestions you might have are welcome."

"Maybe you should go in disguise, like some old man, or you could even pass for a skateboarding teenager. They'd never expect that." Just as she said it, Teri's face lit up. *"That's it!"*

"What's it? Making myself look like a skateboarder?"

"No!" she said with growing excitement. "We'll make you into a Pauline nun!"

Lukas looked at her as if she'd lost her mind.

"That's insane. *You're* insane."

"No, seriously. We'll get you into one of our habits that fits you, and several of us will go with you to Geneva. Nobody would *ever* expect a gaggle of chatty nuns transporting millions in diamonds!"

Lukas set down his fork, folded his arms, and looked at her.

"You know, that's actually not a bad idea. That would

take being in drag to a whole new level, like the Sisters of Perpetual Indulgence!"

They both howled at that, with others in the canteen now looking in their direction.

"We have no time to waste, Lukas. When we're done here, I'll take you to the convent. While you wait in reception, the girls and I will round up a habit that fits you." She sized him up. "What are you, six feet?"

"Yes, exactly."

"Well, our Mother Superior, Sister Mary Bede, is that tall. She's bound to have an outfit that works for you, and she'll think it's a hoot. She'd better join us, too, so you don't stand out. Good thing you don't have a beard."

"I would if I could. Facial hair is discouraged in the Guard."

"Yes, but that would ruin our devious plan, now, wouldn't it?"

"I suppose."

Clearing up their plates and trays, Teri and Lukas left the canteen, bound for the Paulines' convent just outside the walls of the Vatican.

THIRTY-SEVEN

At the confluence of the Rhône River and Lake Geneva lies a seedy area known locally as "Les Paquis," just northwest of the Port of Geneva. While the entire city itself is considered safe, Les Paquis is known for its red-light district, rampant drug dealing, strip bars, pickpockets, and the generally more bohemian population of Switzerland's second-largest city.

It is also the locale for a surplus of rat-infested shipping warehouses, where all manner of international goods are stored while awaiting transit to far-off trading ports.

In one ramshackle warehouse just off the Pont des Bergues bridge, Armand de Saint-Clair sat in a wooden chair facing Julio Guzman and Milo Banducci. Sunlight filtered in through grimy, broken windows, its dusty beams casting long shadows from the boxes stacked high on pallets surrounding the three men.

The Spaniard was cocky, fiddling with a Makarov pistol as he stared at his captive's sullen face.

"When does the American get here?" Banducci asked tremulously, unaccustomed to the likes of kidnapping and extortion. "I want this to be over and done with."

"He'll be along soon enough. He has other business he's attending to," Guzman replied. "Meanwhile, go pray in a corner if you want. You're not cut out for this sort of thing."

Banducci did just that, wandering toward a dark corner of the warehouse as he fretted over how he would handle this ungodly sinfulness in his next confession.

"So, Baron," Guzman began. "We're just waiting for your granddaughter to convince Father Dominic to hand over the floppy disk he found in that damned briefcase—oh, yes, along with the diamonds—then we'll require your cooperation to access the Plutus Vault. You will, of course, remain here as our guest while you assign a subordinate the task of accessing the Vault. As long as Dominic and his colleagues do their part, no harm will come to anyone, least of all you. We will call them again in ..." he glanced at his watch, "another couple of hours or so, when our friend arrives."

Saint-Clair remained silent, glaring stoically at his captor, not a hint of emotion on his face.

After Frederic pulled the Rolls-Royce around to the entrance of the château, Dominic, Hana and Duffy jumped inside while Karl and Marco stayed behind to lay out plans for the baron's rescue.

Their destination was Banque Suisse de Saint-Clair on the Quai du Mont-Blanc, where Hana would introduce Dominic and Duffy to François Trudeau, director general of the bank, for access to the Plutus Vault.

As Frederic parked the car, the others leapt out and hurried inside to find Trudeau. He was in his office studying some papers when Hana knocked on the door. The banker looked up with grave concern on his face.

"*Bonjour*, Mademoiselle. Has the baron been found yet?"

"Sort of, François," she said urgently. "I'm afraid he has been kidnapped, but we need your help in order to free him. These are my friends, Father Michael Dominic and Ian Duffy. We need immediate access to your Plutus Vault in order to retrieve something of great importance. Can you help us with that?"

"*Mon dieu* ... I have not heard talk of that system in many years. *Mais oui*, under the circumstances, I am at your service. Please, follow me."

Trudeau led them down a long, polished marble hallway and into the bank's secure computer room, where several racks of blinking servers sat on stacked black metal shelves. He pointed to a vintage Apple Macintosh II sitting on a small desk in a corner, with an equally old scanner sitting next to it. The quaint scene was an anachronism compared to the other gleaming equipment in the room, but it gave Duffy a warm feeling, like seeing an old friend.

"The Plutus Vault can be accessed using this

Macintosh. Have you the correct keys? Oh, the baron told me to hold this for you." He held out a black 3.5-inch floppy disk.

"I think we do now, yes," Hana said, turning to Duffy and handing him the diskette. "It's all yours now, Ian."

Taking a seat, Duffy toggled the rocker switch on the Macintosh, then while it was booting up, he opened his backpack and removed both the Peter's Chair photograph and Calvi's first floppy disk. Turning the scanner on, he lifted the cover and laid down the photograph on the scanning glass, then closed the cover.

"Amazing how we're so used to instant access now," he groaned. "These ancient machines take forever, but I do confess a lifelong fondness for them."

Once the system was ready, he inserted the diskette into the disk drive on the old computer. After a few moments of waiting while the drive issued mechanical noises, a username and password prompt finally appeared on the display.

Duffy froze for a moment. "François, do you have the login credentials for this computer?"

"*Oui*, I believe I do. They must be here somewhere ..." The banker took out his phone, opened his secure password app, then searched for 'Plutus Vault.' Finding the data, he handed the phone to Duffy.

"Whew!" the Irish lad exhaled. "I was hoping that wouldn't be an issue. Nice going, François."

Entering the credentials onto the Macintosh, moments later the Plutus Vault interface appeared on the display.

After spending some time getting accustomed to the

program, Duffy found the scanning option, then initiated the recreation of the concealed pixel map on the image of Saint Peter's Chair, which revealed the location and color value of every pixel.

The program then accessed the floppy disk to retrieve the originating Key-Part A, then a message appeared on the display to "insert Key-Part B." Duffy slid the diskette into the drive and pressed Enter.

In a matter of moments, the original coded statistics were magically reassembled into a document that appeared on the display.

Finally, the Dictum Covenant was now viewable.

Duffy looked up at Dominic and Hana with a wide grin on his face. "It worked! We've got it!"

"Can you print it out?" Dominic asked, his excitement growing at their unexpected success.

"You bet," Duffy said, turning on the printer attached to the system. He fiddled with a few menu options, then the printer started up, producing a single page.

As he read the printed document, the hair on the back of Dominic's neck stood on end, then a chill made him shudder.

Beneath a religious-themed coat of arms—featuring a shield, the Keys to the Kingdom of Heaven, a bishop's mitre with fringed lappets, the initials of both organizations, and the same raptor that is mounted on the entrance door of Opus Deus's headquarters—was the title "Dictum Covenant" and the Opus Dictum motto written in Latin, and below that, the contents of the covenant itself in Italian:

Dictum Pactum

"Ad aedificandum Regnum Dei in Terra"

Considerato che il Vaticano, e il suo Santo Padre, sono stati contrari agli interessi della Massoneria Italia e agli interessi della Santa Prelatura dell'Opus Deus, in quanto ai cattolici è vietata l'appartenenza massonica, e il Vaticano ha posto una gravosa supervisione e regolamentazione sulla finanze e investimenti della Santa Prelatura dell'Opus Deus, impedendo ad entrambe le organizzazioni di realizzare le loro missioni comuni per costruire il Regno di Dio sulla Terra.

Pertanto, l'undicesimo giorno di novembre, nell'anno di nostro Signore millenovecentottanta, questo Nasce l'Alleanza Segreta tra il Grande Oriente d'Italia, la Loggia Propaganda Due e la Santa Prelatura dell'Opus Deus, proclamando quanto segue, vale a dire: Il presente Patto prevede la preparazione e insediamento di un Pontefice cattolico romano con duplice omaggio ad entrambe le entità firmatarie del presente Patto. Sotto pena di morte, il Santo Padre così eletto dovrà svolgere le proprie funzioni secondo i comuni dettami del sia Propaganda Due che Opus Deus.

A tal fine, entrambe le organizzazioni hanno impegnato il loro tempo, talento e tesoro.

Qualsiasi membro di una delle organizzazioni cui viene mostrato questo Patto non deve mai rivelare il suo contenuto o essere soggetto alle punizioni di ciascuna organizzazione per coloro che violano il giuramento. Inoltre, tale membro deve eseguire gli ordini dei suoi superiori nell'organizzazione per attuare questo Patto con qualsiasi mezzo necessario.

A tal fine, la Prelatura dell'Opus Deus promette Oro, 16 lingotti, a 12,4 chili ciascuno.

A tal fine, il Grande Oriente d'Italia, Loggia Propaganda Due impegna Diamanti, 500, Taglio Asscher, 10 Carati ciascuno.

Questo tesoro deve essere usato per influenzare questo Patto, con qualsiasi mezzo necessario.

Per Propaganda Due   Per Opus Deus

As he read aloud, Dominic translated it for the others:

Dictum Covenant
"To Build the Kingdom of God on Earth"

Whereas, The Vatican, and its Holy Pontiff, have been adverse to the interests of Massoneria Italia and the interests of the Holy Prelature of Opus Deus, in that Catholics are prohibited from Masonic

membership, and the Vatican has placed burdensome oversight and regulation over the finances and investments of the Holy Prelature of Opus Deus, preventing both organizations from realizing their joint missions to build the Kingdom of God on Earth.

Therefore, on the eleventh day of November, in the year of our Lord one thousand nine hundred and eighty, this Secret Covenant was formed between the Grand Orient of Italy, Lodge Propaganda Due and the Holy Prelature of Opus Deus, proclaiming the following, to wit:

This Covenant shall provide for the preparation and installation of a Roman Catholic Pontiff having dual obeisance to both signatory entities to this Covenant. Under penalty of death, the Holy Father so chosen shall execute his duties in accordance with the joint dictates of

both Propaganda Due and Opus Deus

To this end, both organizations have pledged their Time, Talent, and Treasure.

Any member of either organization shown this Covenant shall never reveal its contents or be subject to the punishments of either organization for oath breakers. Furthermore, such member shall carry out the orders of their superiors in the organization to effect this Covenant by whatever means necessary.

To this end, the Prelature of Opus Deus pledges Gold, 16 bars, at 12.4 Kilos each.

To this end, the Grand Orient of Italy, Lodge

Propaganda Due, pledges Diamonds, 500, Asscher Cut, 10 Carats each.
This treasure to be used to affect this Covenant, by whatever means necessary.

Beneath it were two signatures, one for each organization, the names of which he couldn't make out.

"*Under penalty of death?!*" he exclaimed. "A pope who accepts that his very life is forfeit if he doesn't comply with these two organizations! This is a stunning indictment against both P2 and Opus Deus! It's shocking to me that it was ever put in writing; no wonder they hid it so securely.

"It does appear to bind both parties to work together, but obviously it's not something that was ever destined to be resolved in a court of law ... more like trial by *omertà*, the code of silence. And it's such a bizarre objective—yet one that would give them total control of the Vatican! I have to suppose the papabile they present this to—their chosen papal candidate—would have to want the job pretty badly in order to accede to such a formidable resolution. But that person would have the full force and unlimited resources of two wealthy and powerful organizations to achieve their combined goals. My god, I've never seen anything so inconceivable!"

"All the more reason to make it public, Michael," Hana proposed.

Dominic considered this as he reread the document. "Yes, but not yet. We can use this as a bargaining chip if we need to, especially to free your grandfather."

"If they even know we've *seen* this," Duffy pointed out

apprehensively, "wouldn't you think they'd take measures to eliminate us from the equation? After all, they *have* shown how ruthless they can be."

"We just need to protect ourselves, and this document, in case anything happens to one or all of us," Hana said, turning to the Swiss banker. "François can help us with that."

"*Absolument*, Hana," François confirmed proudly. "I would be privileged to keep it here in our vault, and should anything happen, I will release it to Vatican authorities at once."

"Meanwhile, we'll take a copy with us," she added, "to show them we mean business."

"For now, let's get back and discuss things with Marco and Karl," Dominic said. "They may already have come up with a rescue plan."

THIRTY-EIGHT

S ome two dozen burly men in loose, dark suits and shoulder-holstered weapons that were discernible only to the trained eye wandered about the Rome Termini train station, closely examining every person they encountered. Several men were positioned on the upper mezzanine, allowing them to observe anyone below looking the part of a courier carrying millions of euros' worth of diamonds. There was bound to be nervousness in such a person, they reasoned, but the courier could be literally anyone. Lives of suspicion had trained these men to be wary, so they presumed to know what they were looking for.

Many of the men carried and presented official police badges, and many were indeed official police officers—on the payroll of Cosa Nostra. The others had been "loaned" badges by their official associates for the operation. Suspicious people were being briefly detained, their persons and bags searched, as all stops were pulled out in the hunt for Don Alfredo Costello's long-lost treasure.

It was five o'clock in the morning and already the terminal was brimming with activity, with hundreds of people boarding trains on the station's thirty-one tracks.

The mafiosi paid particular attention to those boarding the Frecciarossas to Milan, where those going on to Geneva would transfer to other trains. Complicating the matter was the fact that several trains were departing for Milan that morning, seven alone that were conveniently timed to go on to Geneva. Don Alfredo also had men in both of those distant cities, waiting to carry on the mission should earlier searches fail.

At five forty-five a lively cluster of six chattering Pauline nuns dressed in their trademark blue-and-white habits and low-heeled black shoes, each carrying shoulder bags, laughed and talked animatedly as they crossed the broad terminal, pushing their way through the crowd on the way to their waiting train. One in particular, an especially tall nun named Sister Mary Bede, seemed to be in charge, herding her flock of sisters on to Platform 22 and Frecciarossa 9506 bound for Milan, departing at six ten. Another very tall nun mingled in the center of the others, his head down, doing his best to hide the thick blond hair on the back of his hands and the SIG Sauer pistol strapped inside his belt under the habit.

So stupid! I should have shaved my hands, Lukas groaned to himself.

Two of Don Alfredo's men standing at the boarding steps looked at each other with uncertainty as the group of sisters approached. Was it appropriate to search nuns?

Was there even a remote chance *they* could be carrying the diamonds?

Apparently they decided it was not respectful. They let the nuns pass.

As they made their way up the aisle of the car to find six empty seats together, Sister Teri jabbed her elbow into Lukas's ribs.

"That was the most fun I've had being a nun since taking my vows!" she whispered. The others stifled their laughter along with her, each of them thrilled to be part of such a covert operation.

As he took a seat near the window, Lukas looked around to see if any suspicious characters might have joined them. Having safely passed the worst part, he began breathing easier.

He turned to Teri, who sat next to him. "The hardest part was raising my voice to sound like a woman," he whispered. "But I have to admit, these habits are pretty comfortable!"

Another round of suppressed laughter erupted as the train slowly moved out of the terminal and on to Milan.

As the Frecciarossa entered the Milan Centrale Station nearly four hours later, Lukas looked out the window and saw, as expected, more of Costello's men waiting for passengers to disembark. *These guys are relentless,* he brooded.

As before, the nuns feigned a boisterous conversation, clustering around Lukas to shield him from attention as he kept his head down and hands hidden. Sister Mary

Bede directed them to Platform 12 for the next EuroCity train to Geneva, which was just about to depart. The conductor yelled *"Tutti a bordo!"* as the final warning for passengers to board.

With too many Geneva-bound trains for the mafiosi to monitor, there was only one searcher standing at the entrance of their platform. This guy didn't care whether they were nuns or not. Since he had been told that a priest was involved in the scheme, maybe the *nuns* would make good mules.

Flashing his fake badge, he instructed them to open their bags.

Sister Mary Bede was indignant. In a loud, screeching voice, she admonished the goon. "How *dare* you question us and demand we show you our bags. We will do no such thing!"

Just as the man was about to shout and signal for an associate across the terminal to join him, Lukas stepped forward and, with the clustered nuns serving as cover, gut-punched the guy hard, then as his head naturally fell forward, Lukas delivered a swift upper cut and pushed him down onto the empty tracks on the opposite side of the platform. His head landed on the iron rails, knocking him out.

The nuns quickly ran to board the train just as it started moving out of the station. Finding their seats, they all looked out the window, now silent, uncertain and shaken. Other concerned people had already started calling for help for the unfortunate person who had just fallen off the platform.

"Do you think he's dead?" one of the younger sisters asked Lukas, her clear eyes open wide with worry.

"No, he'll just be out cold for awhile. But now—" He stopped as Sister Mary Bede motioned to the nuns, and they all bowed their heads as she recited a quick prayer for the man's eventual recovery. And his salvation.

Lukas, too, bowed his head but with less sincerity than he knew the sisters held in their hearts. When they looked up, he continued, "—now they know our group of nuns is suspicious at the very least, and they will most certainly stop us in Geneva. Time for me to change into my own clothes, and best if I move away from all of you, just in case they have connections with anyone else on board."

Lukas looked at each of them as he stood up. "Sisters, I am so very grateful for your help in this charade," he whispered. "If there is ever anything I can do to help you in return, you have but to ask. But I swear, you'll never have to wear a Swiss Guard uniform." The nuns muffled their laughter as he waved goodbye and headed for the lavatory.

Having changed into his street clothes and moved to another car toward the front of the train so he would be among the first to disembark when they got to Geneva, Lukas settled in for a nap, the diamonds tucked safely beneath him as he leaned against the window and nodded off.

Six hours later, the EuroCity pulled into the Gare de Genève station. Again, Lukas saw men waiting on the platform, presumably more of Don Alfredo's thugs. But the men paid no attention to others getting off the train, which meant they were likely waiting for a group of nuns to get off.

As Lukas descended the steps, he looked back and saw the Pauline sisters being harassed by four men in dark suits. He smiled as he saw Sister Mary Bede go into her now-familiar ranting mode. He then turned and casually made his way to the taxi stand.

THIRTY-NINE

By the time Dominic, Hana and Duffy returned to the baron's château Lukas had arrived, and he, Karl and Marco leaned over a map of Geneva spread out on the dining table.

"We know where they're keeping the baron!" Marco said eagerly as the others entered the room. Seeing Lukas, Karl rushed over and embraced him.

"How did you find out?!" Hana asked, thrilled with the news.

Marco glanced at the butler. "Frederic remembered he had the baron registered in the Find My app on his iPhone. So, using GPS we found he's being held at a warehouse in Les Paquis, which Frederic tells us is a rather sketchy part of town. But it's nothing the three of us can't handle, depending on what reinforcements they have there. We're planning on going in later tonight, or actually early in the morning, around two or so. It's doubtful they'd be expecting a raid at that time.

"Speaking of news," Karl added, "have you heard about the pope yet?"

Dominic shook his head. "No, we haven't seen or listened to anything since leaving the bank. What happened?"

"His Holiness just announced his retirement! So you *did* know something about that earlier, didn't you, Michael?"

"Well, as I said, I was held to complete secrecy," Dominic admitted, "but yes, I knew it was coming. That just makes our mission all the more important now. You can bet P2 and Opus Deus are lining up their candidate and soldiers as we speak."

"In the meantime," Marco said, looking at Karl and Lukas, "we'd better get some shut-eye now so we're ready for what lies ahead."

Word had spread fast, with newspaper headlines around the world blaring, "**POPE ABDICATES! Conclave To Begin Soon**."

Among the few who were not surprised by the Vatican's announcement, Cardinal Petrini paced his office in the Government Palace, mentally preparing for the rigors of a conclave and even the prospect of becoming pope himself, as His Holiness had alluded to in their previous conversation.

Having announced his decision, and in line with tradition, at eight o'clock that evening the pope was considered to have officially retired, and the Vatican went into an operational mode known as *sede vacante*, the Latin expression meaning that the seat of Saint Peter is currently vacant. In the *interregnum*—that period of time between one pope leaving and another pope taking over —all major positions throughout the Vatican, with few exceptions, ceased to perform their duties. Nearly everything went into shutdown.

In the meantime, just one person, the Cardinal Camerlengo, or Vatican chamberlain, effectively ran the entire city-state himself, with the assistance of the office of the Apostolic Chamber. Together they ensured that the conclave to elect the next pope would be conducted according to sacred tradition, and that the minimal machinery to run the Vatican performed as efficiently as it could under the constraints of a papal vacancy.

All cardinals from around the world had been called to Rome to attend the approaching conclave. Even those over the age of eighty, who were ineligible to vote, were eager and welcomed to be part of the excitement. Before long, waves of black and scarlet would be spotted throughout airports and train stations as nearly two hundred cardinals descended on the Eternal City.

The conclave was about to begin.

Don Silvio Pollastri was brimming with anticipation. At long last, everything was coming together to carry out the most secretly brazen papal election in modern history, and his hand would be at the center of it, the puppet master controlling his marionettes.

Apart from the funds they had accumulated for the venture, they also had the gold from Calvi's safe deposit box, now safely stored at Villa Rosso. And provided things progressed as planned, he would have the diamonds from Dominic any time now in exchange for Baron Armand de Saint-Clair.

But they had to reach certain of the cardinal electors before they went into the conclave, at which point they would be sealed inside the Sistine Chapel *cum clave*— "with a key"—and thus unapproachable for his beneficial offerings in exchange for a vote for Cardinal Alastair Wolsey, the man who would be Propaganda Due's and Opus Deus' carefully groomed choice to be the next pontiff.

Already Pollastri's loyal corps of priests and bishops in and around the Vatican—those jointly pledged to the work of both organizations—had influenced many of the more important cardinal electors: Baltazar Antić from Zagreb, Franco Beneventi from Sicily, Anatoli Sokolov from Romania, and others. Each of these men, and many more, would cast their votes in the conclave for Cardinal Wolsey in exchange for treasure or favor.

There was no way his plan could fail, he assumed, for every man had his price.

Pollastri knew that Cardinal Enrico Petrini would be a challenging man to beat, for he had the blessing and personal support of the Holy Father, not to mention his prominent reputation among the College of Cardinals as a result of his widely-praised effectiveness as secretary of state.

But Pollastri also had a plan for managing that

particular obstacle. Once the other cardinals learned that Petrini was the father of Michael Dominic, he would have no choice but to withdraw from papal consideration to prevent disgrace to Holy Mother Church. Depending on how the votes were turning out during the conclave, at the appropriate hour one of P2's loyal brethren in the Sistine Chapel would broach the matter with his fellow electors.

Of course, such politics were expressly forbidden by the rules of the conclave, as was self-promotion. For centuries it had been considered poor form for one to campaign for himself for the position of pope. But from a practical standpoint, one could not be prevented from voicing his own *opinions* one way or another, for himself or on behalf of someone else. Typical of Vatican culture, gossip was deemed just another of the methods in which the Lord moved in mysterious ways.

CHAPTER
FORTY

It was three o'clock in the morning. Marco Picard crouched on the roof of a two-story warehouse in Les Paquis, across the street from the building that had appeared on the baron's Find My app when Frederic had logged into his boss's iCloud account. Clearly, whoever had the baron had not realized that using his iPhone to call Hana would register the location of the device. Also, whoever it was spoke Italian with an American accent. Marco's unsettling suspicions were festering like a cerebral ulcer.

Dressed in black from head to toe, he peered through the lens of a thermal night vision scope into the windows of the single-story warehouse across the street, most likely where Armand de Saint-Clair was being held. In the alley next to the warehouse a Fiat Strada was parked, facing away from him. He could see in the thermal scope that the engine was still warm. The door to the warehouse had been opened and two men had stepped out and were getting into the Strada. He had missed them as they exited the building, and now they had their backs to him. But another man was still standing at the door, and this man was clearly in view.

As he stared in shock, Marco recognized him—his old buddy Rusty Brinkman. *Rusty?! The American working with P2? How could I have been such a fool as to have missed that?*

Rusty closed the door as the other two men drove away. Marco couldn't reconcile the deep sense of anger and betrayal plaguing him. *Too many thoughts in your head, Marco. Too many distractions. Not the way to start a mission. Get back in the game.*

He focused on the warehouse. Through the wall of dirty windows he saw palletized boxes standing in stacks, many eight feet high, laid out on a grid pattern on the floor with only enough space between them for a small forklift to turn. Off to one side, lights glared. One shadow moved around. The rest of the warehouse was dark.

Marco went back down the fire escape on the opposite side of the building and down the alley to the front. He looked up and down the street, then darted across it and into the alley next to the warehouse. A single steel door joined the cinderblock wall of the warehouse facing the alley. Marco tried the doorknob. It was locked. Taking out a small lockpick set from his vest pocket, he inserted the tensioning lever, then set about raking the tumblers with a pick. Thirty seconds later the lock turned, and Marco cracked open the door. He pocketed the pick set and took out a small, plastic tube of gun oil from his compact cleaning kit. He applied a few drops of oil to the inside of the hinges. No sense announcing his presence with a squeaky hinge. Tonight was all about stealth.

Taking out his Glock 19, he looked through the crack between the door and the wall with the thermal scope in his other hand. Nothing. He placed his back against the wall near the hinges of the door, and slowly pressed the door open with the hand holding the scope, his Glock at the ready. Bringing the scope back up, he scanned through the opening. Still dark. He entered, moving swiftly across the opening where he would be exposed in silhouette, and blended into the maze of stacked boxes.

Marco moved carefully, treading silently on the concrete floor. At each intersection he used the scope to slowly scan the opening as he moved from a position of cover into the opening, or "slicing the pie" as they called it in Special Forces. Cautiously, he crept closer to the corner of the warehouse where the lights still blazed.

Marco finally got to a position where he could see into the lighted area. The baron sat in a wooden chair, his wrists and ankles duct taped to the arms and legs of the seat, facing in Marco's direction. The French commando put the thermal scope in his pocket and shifted the Glock to his left hand to take advantage of the available cover on his right side, keeping most of his body behind the boxes as he pointed the Glock at Rusty.

"Sorry about this, old man," Marco heard Rusty say, "but your granddaughter and her friends have not been forthcoming with what we need. We have no choice but to have you convince them to cooperate. When they do, you're free to go."

"Actually, he has other plans now," Marco jeered as he leaned into the opening, aiming his Glock at Rusty.

Rusty spun to face Marco. "Yeah, I was expecting you might show up. Planned on it actually." At that moment, Marco heard the clicking of a hammer being cocked on a pistol at the back of his head, the muzzle firmly pressed against him.

"Drop the gun and put your hands up," Julio Guzman quietly threatened from behind him.

Marco put his right hand up, his arm bent at the elbow. He began to lower his left hand toward the floor, as if to drop the Glock. He shifted his head slightly to the right, deftly shoved the muzzle of Guzman's pistol toward his left side, then swiftly spun to his right, using his raised right arm to push the pistol away from his head. As he completed the turn, his left hand came around and put two rounds into Guzman's chest. The Spaniard dropped his pistol as he crumpled to the ground.

Marco whipped back to the open area, seeing Rusty draw his revolver as he bolted through an opening between boxes on the other side. Marco ran to check on Saint-Clair.

"Baron, where's your iPhone?" he whispered frantically.

"They took it from me," Saint-Clair said. "I think it's over there, on one of the boxes."

"I'll be right back, sir."

Running to where the baron had indicated, Marco found the iPhone. He dropped it into his vest pocket.

Marco stepped over to the gap between the pallets where Rusty had escaped. Rusty's steps echoed away to his right a couple rows ahead. He took a parallel path, hoping to cut him off. As Marco got closer, he heard the footsteps stop. He waited a moment as he got to the closest intersection where the sound had stopped. Crouching down, he took a quick glance around the boxes from knee height. Just as he pulled his head back, a shot rang out from behind him. Rusty had moved further beyond Marco, expecting him to come into view at normal height.

Marco rolled back and came to his feet, moving quickly to put boxes between himself and Rusty. *Time for this to end.* Marco took out the baron's iPhone, opened the FaceTime app, raised the volume, and set it between two of the boxes. Then he moved away down an aisle of boxes.

"I'm not going to let you get away with this, Rusty," Marco said, using the FaceTime function on his own iPhone talking through the baron's iPhone speaker, now several meters away.

"We already have, Marco. You have no idea what you're up against." Rusty's voice was getting closer.

"But kidnapping and possibly torturing an old man, Rusty? That's not the soldier I knew." Marco's voice had come from around the corner. Rusty circled wide, pointing his revolver at where his old friend's voice had come from.

But all he found there was an iPhone. With perfect timing, Marco leapt up at Rusty from behind on the latter's right side. He grabbed over the top of Rusty's revolver with his left hand, seizing the cylinder and making the gun inoperable so long as he kept the cylinder from rotating. Marco pulled the revolver up between them to the left, trying to wrench it away. But as Marco brought his Glock 19 around to fire, Rusty took hold of it with his left hand from underneath and pushed it just off line enough that when Marco pulled the trigger it missed its mark. Rusty's grip on the slide of Marco's pistol slowed its rearward travel and the weapon jammed, a fired cartridge case protruding from the ejection port like a stove pipe. Marco's pistol was out of action until he could clear the jam, and Rusty hadn't let go.

"See, those jam-o-matics just aren't reliable in close quarters, asshole," Rusty goaded as he tried to twist his revolver out of Marco's grip, while still holding on to the front of Marco's pistol with his other hand. The powerfully built American had the strength, but the Frenchman had the agility.

Marco let go of the 19, startling Rusty. Instantly reaching behind his back, Marco drew his Glock 26.

"Two is one, one is none. Always have a backup," Marco taunted, pointing the subcompact pistol at Rusty's heart and pulling the trigger.

Rusty's two hundred pounds fell stiffly to the floor, his head cracking on the concrete. As he breathed heavily, Marco's muscles began to relax—then tensed again when he heard the click of a pistol just behind his head.

"You should have taken your own advice, smart guy. You came in here alone, without backup," Milo Banducci boasted, nervously pointing a Beretta 9mm at Marco's skull.

But before Banducci could pull the trigger, a hand knocked his pistol up and the banker was hit with two rounds from Karl's SIG. Milo's body toppled to the floor.

"Oh, he had backup," Karl smirked. Lukas was right behind him, his own weapon drawn.

"See Marco," Karl chided, "shoot first, chitchat later. All that talking to people who need to be shot is going to get you killed someday."

"You know, I could have used you guys with the other two as well," Marco quipped.

"We couldn't get to you until Milo moved. He was guarding the other door and neither of us had a shot or a way in until he left.

"So, what do we do with all these bodies?" Karl asked.

"Who cares?" Marco said flippantly. "They made their concrete beds. Let them lie in them."

Running back to where the baron was tied up, Marco took out his tactical knife and cut the man free of the duct tape. He helped raise the old man up, then steadied him as all four walked toward the exit.

"Marco," Saint-Clair said, clearly exhausted, "thank you, so very much. I owe you more than my freedom. I assume Hana is safe?"

"Yes, sir, she's perfectly fine. Let's get you someplace safe and warm. And a shot of whiskey wouldn't hurt, either."

"Make it a tumbler of scotch and you've got yourself a raise."

FORTY-ONE

The sun was just starting to rise when Marco, Karl and Lukas walked in the front door of the château, a haggard-looking Armand de Saint-Clair with them.

Sitting at the dining table worrying, Hana leapt out of her chair and ran to them when she saw all of them enter.

"Grand-père! You're safe!" she cried. As she embraced him tightly, he leaned into her, patting her back.

"*Oui, mon petit.* Thanks to these good men, I am fine now. You are very lucky to have such capable friends."

"One of which is my cousin," Hana said, hugging Karl then each of them in turn, thanking them for their bravery and accomplishment.

"Good to have you back, Baron," Dominic said, extending a hand. "Especially now, since time is so crucial. You likely haven't heard yet, but the Holy Father has retired, the Vatican is now in *sede vacante*, and the conclave to elect a new pope will begin soon. That means

P2 and Opus Deus are probably positioning their candidate as we speak. Though everyone believes Cardinal Petrini to be the likely choice among the *papabile*, we cannot trust the ways and means of those two organizations to get their own man installed."

Dominic explained to him about the discovery of the Dictum Covenant and its onerous objective, and that they somehow had to get the attention of all the cardinal electors before the conclave began, to brief them on P2's Masonic intentions and Opus Deus's far-right agenda.

"Do you know yet who their preferred candidate might be?" the baron asked.

"We have our suspicions, but nothing concrete yet. I'm going to speak with Cardinal Petrini about that and see if he can shed any light on the matter. Until then, I'm not really sure what we can do."

"Well, whatever you do, it can't be much help doing it from here in Geneva," the baron replied. "Why don't you all take my plane back to Rome? It's always ready and fueled, and it is at your disposal for as long as you need it."

Dominic looked at the others, clearly pleased at the thought of saving so much time. Flying from Geneva to Rome would only take an hour and a half by private jet.

"Thank you, sir, that would help tremendously." Looking around, he added, "Everyone ready to go?"

"Just give me ten minutes," Hana said. "Frederic, can you pull the car around and have the pilots file a flight plan?"

"Of course, Mademoiselle," the butler said, smiling at the bustle of activity.

As they packed up their things, Dominic grabbed the Covenant and related documents, as well as the diamonds, and tucked them into his pack.

After they all settled themselves in the Rolls-Royce, Frederic drove the team to Geneva Cointrin International Airport, where the baron's Dassault Falcon 900 was waiting to whisk them to Rome.

Furious that his kidnapping plan had been foiled, Silvio Pollastri was now down three good men, and he still had not gained possession of the diamonds.

"I'm telling you, Guillermo, I am not at all happy with this development," he seethed to Bishop Silva on the phone. "Saint-Clair is now free, and Dominic's people not only still have the diamonds, but they have the Dictum Covenant as well—the only evidence that can destroy our plans. We *must* put a stop to him!"

Sitting behind his Cassoni Pegaso desk, absently admiring its beauty, Silva remained calm but concerned as he puffed on a Ducados. Tiny fragments of white ash fell onto his black cassock, which he casually brushed off.

"Yes, Don Silvio, I agree with you. I will take the appropriate steps here as soon as possible. As you can imagine, the conclave requires a great deal of my attention right now, but we will find a way to stop whatever actions Father Dominic intends to take. On that you have my word."

"With due respect, Excellency, your word may not be

good enough. I will send a team of my own men down to assist you as needed."

Silva sighed. "That may only add to the complications we're already facing, signore. But if it would make you more comfortable, so be it. Admittedly, with Julio Guzman now gone, I could use someone more versed in security precautions."

"I will send my best man for that job: Vito Santini. He will soon be in touch with you personally. Until then, I insist that you keep me updated." Pollastri ended the call.

After considering the situation for a while, Silva pressed the intercom button on his desk phone. When his secretary picked up, he said, "Please find Signor Dante and send him in at once."

Fifteen minutes later there was a knock on the door and Dante entered.

"Have a seat, Fabrizio," Silva instructed. "We have need of your services. I want you to pay a visit to Cardinal Petrini, soon. Tell him these things ..."

When Silva had finished, a wicked smile creased Dante's face.

"This would give me more satisfaction than you realize, Excellency," he said. "Thank you for such a rewarding mission."

FORTY-TWO

F ather Bruno Vannucci sat at his desk in the Government Palace, bored with the routine paperwork assigned to him in his job with the Congregation for the Causes of Saints. He missed the days when he was Cardinal Dante's personal secretary nearly two years prior, in the offices of the Secretariat of State, when he had enjoyed real power as a Vatican player. Now he just pushed paper in a job he cared little for.

Stubbing out yet another cigarette with his bony, nicotine-stained fingers, he looked out the window at the Vatican gardens. A recent rain had brightened all the foliage but a low cloud layer still made for a gloomy day as he yawned and turned to his next tedious project.

The telephone on his desk rang. Picking it up, he answered, "*Pronto, Vannucci qui.*"

"*Buongiorno*, Bruno," a deep, cautious voice said in greeting.

"Cardinale! ... I mean, Signor Dante! I am so happy to hear from you! How are things going?"

"Things are fine, Bruno, but I have no time for small talk just now," Dante said in a low voice. "I have an urgent request of you, though. Can you get me in to see Cardinal Petrini as soon as possible, hopefully today?"

"Oh, I do not know if that is possible, signore," Vannucci lamented. "His Eminence is very busy, what with the conclave coming up."

"But you *must try*, Bruno," Dante implored, his voice more desperate, even menacing now. "It is crucial that I see Petrini immediately! Make an appointment in your name—I doubt he would consent to seeing me, anyway—but tell his secretary it is of vital importance."

As was his nature, Vannucci paused in fear: fear of both Dante and Petrini, and of how this might reflect on him in either man's graces. Petrini currently held the greater position of power, to be sure; yet Dante made Vannucci tremble.

"Alright, signore, I shall do what you ask. I will call you back when I have arranged for such an appointment."

"*Grazie*, Bruno. One day I shall provide a similar accommodation to you. I look forward to hearing from you soon. Don't bother calling, just text me at this number with the details." Dante ended the call.

Vannucci then called Father Bannon, Cardinal Petrini's secretary. After nominally explaining to the good-natured Bannon his need for a visit, Vannucci was told the cardinal could see him for five minutes first thing tomorrow morning.

Vannucci sighed, anxious about the subterfuge. He lit another cigarette, contemplating whether or not to comply with his former boss's request.

His skeletal hands now shaking, he picked up his mobile phone, entered Dante's number in the text message, then passed on the time for the appointment and that he would meet him at Saint Anne's Gate and escort him into the city a few minutes beforehand. Then he would take him up to Petrini's office—and wait for the consequences.

Villa Costello was hardly the typical Sicilian country house. High on the coast overlooking the Mediterranean, it was surrounded on three sides by rows of lush citrus trees, ancient olive groves, blossoming almonds with their fragrant vanilla perfume, and an abundance of rural tranquility not far away from the bustling city of Palermo. The main aspect setting it apart from neighboring estates was the proliferation of armed guards patrolling the property, a necessary accommodation for Don Alfredo Costello's line of work.

One of the *padrino's* most valued employees, Federico Vallardi, sat in his office on the compound focusing on the singular craft at which he excelled: the forgery of counterfeit documents. Passports, birth certificates, driver licenses, bank checks—whatever type of official papers needed in service of Cosa Nostra's operations was handled by Vallardi's steady and capable hands.

His current project was one of the rarest types of documents he had ever come across, and this particular task would be a first for him: an internal security badge for Vatican employees. Fortunately, one of their associates in the Vatican Museum was able to purloin one of the rare passes for Vallardi's use in duplicating it.

Peering into his microscope, he expected and recognized the use of nonstandard safety paper with polyester threads woven throughout, not dissimilar to that used by mints in creating currency, and also used by organizations having high-security needs. In this case, then, he would have to use the same badge to provide Vatican access for Vito Santini, Don Alfredo's most accomplished special operative, who was assigned to the upcoming mission.

First, he took a high-resolution scan of the entire badge, mainly to acquire exact duplicates of the safety paper. Then, using state-of-the-art desktop publishing software, he inserted Santini's photo over the existing image of the prior owner. He did the same with a fake name and Santini's actual signature of that name. Then he printed the badge using an advanced color photocopier.

Taking a sharp specialized knife in hand, he carefully cut out the parts of the pass needed for the exchange. Trimming Santini's photo into the same exact space was relatively easy for a man so accomplished, as was ensuring that the wavy lines of the safety paper containing the name and signature matched those of the previous elements. Placing it under the microscope again, he minutely repositioned each segment to line up perfectly. Now it was ready to be laminated.

Placing a sheet of plastic laminate over the top of the badge, he fed both items into a thermal laminator, and a few moments later the badge was complete.

Apart from the forged elements, it was indistinguishable from the original.

FORTY-THREE

I t was a brisk morning, and Father Bruno Vannucci stood shivering at Saint Anne's Gate, cursing himself for not bringing a coat as he waited for Fabrizio Dante to arrive.

Soon a black Mercedes sedan pulled up to the gate's entrance, and Dante stepped out of the back door. As the car turned around and sped away, Vannucci signed his guest in at the guard station, then he and Dante headed toward the Government Palace to meet with the Secretary of State.

As they stepped into the elevator, Dante punched the button for his former office on the fourth floor.

"Are you quite certain this is a good idea, Eminence?" Vannucci asked, rubbing his hands nervously.

"Oh, Bruno, you're such a neurotic. One of your least appealing traits, by the way. Once I'm inside with Petrini, he will have no choice but to listen to what I have to say. You will be the least of his problems."

Struck by Dante's admonishment, Vannucci sniffed and held his tongue. How much longer would he allow himself to suffer the indignities this man threw at him?

The elevator doors opened into the foyer of the Secretariat of State's office. Father Nick Bannon was at his desk speaking with someone on the phone when he looked up and, with some surprise, saw Dante heading toward Petrini's office door.

Vannucci silently signaled if it was alright to go in. Unable to stop listening to the caller, Bannon was torn. The cardinal would not be expecting his longtime nemesis to show up unannounced.

Dante solved his dilemma, though, by simply opening Petrini's door and going inside the office, shutting the door behind him as he left Vannucci standing there with a distressed Bannon still talking on the phone.

Enrico Petrini looked up from his paperwork. "What the hell are you doing here, Dante?!"

"I will be taking Father Vannucci's place for his appointed meeting with you, Eminence. And before you call for your secretary, I would urge you to listen to what I have to say, for you will find it of significant interest."

"I suppose since you're here now I don't have much choice, do I?" As he said this, Petrini subtly reached across his desk and punched a button.

"That's the spirit," Dante quipped. "Now, let's get down to business. With the Holy Father stepping down, I've no doubt you're in line to take over as pope, should the Holy Spirit so guide the cardinal electors. I am here to simply ask—no, *insist*—that you remove yourself from consideration."

"And why would I want to do that, Fabrizio? The Holy Spirit seems to be persuading me otherwise."

Dante had been relishing the anticipation of this moment for years. "Well," he said with a slick smile, "I don't believe the other cardinals would take well to someone whose bastard son is now in charge of the Apostolic Archive, do you?"

Though he should have expected this from Dante, Petrini was still shocked at hearing the words. He stood up from his desk and walked to the window.

"You should know that the Holy Father is aware of my situation and has given me both his blessing and absolution. That occurred over thirty years ago, Dante. With the pope's support, I have nothing to fear. And certainly not from someone as vile as you, an ex-con. How was life in prison, by the way? Were the conditions as awful as one might imagine in that rat-infested cell of yours?"

Irritated by Petrini as ever, Dante would still not take the bait.

"The pope will have little influence in the matter now," he said, "and of course, like you, he is ineligible to vote. We are already lining up our candidate, who is sure to be elected the Church's next pontiff."

"And who might that be?" Petrini asked. "And who are 'we?'"

"Cardinal Alastair Wolsey, if you must know. And the 'we' I refer to is Opus Deus, an order you do not want to have as an enemy."

"Isn't blackmail a violation of your parole conditions, Fabrizio? Perhaps I should have a word with the Carabinieri about *your* situation."

"It's your word against mine, Eminence, and I have some very powerful friends now, friends with connections even inside the Carabinieri."

"Oh, I doubt even Opus Deus can get you out of this." Petrini returned to his desk and picked up a mini-recorder sitting there, its red light blinking.

"As you see, two can play at your deceitful game." The cardinal smiled at his prescience.

Dante stared at the recorder, shocked that he had been played. He lunged for the device.

"*Uh uh* ..." Petrini blurted, snatching the recorder away from Dante's hands. Then he shouted, "*Nick?* Could you come in here, please?"

It was but seconds before the door flung open and the young, fit Father Bannon stood there, primed to handle anything his superior might require.

"Signor Dante was just leaving. Could you escort him out of the building and make sure he finds his way back to Saint Anne's Gate?"

"It would be a pleasure, Eminence," Bannon said, holding the door open for the unwelcome guest. "This way, signore."

Furious, Dante swept out of the office, past Vannucci and down the four flights of stairs. Bannon followed him the entire way to the gate, where he instructed the Swiss Guards that Dante was never to return.

Meanwhile, Petrini looked harshly at Father Vannucci, who stood in the foyer quivering.

"Bruno, I'm afraid your services here are no longer required. Pack up your things and return to your order for a new assignment, which will *not* be in Vatican City."

~

The Dassault Falcon was on final approach to Rome when Dominic got up and moved to a seat near Hana.

"My own plans are pretty clear right now, revealing the Dictum Covenant to Cardinal Petrini and helping with the fallout," he said, "but what are you two up to over the next few days?"

"Not much," Hana said. "Karl is giving us a private tour of St. Peter's Basilica and Castel Sant'Angelo the day after tomorrow, something I've never done in all the years I've visited Rome. Hopefully, Lukas can join us, too." She turned to Marco.

"First, though," Marco said, reaching for Hana's hand, "I'm going to pay a visit to Cassandra, Rusty's wife, and explain things to her. Even though Rusty betrayed me, he was my closest friend for years. We have a history, and I owe him that one thing, to inform his wife of his death. Hopefully she'll understand the circumstances."

"That's really noble of you, Marco," Dominic said. "A lesser man wouldn't take the time, I expect." Touched by the tenderness of the moment, Hana wrapped her arm around Marco's, proud of his integrity.

The jet touched down on runway 16R of Leonardo da Vinci–Fiumicino Airport just before noon and taxied to the private Signature terminal. There, Dominic, Hana, Marco, Duffy, Karl and Lukas loaded their gear into the waiting transit van they had arranged for while in-flight.

The van first stopped at the Rome Cavalieri to drop off Hana and Marco, then took the others directly to the Vatican. Dominic was anxious to share the Dictum Covenant with Cardinal Petrini in an effort to suspend the conclave until all cardinal electors were able to read the damning document. They also had to find out who P2's preferred candidate would be, something best left to Petrini, he imagined. But things were moving quickly now. He only hoped he would be in time.

CHAPTER

FORTY-FOUR

Following centuries of tradition, with the College of Cardinals gathered around him, the Cardinal Camerlengo had taken the Ring of the Fisherman from the finger of the now retired pope, and with a small silver hammer and chisel, carved an "X" across the gold papal insignia, disfiguring it such that it could no longer be used for signing and sealing official papal documents and symbolizing an end to the pope's authority.

Now gathered in St. Peter's Basilica, the cardinal electors were given the first of two sermons they would receive as part of the official conclave ceremonies. The first of these sermons spoke to the current state of affairs of the Church, followed by the specific expectations for an incoming pontiff based on the Church's needs and goals, and the qualities such a person should possess in order to carry out those duties. Then they celebrated Mass preceding the start of the conclave.

While Mass was taking place, *la Cappella Sistina*, the Sistine Chapel, was being prepared for the convocation. Trusted security technicians using nonlinear junction detectors swept the room for "bugs"—counter-surveillance and eavesdropping devices employing infrared, microwave or radio frequencies. Thermal imagers were then brought in to intercept devices broadcasting on low wattage. Across all of Vatican City, Wi-Fi access was blocked, and wireless signal jammers were deployed inside the chapel itself to prevent any cardinal elector from sending or receiving electronic communications. Absolute secrecy was to be observed at all times by anyone going into or out of the venerated room, including food service attendants, doctors and nurses, and the very few other authorized personnel permitted ingress to or egress from the Sistine Chapel while the conclave was in session.

Following Mass, the cardinal electors gathered in the Pauline Chapel of the Apostolic Palace, singing the *Litany of the Saints* as they formed a two-by-two procession on their way to the Sistine Chapel. Once there and seated inside, the cardinals took an oath to abide by the rules and procedures of the conclave and to maintain confidentiality throughout the process.

The master of papal liturgical celebrations then ordered that all outsiders be expelled from the chapel, and the centuries-old wooden doors were chained and locked, with two Swiss Guards, Corporal Finn Bachman and Sergeant Dieter Koehl, standing outside as sentries to ensure total security.

The conclave had begun, *cum clave.*

Exiting the airport transit van from the airport just outside Saint Anne's Gate and showing their badges, Michael Dominic and Ian Duffy walked hurriedly through the entrance and up Via di Belvedere toward the Archives building. Karl and Lukas went straight to the Swiss Guard barracks to report in for duty.

"We may already be too late," Dominic said to Ian as they broke into a quick jog. "Once those doors to the chapel are closed, no one is allowed in."

"But can't we get a message to Cardinal Petrini somehow?" Duffy asked.

"Actually, being over the age of eighty he's ineligible to vote, so he won't be part of the conclave—though he could still be elected pope. He's our only chance. We'll have to pray that the Cardinal Camerlengo will make an exception and hear our case.

"Ian, when you get to your office can you find and print out copies of the original Calvi documents we got from the briefcase? Make a hundred and twenty copies, just of the important pages I've flagged. Oh, and for good measure, print out a photo of that gold from the safe deposit box. I'll need all the ammunition I can muster for the kind of accusations I'll be making to the cardinals, *if* I'm permitted access. And make it fast."

"You bet, Michael. I'll bring them to your office when I'm done."

Once they reached the Archives building, each went

his separate way: Dominic to his office, Duffy to his own, farther down in the digitizing lab.

Taking a seat at his desk, Dominic removed the Dictum Covenant and other papers from his backpack and began sorting and preparing them for presentation to the cardinal electors and laying out in his mind how he would accomplish this nearly impossible task. Remembering that bag of diamonds was still in his backpack, he pulled them out and stood to open the large safe next to his desk, then tucked them securely on an interior shelf and closed the door.

Minutes earlier, after exiting the taxi, his black cassock fluttering in the midday breeze, Vito Santini presented his "official" Vatican badge to the Swiss Guard at the gate.

"Welcome, Father ..." the guard glanced at the ID, "Santini. I do not recognize you. Are you new to the Vatican?"

"Yes, my son," said the well-built Italian in his forties. "I was recently assigned to the Apostolic Archive. I will be working with the prefect. Perhaps you know him, Father Michael Dominic?"

"Actually, Father Dominic just arrived a few minutes ago. Do you need an escort to the Archive?"

"No, I'm sure I can find my way there with the instructions he gave me. Thank you, though. Ciao."

Remembering the route given to him by one of Cosa Nostra's moles in the Vatican Museum, Santini proceeded to the entrance of the building where the Secret Archives were kept. He felt beneath his cassock to make sure his Beretta M9A3 and Gerber switchblade were readily available and played the plan through his mind again. He had timed his arrival within the two hours when all Italians traditionally take lunch, when most of the staff presumably would be gone and he would hopefully find Dominic alone.

Entering the Archive building, he turned right and went down the long marble hall to the prefect's office. As he passed the open door and glanced inside he saw a handsome, young priest standing next to a large open safe. *That must be him.*

As he continued reconnoitering the building, making sure few others were around—and rewarded by their absence—Santini turned back toward Dominic's office. Walking in, he closed the door behind him.

Now sitting at his desk, Dominic looked up, disturbed. "May I help you?" he asked the visitor, glancing at his watch. "I'm in a bit of a hurry just now."

Santini approached him, reached under his cassock and withdrew the Beretta, then took a seat across from Dominic as he casually attached a silencer onto the pistol.

"I'm afraid I'll need your full attention, Father Dominic. I am here for the diamonds. Just hand them over and I'll be on my way, no problems. Are we clear?" Santini gently waved the Beretta in his lap to reinforce his intentions.

"I ... I'm not sure what you mean ... diamonds? What diamonds?" Dominic feigned.

"Neither of us has time for games, Father. The diamonds do not belong to you. They belong to my employer, La Cosa Nostra. As you can guess, nobody stands in the way of *la famiglia*. I just saw you put the diamonds in your safe a few minutes ago. And I expect you to give them to me. *Now*." He held the pistol up and aimed it directly at Dominic's face, hoping his guess about the diamonds was correct.

Dominic's mind raced. *How could he have seen that? And the* Mafia?! *Definitely not anything I want to take on ... Besides, the damned diamonds are nothing compared to allowing Opus Deus and P2 to take over the Catholic Church.*

Staring at Santini, Dominic sighed. "Fine. These have been more trouble than they're worth. To me, anyway."

Standing up, with Santini watching him guardedly, Dominic entered the combination to the safe, opened the steel door, and withdrew the purple bag. Closing the safe, he turned around and handed Santini the diamonds. The mafioso opened the bag to inspect its contents. Satisfied, he looked up at Dominic.

"Now see? That wasn't so hard, was it? You made the right decision, Father, and for that, you get to live. But I will need to tie you up, I'm afraid."

"Is that really necessary?" Dominic asked, anxious to reach Petrini before the conclave went into lockdown.

"Unless you pinkie swear you'll not call the Swiss Guards until I'm well beyond the Vatican? Forgive me, but in my business, trust is not something one can so easily rely upon."

Again reaching beneath his cassock, Santini pulled out a coil of twine he had in his pocket, just enough to secure Dominic to his chair. He also had a strip of duct tape lined with adhesive paper. Removing the strip, he wrapped the tape across Dominic's mouth.

Locking and closing the door behind him, Santini walked quickly back to Saint Anne's Gate, waved to the guard, and hailed the first taxi he found.

His job here was done.

CHAPTER
FORTY-FIVE

Accompanied by Hana—for a woman's support with a potentially grieving widow—Marco hailed a taxi from the Rome Cavalieri, which took them across the Tiber River to central Rome and the historic Monti neighborhood. Getting out at the Piazza della Madonna, he paid the driver, then they both walked across the piazza to Cassandra's 17th-century townhouse.

Marco took a deep breath before knocking on the door.

"You'll be fine, and I'm here to support you," Hana reassured him. "She knows you loved Rusty, but the circumstances called for an instant and justifiable reaction. He just chose the wrong side."

As they were talking, the door opened before he had even knocked.

"Marco! *Buongiorno!*" Cassie said happily. "I saw you both from the window and ran to the door. Please, come in."

"Hi, Cassie," Marco said somberly. "Oh, this is my friend Hana, who I told you about at dinner."

Reaching out, Cassie pulled her in for a warm embrace. "It is such a pleasure meeting you, Hana. Based on Marco's elaborate storytelling, it feels as if I already know you."

Hana smiled modestly as she returned the hug.

"Unfortunately, Rusty is not here," Cassie said. "He had some business in Geneva and I imagine he is still there."

Marco felt crushed by her exuberance, especially knowing that what he was about to tell her would change her world.

"Cassie, that's why we've come. I'm afraid I have some terrible news. Can we sit down?"

Cassie's demeanor changed instantly to one of concern. "Of course, come in, we'll sit here. May I offer you some tea, or ...?"

"No, thanks," Marco said, a sorrowful look on his face. "We just returned from Geneva ourselves, and ..."

He explained about the abduction of Hana's grandfather, the diamonds, a brief summary of Propaganda Due and their odious mission, and finally, about Rusty's attack on him and his having to defend himself.

"Rusty was killed as we were grappling for control of the weapon, Cassie. I'm so very sorry."

Cassie's face turned from concern to grief as Marco finished. She put her head in her hands and began to sob. Marco stood and walked toward her. Cassie stood to meet him. She put her arms around him and her head on his chest, still crying. But Marco sensed something else, too. His instinct drew an uncertain caution.

"I know... I know..." Cassie said with a now firmer voice. Marco felt her tense up. Then she whispered into his ear, "Rusty told me what he was doing, you bastard. We worked on that mission together."

As Cassie's hands went around Marco's waist, he felt her hand land on the grip of his Glock, tucked in his waistband at the small of his back. Reflexively, he started to move just as Cassie reached under his jacket, grabbed the gun, and began pulling it around him.

Instinctively, Marco closed his left arm to trap Cassie's arm against his side. He swung his right elbow across her face, and twisted to his left to pull her in closer.

Then, with a grip on her right wrist, Marco reversed direction, using his left hand to swing Cassie's right arm up and over in front of him. In the same instant, Cassie fired the gun.

Hana screamed.

Marco drove his forearm down on Cassie's elbow, breaking her arm. She dropped the gun, shrieking in pain. Marco impulsively drove his right fist into her throat. He felt the cartilage shatter. She fell to the floor.

"Hana!" Marco shouted, looking around the room for her. He found her on the floor, huddled behind the couch in a fetal position, crying.

Marco dove to her side. "Are you okay? Were you hit?"

Hana shook her head, but couldn't speak. Marco ran his hands quickly over her form—no blood. But her eyes stared at him in the shock. Then he checked on Cassie.

The blow to her neck had proven fatal. As he lifted

her, her head lolled back like that of a broken doll's, her eyes wide open, staring at ... nothing. He laid her on the couch.

"Damn. I did not intend for this to happen ...

"Come, Hana," Marco prompted. "We have to get out of here."

As the taxi took them back to the hotel, Hana and Marco both stared out the window, not speaking. She could not help but reflect on the ease with which Marco could dispense violence. He was the most dangerous man she had ever met. He could be caring most of the time, and exciting to be with, but at the same time he had a natural capacity to inflict harm. That scared her. Was he really someone she wanted to spend her life with? Death seemed to follow him.

Hana had finally come to realize that she was torn between the man she could have but wasn't sure she wanted, and the man she wanted but was sure she couldn't have.

FORTY-SIX

S itting at two long tables, one facing one another in the great Sistine Chapel, each of the cardinal electors had before him two simple, folded cards, at the top of which were printed the Latin phrase, *Eligo in Summum Pontificem*—"I elect as Supreme Pontiff"— below which was a single line.

The first round of balloting, called a scrutiny, had begun. Each cardinal entered the name of the person he wished to elect as pope. Then, one by one, each man walked up to the front of the Sistine Chapel to a small altar beneath Michelangelo's majestic fresco of *The Last Judgment*, uttered a solemn oath in Latin, then dropped his ballot onto a brass salver which he then tipped to let the ballot fall into a large brass urn beneath it. This procedure continued for all one hundred and twenty cardinal electors in the room.

Three randomly chosen cardinals acted as

"scrutineers," delegated to count the ballots to ensure the number of votes did not exceed the number of electors. Assuming there were no irregularities, the ballots were then opened and read, the name shown on each one recorded in a journal, and then the results of the vote were read aloud. If at least two-thirds, or 80, of the ballots were in support of one name, that person would become the next pope.

The two leading contenders in the first scrutiny were Cardinal Enrico Petrini with 54 votes, and Cardinal Alastair Wolsey with 57 votes. In time, the smattering of other names would diminish as the outlier cardinals eventually grew frustrated with their minority, or were otherwise guided by the Holy Spirit to back one of the leading candidates.

In this case, the two-thirds rule for the first scrutiny was not met. The ballots were bundled together, one of two distinctive chemicals was added to the papers, and they were burned in a special stove installed for the time-honored ritual. The chemical added for this batch produced a thick, black smoke which poured out of a temporary chimney installed on the roof of the Sistine Chapel.

Seeing the black smoke, thousands of faithful gathered in St. Peter's Square for the event groaned with dismay. There would be no new pope yet.

After a brief period for prayer, reflection and dialogue, another scrutiny would soon take place.

~

After printing out the specific Calvi documents Dominic had requested, Ian Duffy placed them in a box and left the lab, bound for the prefect's office.

When he was almost there, he suddenly realized he'd forgotten about the photograph of the gold. He sighed, then went all the way back to the lab to find the image on his computer. Once he located it, he printed it out and added it to the stack in the box, then left the lab to join Father Dominic in his office.

Reaching the office, Duffy knocked on the door. There was no answer. He tried the handle but it was locked. *Odd*, he thought. *He told me to meet him back here. Maybe he already left for the Sistine Chapel.*

He knocked again and had started to turn away when he heard a faint, muffled sound. He put his ear to the heavy wooden door. Yes, there was a distinct sound inside, as if someone were trying to shout through a pillow or something, he reasoned. Duffy had a bad feeling about this. But he didn't have a key. And as there were no windows into the room, he couldn't see inside.

Setting the boxes down, he ran off to find Father Laguardia, the only other person he knew who had a key to the prefect's office. But everyone was at lunch! Maybe he was in the canteen.

Duffy ran out through the doors beneath the Tower of the Winds and toward the commercial area where the canteen was located. Rushing inside, he did find Father Laguardia, eating his meal with a few other priests.

"Father," he stammered breathlessly, "I fear Father Dominic may be locked in his office and unable to open his door. I'm sure something's wrong. I can hear what sounds like muffled shouting. Can I borrow your key to his office?"

Laguardia did not hesitate. Reaching into his pocket, he detached Dominic's office key from his ring and handed it to Duffy.

"Thanks! I'll get it back to you later." He rushed out of the canteen and back to the Archives building.

Reaching the door, he thrust the key into the hole and turned the knob. Seeing Dominic tied up to a chair laying on its side, he raced to lift him up and untie him after first removing the duct tape from his mouth.

"Thank God, Ian! I don't know how he got in here, but some Mafia goon took the diamonds from me at gunpoint and bound me to this chair. I was trying to reach the phone when I fell onto the floor and couldn't get back up. I figured you'd find me eventually, but I've got to get to Cardinal Petrini. Now!"

Back in the Sistine Chapel, the second scrutiny had just taken place. After the scrutineers counted this round of ballots, the votes for Cardinal Petrini stood at 56. Cardinal Wolsey pulled in 61 votes.

Again, black smoke emerged from the chimney. Again, the great crowd moaned, then dispersed to return in the morning, awaiting their new pope.

The first rounds of balloting being done for the day, the doors of the chapel were unlocked and opened, and the quietly murmuring cardinals were surrounded by a squad of Swiss Guards and escorted down through the papal gardens to Domus Santa Marta, the Vatican's special guest house which had been prepared to domicile all cardinal electors during the conclave, ensuring privacy and continued secrecy.

FORTY-SEVEN

H is backpack slung over his shoulder, Dominic raced down the long hallway through the numerous rooms of the Vatican Museum and on into the Sistine Chapel only to find it vacant, the cardinals now having retired to Domus Santa Marta for the evening.

Aware that not even Petrini could reach anyone participating in the conclave, Dominic was frustrated. All this effort, only to be prevented from relaying such crucial information to Church authorities when they needed it most. Too much was at stake. Too much hung in the balance to simply *not* do something.

He set off to find Cardinal Petrini. Hopefully he would know of some way of breaking the sacred traditions of the conclave.

. . .

Enrico Petrini sat in his apartment in the San Carlo Palace, looking out over the gardens of Saint Martha's Square, alternately drawing on his pipe and sipping from a tumbler of Puni Alba Scotch. As he took in the rich, cherry aroma of the toasted Cavendish and Burley tobacco blend drifting throughout his lavish sitting room, he reflected on the days ahead. He could actually be elected pope within a matter of hours. He wondered if that was the job he really wanted.

He recalled his old friend, Albino Luciani, who became Pope John Paul I and who, when accepting his election, pleaded to his fellow cardinal electors, "May God forgive you for what you have done." Petrini felt much the same, humbled by the prospect of being handed the role of Supreme Pontiff.

But he was getting ahead of himself. If what Dante had said was true then the fix was in, and there was nothing he could do about it. That scoundrel Wolsey would most likely win the election, bought and paid for by P2 and Opus Deus. Being under eighty, Wolsey would be participating in the Conclave, and his very presence would hold some sway on those gathered for this most sacred of votes.

From a distance, he heard a knock on his door. Knowing one of the nuns would answer it, he waited to see who his visitor was.

"Your Eminence, Father Dominic is here to see you," Sister Francesca announced. "He said it is quite urgent."

"Yes, please bring him in, Sister. Thank you."

The young priest entered the sitting room, his

backpack slung over his shoulder. Petrini stood to embrace his son.

"Dear Michael, how are things?"

"Eminence," Dominic began excitedly, taking a seat and removing the documents from his pack. "We've got to stop the conclave. Or at least get critical information to the electors about the grave mistake they'll be making if they don't hear these details of a terrible conspiracy."

He explained to Petrini the events of the past several days: of Baron Saint-Clair's kidnapping, of the diamonds being stolen from him at gunpoint, and finally, of the discovery of the Dictum Covenant and the plan for someone of P2's choosing to become pope. Petrini reacted viscerally to being shown the incendiary documents.

"This is nothing short of shocking, Michael! I got an unexpected visit by Fabrizio Dante yesterday, who tried to blackmail me into stepping down in favor of Cardinal Wolsey, Opus Deus's chosen candidate. Obviously, they're now working hand in hand with Propaganda Due."

"So it's *Wolsey* they're lining up!" Dominic exclaimed. "I thought as much. Are you aware he's the father of Isabella Stewart Hastings, the new president of the Vatican Bank?"

"I was not," Petrini said, a slight look of fear on his face. "But that's not something you or I should really bring up, is it? At least not until it becomes absolutely necessary ... in the event, say, they bring up our own relationship."

"I agree that's the more prudent course, yes."

"We must get this information to the cardinal electors at once, Michael. But as they are in lockdown, that may prove impossible. My god, I just cannot believe this."

The two men sat thinking of ways around the predicament until Dominic looked up, his eyes bright with an idea.

"Wait ... The cardinal electors celebrate Mass each morning before the day's conclave begins, don't they? What if *you* were to be the celebrant? That would give you the opportunity of addressing the entire assembly at Mass, during the sermon! Surely, they would have to believe you, of all people!"

Taking a draw on his pipe, Petrini considered this.

"I don't think it would be appropriate for a papabile to celebrate a conclave Mass. It could be considered contrived and potentially influential to the electors. No, it's a very good idea, Michael, but I think *you* should be the one to do it. You can also speak to the matter much better informed than I could.

"The real problem might be when you attempt to speak to the electors during the sermon. You'd have to do it quickly, lest risk being yanked offstage like some vaudevillian performer, most likely by Swiss Guards. But at least you might have a few moments to impart the dangers they would be facing."

"I'm game. I can do this. So how do we go about it? Can you find out who is performing tomorrow's Mass and see if I could act as his replacement, or even concelebrant?"

"Yes, I believe Monsignor DeSantis is scheduled for

the morning Mass. I can speak with him and have you stand in for him. It's a wonderful plan, Michael. Let's hope it works."

CHAPTER

FORTY-EIGHT

With a detail of eight Swiss Guards flanking them, the Cardinal Camerlengo led the procession of the 120 cardinal electors from their residence at Domus Santa Marta to St. Peter's Basilica for Mass preceding the day's conclave.

Father Michael Dominic nervously prepared himself in the sacristy, Cardinal Petrini having persuaded Monsignor DeSantis to let Dominic serve as his replacement for the special morning service.

Not only did Dominic carry the burden of trying to get his important message out, he also felt a certain privilege to be serving Mass to members of a papal conclave: not an event that happens very often, and yet one with historic implications. It was a great honor, he thought, to be doing both these things. He only hoped his gambit would pay off, and the cardinals would see that Wolsey had to be excused from the *papabile* for his apparent collusion with outside forces. Dominic hated knowing this would come off as a political maneuver, since everyone knew how close he was to Cardinal Petrini. But too much was at stake to worry about personal issues at this point.

As the altar servers and sacristan prepared for the entrance procession, Dominic said a silent prayer, pleading for strength and clarity of purpose during Mass and his potentially explosive sermon.

With the conclave in progress, duties of the Swiss Guards were fairly light—there being no pope to protect at the moment—and most other traditional duties were suspended until a new pope was named.

Meanwhile, Karl Dengler was looking forward to escorting his cousin Hana and their friend Marco for their private tour of Castel Sant'Angelo and St. Peter's Basilica.

Marco and Hana had arrived at Saint Anne's Gate promptly at nine o'clock. Greeting them, Karl suggested they first visit Castel Sant'Angelo, since Mass for the cardinal electors was taking place in St. Peter's.

"Hey, did Father Michael tell you he's celebrating the conclave Mass this morning? I passed him briefly on his way to the sacristy and all he said was, 'I'm the celebrant for Mass this morning. You should know, I plan on exposing Wolsey and the Dictum Covenant to the cardinal electors, so be ready for all hell to break loose. And pray for me.' Then he sped off. I have no idea what will happen, or if they will even allow him to speak. There's so much riding on him right now. I wish we could be there for him, but all conclave activities are closed off to everyone else."

Hana was now concerned. "Oh, Karl! No, he didn't mention it. But I'll bet things are moving pretty fast for him just now. I wish there was something we could do to help. For him to be revealing such a vile conspiracy by himself must really be tearing at him. I'm for postponing the tour and seeing if we can help somehow."

"Michael is made of stronger stuff," Marco said. "He'll do just fine, *if* he's even given the chance."

"Well, I agree with Marco. There isn't anything we can do—we can't even get near the action. Besides, we'll know soon enough," Karl replied. "It's a good thing you're here now, regardless, so we can be there for him later. So let's get on with the tour, then visit Father Michael afterward and see how things turned out. Sound good?"

"You bet," said Marco. "I am really looking forward to the tour, especially with such a seasoned guide."

Hana sighed, resigning herself reluctantly to their logic.

Karl led them through the long, covered corridor called the Passetto di Borgo, an elevated stone walkway connecting the Vatican to Castel Sant'Angelo. Karl began telling them of its history.

"Originally built as a mausoleum for the family of the Roman Emperor Hadrian in 139 AD, the castle sits at the end of the Ponte Sant'Angelo bridge and is connected to the Vatican by this covered walkway.

"The castle was converted into a fortress in the fourteenth century, serving as popes' protection from armed forces invading the Vatican. During the sack of

Rome on May 6, 1527, forty Swiss Guards rushed Pope Clement VII across the Passetto di Borgo to the safety of Castel Sant'Angelo, while back in the Vatican one hundred forty-seven of their brother Guards fought mightily to protect their pope and defend the city. Tragically, all one hundred forty-seven of those brave soldiers lost their lives in that valiant effort. Since then, the sixth of May has remained a sacred day for the Swiss Guard: the day when new candidates are sworn into our corps during a most solemn ceremony."

Karl was proud of his corps' heritage, and it showed. Every guard honored the great sacrifices his comrades had made on that terrible day.

Mass had begun. Dominic had already taken the cardinals through the Introductory Rites—the Greeting, the Penitential Act, the Kyrie and the Gloria—and began reading the Liturgy of the Word.

As he stood before this unique congregation, about to deliver his explosive homily, Dominic's heart began to race. His mouth was dry, and he paused to take a sip from the bottle of water at his side.

"A reading from the Holy Gospel according to Luke." Dominic stammered. He intentionally chose Luke, Chapter 10 for its treatise on power, hoping it would serve as an appropriate introduction to the ad hoc "sermon" he was about to give.

He began reciting the Gospel, concluding with the nineteenth verse: 'Behold, I give unto you power to tread on serpents and scorpions, and over all the power of the enemy: and nothing shall by any means hurt you.'"

He put down the Bible and looked out over the assembled cardinals.

"Your Eminences, I truly beg your forgiveness for what I am about to say, for it gives me no pleasure to inform you that there is a terrible conspiracy taking place during this very conclave, one designed to influence your votes in favor of one particular cardinal."

Gasps of consternation echoed throughout the great basilica as Dominic spoke and kept on speaking with no let up.

He held a single piece of paper, the original Dictum Covenant, high above his head for all to see. "I have evidence here that proves beyond a shadow of a doubt that the united forces of both Opus Deus and the forbidden Masonic Lodge Propaganda Due have jointly chosen Cardinal Alastair Wolsey as their preferred candidate for the papal office."

Several cardinals hung their heads down nervously, expecting the worse—their own names being read as having been influenced by gold or diamonds or special favors.

As he continued speaking, Swiss Guards on both sides of the lectern started to approach him, glancing at the Cardinal Camerlengo for the order to apprehend him. Dominic's pace accelerated.

"Their chosen candidate is bound by this document— under penalty of death!—to abide by the dictates of both organizations. During our efforts to ensure that this was a true and accurate document, operatives from both Opus

Deus and P2 have resorted to kidnapping, blackmail and extortion to stop us from learning and exposing the truth."

In the middle of the congregation, Cardinal Wolsey stood up.

"This is outrageous!!" he shouted. "I insist that this man be removed from this sacred place at once. Whatever he is saying makes no sense whatsoever. He is obviously delusional!"

Pandemonium reigned throughout the assembled cardinals, each turning to one another in surprise, indignation or admiration at what they were hearing.

"Let the man continue speaking," one of the cardinals proclaimed loudly. "Let us see this evidence."

But the Cardinal Camerlengo—an ardent Wolsey supporter—gave signals to the Swiss Guards that Father Dominic be removed from the church immediately.

As the guards moved to apprehend Dominic, the great doors at the back of the basilica opened and a cadre of Swiss Guards armed with halberds escorted two men into the chamber: Cardinal Enrico Petrini and the newly retired Pope Emeritus in his singular white cassock.

A sudden hush fell over everyone when the pope spoke loudly and with conviction as he walked up the main aisle toward the altar. The only other sounds in the basilica were those of the footsteps of the pope's entourage and the whisperings of the stunned assembly.

"What Father Dominic is telling you is the truth, my brothers. I have been shown these documents and believe our Holy Mother Church is in grave danger at this very moment. It is important that you hear him out."

Suddenly, while all other eyes were on His Holiness, Cardinal Wolsey broke ranks and ran up to where Dominic stood at the lectern.

"You fucking sonofabitch! Give me that!" Wolsey snarled, then grabbed the Dictum Covenant from Dominic's hands and ran toward the exit off the northern transept chapel. In moments he was out onto the Passetto di Borgo, escaping through the passageway toward Castel Sant'Angelo.

Uncertain how to react, Dominic stood there for a minute, appraising how he should respond.

Then he ran off in pursuit of Wolsey.

FORTY-NINE

A s they walked through the warren of great and small rooms, hallways, and dark, narrow stairways of Castel Sant'Angelo, Karl, Hana and Marco took in the elegantly carved columns and arches, and magnificent ceiling murals featuring angels, cherubs and several ancient popes and other notable historical figures dominating each room.

Numerous glass cases displayed swords, halberds and other weapons of war, with steel suits of armor and battle shields standing in various corners, as if they had just been removed and hung by the soldiers wearing them.

"Here in the Sala dei Festoni is where the original papal archives were located in the eighteenth century. The vault, designed in 1545 by Luzio Luzi, depicts stories of Ancient Rome with the emblems of the pope's family, the Farnese, here in the center. You see here? The lily and the lady with the unicorn? Luzi was inspired by the great

Italian painter Raphael, and was particularly influenced by Nero's Golden Palace, which was recently unearth—"

Suddenly Karl stopped talking as he heard a loud flurry of running footsteps approaching them, coming up the Elliptic Ramp and into the Sala dei Festoni. Cardinal Wolsey was the first to appear, gripping a piece of paper, his face beet red and his lungs laboring for air. With wild eyes he looked at Karl and the others as if they might help him, but he raced past them into the Cell of the Roman Sepulchral Urns and on into the Loggia of Pope Paul II.

Dominic was right behind him, arriving several seconds later, and behind him a pack of Swiss Guards also were in pursuit, but of whom was unclear to the onlookers. Were they after Wolsey or Dominic?

Karl and Marco were the first to react, swiftly following Dominic and the others to see what the commotion was about. Now alone in the room, Hana decided to run after the others.

As she reached the Loggia of Pope Paul II, she saw everyone gathered around Cardinal Wolsey, who stood precariously on the ledge of a large, open window facing out onto the gardens two stories below. Standing just below Wolsey was Dominic with the Swiss Guards behind him.

"Stop where you are, all of you," Wolsey screamed maniacally, his chest heaving from the exertion, eyes fired up with hatred. He stared balefully at Dominic.

"You!" he spat. "You just *had* to get involved, didn't you? You understand *nothing*! The good we would have brought to the Church... you and your self-absorbed righteousness are what's causing this Church to fail! The Vatican is overrun with sanctimonious—"

Dominic reached out to pull him back in. He caught hold of the cardinal's arm, then leapt up onto the ledge to prevent Wolsey from falling or jumping.

"Let go of me!" the cardinal cried.

"Let him jump," said Marco, watching with amusement from behind the Swiss Guards. "He's not worth saving."

Hana looked up at Marco, again disturbed by his callousness.

"Eminence," Dominic pleaded, "let's get down from here and—"

It was too late. Wolsey had leaned out of the window too far and the weight of his own body started to pull him down. He reached out to Dominic, reflexively grabbing him for support. Panicked, Dominic reached back furiously to grab hold of the window frame, anything to find purchase and keep him from falling too.

But there was nothing there.

He felt as if everything was happening in slow motion, he and Wolsey falling down through the air, the fast approaching ground seeming to take forever to reach.

Wolsey's body hit first, falling onto the stone walkway of Pope Boniface IX. Dominic heard a crunch of bones as he fell directly on top of the cardinal.

Then everything went black as he lost consciousness.

FIFTY

Hana screamed. The Swiss Guards were the first to react, scrambling out of the Loggia, back down the Elliptic Ramp and out to the garden. Karl, Marco and Hana ran after them, praying their friend was alright.

When they finally made it to the garden and reached the bodies, Karl, the most senior Guard among the others, took charge. He felt for a pulse on both men.

Wolsey was dead.

Dominic did have a pulse, but it was faint. While she had been following the others, Hana had the good sense to dial 118, calling for an ambulance.

"Michael was lucky to have landed on Wolsey, cushioning the fall," Marco said. "But he'll need immediate medical attention." As gently as he could, and mindful of possible cervical spinal cord injury, Marco did a battlefield medical assessment.

He lifted Dominic in position as best he could and

pulled his jaw down to maintain an open airway. The priest was breathing, but shallowly. His pulse was weak and thready. Marco then checked for obvious signs of injury: no bleeding, no fractures. But most worrying was that Dominic's right pupil was dilated and nonreactive to light, a common sign of head injury.

"Don't move him, let the EMTs handle that," he advised. "Has anyone called for an ambulance?"

"Yes, I did," Hana nodded. "They should be here any time now." Tears streamed down her cheeks as she stared at her friend lying there. *Please, Michael. Come through this. Don't leave me now.*

The two-tone wail of an emergency vehicle was fast approaching. Marco ran out to Lungotevere Castello, the main street in front of the castle, and, seeing the ambulance, waved it down.

Two EMTs jumped out of the van, ran to the back to grab their gurney and medical equipment, then hustled to the bodies, not far from the road.

As one EMT called for a coroner van after determining that Wolsey had indeed been killed by the fall, the other knelt down to conduct a rapid trauma assessment on Dominic, looking for contusions or abrasions, punctures, penetrations, swelling .... Finding nothing apparent, she performed a field electrocardiogram, then started him on IV fluids to counter shock. Carefully strapping a neck brace onto him, the two EMTs gently transferred him onto the gurney.

Wheeling him back to the ambulance, they hoisted the gurney into the cabin.

"I'm going with him," Hana said resolutely, jumping

into the cabin next to Dominic. "You can both meet me at the hospital." The EMTs slammed the doors shut, took their respective places in the vehicle, and with lights flashing and siren blazing, took off for the nearest hospital.

Rushed into the emergency room of Ospedale di Santo Spirito, a few blocks away from Castel Sant'Angelo, Dominic was transferred from the gurney to an ER bed, with a trauma team attending to him. Hana was told to wait in the visitor's lounge while they worked.

The doctors first did a basic exam for limb movement, looking for neurologic injury and any obvious fractures, then ordered a head CT scan and basic blood workup. The cervical spine exam proved negative for fracture—thankfully, given the height of the fall. They also did a CT scan of his abdomen looking for torn aorta, contused kidneys, or other vital organs that might have been damaged. The tests were being evaluated.

It wasn't long before Karl and Marco arrived and joined Hana in the visitor's lounge. She hugged both of them, but gave Marco a cool, halfhearted embrace, still feeling wounded by his lack of compassion—even for a nemesis like Cardinal Wolsey.

A couple hours later a doctor in scrubs approached them, removing his mask. Stepping forward anxiously, Hana asked, "How is he, doctor? Will he be alright?"

"Well, Father Dominic has a closed head injury with a small cerebral hematoma, which is a layer of blood between the brain and the skull. His head may have hit the other victim's head as he fell, we just don't know. The hematoma causes some pressure on the brain and is more severe than a simple concussion, but it is probably not life-threatening. It could certainly cause him to be confused and slightly foggy for a time, especially with the morphine we're giving him now for pain. We must simply wait for his body to reabsorb the stray blood, but he's strong and his body is fighting for itself. If the swelling subsides, he could be ready to leave the hospital in a few more days. We'll know more tomorrow."

"Oh, thank God," she said, burying her face in both hands. "Can we see him now?"

"Yes, but only for a short time, please. He's in and out of consciousness, and if he doesn't recognize you don't be alarmed: that's typical under the circumstances."

The doctor led them to Dominic's room in the Intensive Care Unit. When she saw him lying there, wires connected everywhere and an oxygen tube in his nose, Hana began weeping again. She rushed to his side, grasping his hand and lightly stroking his arm, then sat on the edge of the bed.

"Hey, Michael ..." she said softly. "It's Hana. Karl and Marco are here, too. Michael ...?"

There was no response. The cacophony of medical equipment—the subtle noises of the BiPAP machine and IV pump and beeping of the heart monitor—were the only other sounds in the room. Hana kept speaking to him, gently trying to waken him.

A few minutes later a nurse came in to tell them that it was time to leave, that the priest needed more rest now. Hana was torn, wanting to stay there until he awakened.

Marco and Karl obediently left the room, heading back to the visitor's lounge. Karl made a quick phone call back to Lukas at the Vatican, updating them on Michael's grave condition.

Just as Hana was about to get up, Michael's eyes fluttered a bit, then opened. Turning his head ever so slightly, he looked into Hana's eyes, then attempted a weak smile.

Staring at her with glassy eyes, he murmured in a barely audible whisper, "I ... I love you ... so much ..."

Hana wasn't sure she heard him correctly. "What was that, Michael? What did you say?"

The nurse was now adamant. "I'm afraid you really must leave now, signorina. Please."

Dominic's eyes closed and he drifted back into the netherworld of a morphine drip.

Hana finally stood, looking down at her friend's bruised body. Her heart seemed as if it would burst right there.

But she was certain of one thing. She had heard him correctly.

And finally, she knew.

CHAPTER

FIFTY-ONE

B ack in St. Peter's Basilica, the pope and Cardinal
Petrini stood in front of the assembled cardinal
electors and other personnel.

"I am well aware of this being an extraordinary state
of affairs, brethren," His Holiness beseeched, gesturing
with his hands as he spoke. "But I'm afraid what Father
Dominic has told you is absolutely true. Apparently, Opus
Deus and Propaganda Due have been colluding for some
time to interfere with the next conclave, and if it were the
result of my death instead of retirement, I would not be
here now to assure you of these facts myself.

"There are most certainly amongst you many who
have been influenced by either or both of these
disgraceful organizations, and in that regard I would
encourage you to seek absolution in the sacrament of
confession. This is not how princes of Holy Mother
Church conduct her affairs. The days of paid indulgences
are long over, and your sacred duty to elect a new pontiff

must come from your heart and mind, not out of lust for what you might gain from it. That kind of shameful conduct is purely unacceptable.

"Meanwhile the conclave will reconvene immediately, with confessors available in the Sistine Chapel for those seeking absolution."

As the pope was speaking, an aide holding a piece of paper rushed up to Cardinal Petrini, whispered in his ear, then moved away.

Petrini's face turned ashen and he looked down at the floor, emotion taking hold of him.

Slowly he then opened and read the Dictum Covenant the aide had handed him, retrieved from the cold grip of Cardinal Wolsey's dead hand. Finally, here was the proof needed to inform the cardinal electors.

Having finished what he had to say, the pope turned to his Secretary of State. "Is there anything you wish to add, Enrico?"

Petrini looked over the assembly.

"I have just received word that Cardinal Alastair Wolsey is dead, having taken his own life."

The basilica suddenly echoed with gasps and murmurs as the cardinals reacted to the news.

"Moreover, apparently Father Dominic was injured in the skirmish, which took place at Castel Sant'Angelo. He is now in the hospital, fighting for his life." It took all of his strength for Petrini to remain stoic, knowing his son may be having a close call with death. He was anxious to see him.

He held the piece of paper over his head and stared at the congregation.

"This is what Wolsey had taken from Father Dominic, the evidence indicting both Opus Deus and Propaganda Due in their treacherous scheme to influence the conclave. I will read it to you now."

Petrini read aloud the Dictum Covenant. As he recited the proclamation, gasps and whispers again arose from the assembled cardinals. Several remained silent, looking guiltily down at their hands.

"While the diamonds that were originally intended for Peter's Pence have since been stolen from Father Dominic's safe, the gold has been secretly marked. Anyone found attempting to dispose of those ingots will be punished to the full extent of the Church's canon law."

With the basilica now in complete silence, Petrini and the Pope Emeritus looked sternly over the crowd, as if trying to ferret out, or at least to intimidate, those culpable of such infidelity.

"I think our point has been made clear," the Pope Emeritus said. "Now, my brothers, go back to your conclave, and do what's right under the prescribed oaths you have taken."

Eight Swiss Guards escorted the cardinal electors back into the Sistine Chapel. As usual, the first order of business was a sermon, reinstating the qualities of the person who would be pope and reiterating the current conditions of the Church. During the sermon, several cardinals had made their way to the confessionals, where priests heard their secret confessions.

Then the first vote of the morning took place. Each elector wrote down the name of his preferred candidate and folded his ballot twice, then over the next ninety minutes, each cardinal alone made his way to the front of the chapel, placed his ballot on the brass salver, uttered the sacred oath and a prayer, then dropped his ballot into the urn below and returned to his seat.

The three scrutineers at a table in the front of the chapel began: one counting the votes, one noting the names in the journal, and one reading each name aloud.

At the end of the count, the head scrutineer stood up, made the sign of the cross, smiled and uttered the ancient Latin words, "*Habemus papam.*"

"We have a pope."

The voting ballots were bundled together, then a chemical combination of potassium chlorate, lactose, and pine rosin was added to the batch, and they were burned in the special stove.

As white smoke plumed out of the chimney, the thousands of faithful in St. Peter's Square erupted in a great cheer, many in tears, all grateful that they had a new pontiff.

Now they all looked upward, to the top floor window in the loggia of the Apostolic Palace where popes traditionally made their first appearance, and where the world would finally learn who had been elected, as guided by the Holy Spirit. A dark red papal banner was being unfurled beneath the window in preparation for the new Holy Father's emergence.

The Dean of the College of Cardinals had instructed an aide to go fetch the newly elected pope—who, being over eighty years of age, was not among the cardinal electors —and have him appear before the assembled College of Cardinals.

Having done so, the humbled man made his way up the main aisle of the Sistine Chapel, smartly escorted by a cadre of Swiss Guards, then stood before the Dean and Secretary of the College, as well as the master of papal liturgical celebrations.

The Dean asked the man one question in Latin: "*Acceptasne electionem de te canonice factam in Summum Pontificem?*" Do you accept your canonical election as Supreme Pontiff?

Cardinal Enrico Petrini said simply, "*Si, accepto.*" Yes, I accept.

Then the Dean asked, "*Quo nomine vis vocari?*" By what name do you wish to be called?

The pope responded with a single name: "Ignatius."

Pope Ignatius, to be informally known as "Papa Petrini" among Italians, was then taken to a small red room next to the Sistine Chapel known as the Room of Tears: the sanctum where new popes could privately experience the overwhelming emotions typically endured after having been chosen by the Holy Spirit through the hands of mortal men.

Also in that room, a set of pontifical robes had been laid out for the pope—the traditional pure-white cassock, a vestment called a rochet worn over the cassock, and a red mozzetta, a short cape with a hood. As was protocol, the pope dressed himself, donning a red and gold embroidered stole, a white skull cap—or zucchetto—on his head, then he placed around his neck a gold, corded pectoral cross. He was now prepared to greet the multitude of faithful waiting in St. Peter's Square.

Accompanied by the protodeacon of the College of Cardinals, Pope Ignatius was taken to the loggia in the Apostolic Palace. The protodeacon stepped out onto the high balcony to address the hundreds of thousands gathered below, proclaiming in Latin:

"I announce to you with great joy, we have a Pope, the most eminent and most reverend Lord, Lord Enrico, Cardinal of the Holy Roman Church Petrini, who has taken the name Ignatius."

The crowd cheered with unbridled jubilation as Pope Ignatius stepped out onto the balcony, repeatedly waving and giving the people his blessing.

If only Michael were here to experience this incredible moment with me, Petrini thought, as his eyes clouded with emotion.

CHAPTER
FIFTY-TWO

It would be highly unusual for a newly elected pope to leave the Vatican on his first night, so the operation was conducted with the utmost secrecy. Two Swiss Guards—the Holy Father's Personal Protective Detail, the elite of the elite—were dressed in dark suits as they led the pontiff out of the Apostolic Palace through a little used door. The pope's white cassock was covered with a long black trench coat, and his white skullcap hidden under a black fedora. Another of his protective detail, the newly reassigned Sergeant Karl Dengler waited next to a running up-armored Range Rover. With the pope safely ensconced inside, they headed out through Saint Anne's Gate and onto the streets of Rome.

At the hospital, the pope was swiftly escorted through the back hallways and into Michael's room in the Intensive Care Unit, his protective detail staying outside once it was determined that Dominic was alone. Karl, the new guy, stayed with the Range Rover. Almost nobody on the medical staff knew of the after-hours visit, and those that did were sworn to secrecy.

Petrini, now Pope Ignatius, knelt at Michael's bedside and took his hand. "My son, I wish you could have been with me there today, but I only pray now that you will be with me still."

And with that, he wept over his unconscious son as only a father could.

The next morning, Michael Dominic—now awake and fully alert, free of the morphine drip—lay in bed watching reruns of the papal ceremonies on TV, his heart swelling with pride. *Incredible*, he thought, overjoyed but not surprised.

My father, the pope!

His nurse popped her head in the open doorway and asked, "Are you up for a visitor, Padre?"

"Sure," he said softly. Then he smiled weakly as Hana Sinclair walked into the room.

"It's about time! Where have you been?!" he asked humorously.

"I was here when they brought you in yesterday, with Karl and Marco. But you were kind of out of it, loopy in fact, and I was told you wouldn't be able to see anyone until today."

"Ah, so you were here. Sorry, I don't remember that."

"The doctor said you've had a nearly miraculous recovery. You'll be able to go home in a couple days."

"That's great," Michael said, taking her hand and

looking meaningfully into her eyes. "It must be because of who I had pulling for me."

Recalling what Michael had said to her in his hazy state of consciousness, Hana wondered if she should mention it or not. She wanted to, desperately, but felt it might not be fair to him, or even embarrass him. This wasn't the time or place for that.

Instead she said, "Isn't it amazing Cardinal Petrini was elected pope?! And the first American pope! He's the perfect choice, and such a good man." She looked up at the celebrations on the TV.

Dominic watched her, a warm feeling coming over him. "Thanks for coming," he said.

"Are you kidding? I couldn't find a TV anywhere else …"

They both laughed.

"So, what happened with Wolsey?"

"He didn't make it," Hana said. "In fact, you were very lucky to have landed on top of him. His body cushioned your fall. Otherwise …" she started tearing up, "You might not be here with me now."

Dominic reached over and squeezed her hand. "It's alright. I'm here now and I'm fine. More than fine. Grateful. And just a little sore, but anxious to get out of here and back to work. I'm sure the Holy Father will be shaking things up at the Vatican. I want to be there to watch the fireworks!"

EPILOGUE

Among the pope's first acts on Day One was to fire Isabella Stewart Hastings, president of the Vatican Bank, for her collusion with Roberto Calvi's accounts and transfer of gold to the account of Opus Deus. Isabella was not at all pleased, but she did have her financial empire to fall back on, and she could still be of value to Opus Deus in the years ahead.

The new pope had taken scores of congratulatory calls from heads of state and many friends, including his wartime comrades from Team Hugo: Armand de Saint-Clair and Pierre Valois, the president of France.

He had given private audiences for his two favorite Swiss Guards, Sergeant Karl Dengler and Corporal Lukas Bischoff, thanking them for their united efforts to assist Father Dominic in his mission against Propaganda Due and Opus Deus. That same audience included Hana Sinclair and Marco Picard, since the Holy Father knew they were among Michael's favorite friends and partners in so many operations helpful to the Church over the years. The pope also instructed the Commander of the Swiss Guard to promote Lukas to sergeant in recognition of his bravery and efforts on behalf of the Church.

On his second day as pontiff, Pope Ignatius's motorcade made its way the short distance from the Vatican to Ospedale di Santo Spirito. Without having been warned, the now-public presence of the Holy Father took the hospital's staff by surprise, even shock, as he and his entourage were escorted to the Intensive Care Unit and Father Michael Dominic's room.

Papa Petrini went into the room alone. Dominic had just awakened and turned to see who had entered, then tried to stand in respect for the Holy Father. *His* holy father.

"Your Holiness," Dominic said, his eyes moistening with joy, "I can't believe you came to see me! Especially with all that you must need to be doing right now."

"Dear Michael, my son ..." The pope's eyes were misty as well, as he sat on the bed next to the recovering priest. "How are you feeling? Are they taking proper care of you here?"

"Well, after your visit I'm sure I'll be getting all the pudding I want! Yes, Holy Father, I'm feeling fine. I should be out of here in another day or two. But tell me, how does it feel being pope?"

Ignatius looked kindly into Michael's eyes.

"These are early days yet, but I do feel the Holy Spirit

is with me, especially here and now, sitting with you. But check back with me in a couple of months and I'll give you a more informed report." The pope laughed at his own joke, then laid his arm on his son's.

"By the way, what happened to Bishop Silva and Dante?" Dominic asked.

The pope's face betrayed his annoyance. "I am told they received word from someone at the conclave of what transpired, and they were taken immediately to the airport, obviously to evade prosecution. So they are gone for now, though I'm sure we have not heard the last of them. But enough about those two.

"I am so very grateful you are in good health, Michael. Things could have gone so much worse. I am also indebted to you for all your work on that nasty business with P2 and Opus Deus. If not for that, this certainly would have turned out to be a very different situation.

"It's also worth noting, by the way, that we have received a dozen or so bars of gold sent to us anonymously for the Peter's Pence fund. They appear to have your name stamped on them in microscopic letters, as one of my aides discovered. I suspect you had a hand in that somehow?"

"Yes, we'll just leave it at 'somehow' ... Although I'm pleased to hear the recipients obviously had a change of heart.

"That's a good start to your papacy, Your Holiness ... Dad ...."

AUTHOR'S NOTES

Many readers have asked me to distinguish fact from fiction in my books. Generally, I like to take factual events and historical figures and build on them in creative ways—but much of what I do write is historically accurate. In this book, I'll review some of the chapters where questions may arise, with hopes that it may help those who are wondering.

GENERAL: With one or two minor exceptions, all descriptions of the Vatican—its buildings, special rooms, offices and furniture—are as accurate as I can find, having relied on an abundance of maps, floor plans, diagrams, books and articles which I have collected for years. I want readers to actually "be there" as they travel through the story.

The same goes for trains and planes (and their actual schedules, flight numbers and travel times), restaurants, trattorias and caffè shops (and their menus). Among the countless emails and reviews I get from readers, a great many of them appreciate descriptions of the food our characters eat wherever they go. There are a lot of foodie fans out there.

PROLOGUE: The story of Roberto Calvi, his shady dealings with the Vatican Bank and Banco Ambrosiano, as well as his death, are all true. The events surrounding his death as I have described them are factually corroborated, including his missing briefcase—which served as the inspiration for this story. Though, when it was found, it did contain incriminating papers and a forged passport, I added the safe deposit box key as an extra touch, which served the story well.

Propaganda Due (pronounced *Doo-ay,* the number two in Italian), or P2, was a real Masonic lodge, banned by Italian law in its later existence. It is believed now to be defunct (but who really knows ...?). Many priests, bishops and cardinals were known to have been members—an affiliation punishable by excommunication—though there are no known cases of such. The descriptions in the book of P2 and its adherents in the book are all authentic. Apart from a few fictional additions, everything else in the Prologue is true.

CHAPTER 1: The Vatican switchboard and computer networks, as described, are managed and operated by, respectively, the Sisters of the Pious Disciples of the Divine Master and the Daughters of St. Paul, or Pauline nuns, who are also known as the "Media Nuns."

CHAPTER 5: Though there are some structural similarities to the actual personal prelature known as Opus Dei, my "Opus Deus" is a completely fictional entity and has no bearing whatsoever on the interests or activities of the prelature known as Opus Dei.

CHAPTER 11: Regina Coeli prison and its history are accurately portrayed here. Even today, as with most prisons worldwide, overcrowding is a major issue, and for a truly ancient prison in continuous operation whose roots go back nearly 400 years, conditions must be as deplorable as I've described them.

CHAPTER 12: As far as I know, the pope's helicopter is not named Shepherd Two—but when he flies on a specially equipped jet leased from Alitalia, the aircraft is known as Shepherd One. I just took it one logical step forward with the helicopter.

The Swiss Guard do in fact play soccer ("football" or *calcio* in Italian) on the grounds of the Campo Pio XI football stadium not far from the Vatican. Teams indeed comprise both Swiss Guards and Vatican Museum guards, in a sort of fraternal competition. And yes, the pope (at the present time, Francis) does stop by for the occasional game he loves so much.

CHAPTER 16: TSN Roma in Italian is *Tiro a Segno Nazionale*, translated as National Target Shooting range, hence the abbreviation in Italian, TSN. Early readers of this book thought I had the initials confused, so I point that out here for clarity.

The expert descriptions of weaponry here were provided by a devoted reader of my books who has become a good friend, Ron Moore, a guy with a rich background in this and many other areas of expertise.

CHAPTER 21: I found the legend here of Saint Helena quaint, of her having brought an ox cart of earth from Golgotha—the place where Christ was crucified—to seed the grounds of the Vatican gardens, and I couldn't think of not using it.

Again, my thanks go to Ron Moore for his brilliant introduction to me of the micro scribe punch for imprinting infinitesimally small characters onto most anything. It served good use here for imprinting the gold bars.

CHAPTER 22: References to the Vatican's financial statement shown here were actually taken from the Vatican Bank's (IOR's) publicly released financial statement for 2020.

The *Obolo*, better known as Peter's Pence, is in fact the pope's personal fund to disperse as he pleases, traditionally towards humanitarian initiatives and social promotion projects, as well as to the support of the Holy See. On one day each year, Catholic churches worldwide take up a special collection for Peter's Pence, which goes directly to the pope.

CHAPTER 23: Villa Rosso is the fictional home of former P2 Grandmaster Licio Gelli. Its actual name was Villa Wanda, named after his wife, Wanda Vannacci. Since

2013, as of this writing, the villa has been under preventive seizure due to an inquiry relating to the evasion of €17 million in taxes for which Gelli and his family are being investigated. The rest of Gelli's and P2's history here, as well as Operation Paperclip, are all true and in the public record—including the gold found in the geraniums!—though Silvio Pollastri is fictional.

CHAPTER 26: From what I have been told by Vatican insiders, the pope does actually have a hidden button under his desk to summon his aides, presumably (in my writer's mind, anyway) to bring an end to a given meeting, or more likely to summon an aide.

CHAPTER 44: The protocols described here in preparing for a papal conclave are all accurate. The entire Vatican goes into a virtual lockdown mode, and secrecy reigns.

In early drafts, I had Cardinal Petrini as one of the cardinal electors—then realized that, in prior books, I had him serving during World War II, which of course puts him well over the age of eighty, thus excluding him from voting in a conclave. Ah, the challenges of being a series writer...

CHAPTER 46: Again, the conclave procedures described here are fairly accurate, but take much more time than I had allowed (for the sake of expediency).

Thank you for reading *The Opus Dictum*. I hope you enjoyed it and, if you haven't already, suggest you pick up the story in the other books in The Magdalene Chronicles series—*The Magdalene Deception, The Magdalene Reliquary, The Magdalene Veil*—and look forward to forthcoming books featuring the same characters—and a few new ones—in the current *Vatican Secret Archives Thriller* series starting with *The Vivaldi Cipher*.

When you have a moment, may I ask that you leave a review on Amazon and elsewhere? Reviews are crucial to a book's success, and I hope for the *Vatican Secret Archives Thriller* series to have a long and entertaining life.

You can easily leave your review by going to my Amazon book page for The Opus Dictum.

If you would like to reach out for any reason, you can email me at gary@garymcavoy.com. If you'd like to learn more about my background or about my other books, visit my website at www.garymcavoy.com, where you can also sign up for my private readers mailing list.

With kind regards,

Gary McAvoy

ACKNOWLEDGMENTS

Throughout the writing of this book I have been grateful for the assistance of many friends, colleagues, and professionals in specialized areas, without whose help this would have been a more challenging project.

MVP for this book goes to Ron Moore, whose ingenious mind for plotting and truly understanding the depths of my characters—not to mention his brilliant expertise in so many diverse subjects—is a gift. I'm sure you'll see his name again in future books.

To my friend John Burgess, who helped me understand how European football works, giving Karl and Lukas a little fun time between battles.

Grateful appreciation to Andrew Boyd, Professor of Theology and Religious Studies at the Pontifical Beda College in Rome, for his vast knowledge of Vatican—and especially papal—practices.

And credits to Stephanie Wilson for her depth of knowledge on banking procedures, as well as friend, fellow author, and retired physician PJ Peterson for her learned medical knowledge.

To punctilious copyeditor Kathleen Costello, Red Pencil in Chief at GrammarToGo, my thanks for your skill and bravery in battling my dangling participles and disobedient commas. And to my brilliant developmental editor, Sandra Haven, without whose able prowess in how plot and characters come together, I might otherwise be lost in a sea of words.

As always, my thanks to Yale Lewis and Greg McDonald for their frequent early reads and feedback on the manuscript as it continued to develop.

I'm grateful to my intrepid beta readers Launch Team, who got first review of the final draft of the book and gave me their incisive comments. Though too many to mention, I thank each one of you.

And finally, huge appreciation to the many readers of my work. It is you for whom I write, and your letters, questions, reviews, and feedback are genuinely appreciated.